THE
tapestry
OF A
HEART

ERIN ZAK

FIERCE FEMM MEDIA

FIRST EDITION May 2023
PUBLISHED BY Erin Zak
COVER DESIGN: Erin Zak
EDITOR: Jessica Hatch

Copyright © 2023 by ERIN ZAK
All rights reserved. This book is for your personal enjoyment only. This book or any portion thereof may not be reproduced or used in any manner without the express permission of the author.
This is a work of fiction. All characters & happenings in this publication are fictitious and any resemblance to real persons (living or dead), locales or events is purely coincidental.

ALSO BY ERIN ZAK

Standalone Titles
Falling Into Her
Breaking Down Her Walls
Create a Life to Love
Beautiful Accidents
The Road Home
The Hummingbird Sanctuary
Guarding Evelyn

Novella
Closed-Door Policy

Co-Write
Swift Vengeance, with Jackie D and Jean Copeland
GLITCH, with Jackie D

ACKNOWLEDGMENTS

For those of you who know me, this book will probably feel like I've included a lot of myself in it. You won't be wrong. I think it's incredibly difficult to write *without* including the things you're going through and the things you're learning. After all, aren't we supposed to write what we know? And what I know, right now, is that finding happiness has been the most rewarding, and excruciating, experience. That's how I wrote Finnley. She struggled to realize how miserable she was. Once she figures it out, well… I won't spoil it for you.

Now for the people who made this possible. Thank you to Gail. You are amazing and I love you more than I ever thought was possible. Your support, kindness, and love have made me a better person. Thank you to my editor, Jessica. I don't know if you'll ever understand how much I have enjoyed developing my craft with you. All you've done is made me better. And I am so very grateful. Thank you to my beta readers. This book wouldn't be what it is without your guidance. Thank you to my best friends. Jackie, where would I be without you? Melissa, you're important and part of the reason I am so much happier. Stacey, my bird, you're simply remarkable. Stacy, you bring me so much laughter and love. Julie, you make me so happy that I'm in your life. Mel, Sheri, Jen, Valeri, Charlotte, you ladies make me smile on a daily basis. Lerin, my longest friend, thank you for hanging in there with me. Maggie, Aurora, Dena, thank you for staying.

And, last but never least, thank you to my readers. I quite literally would not be here without your love and support.

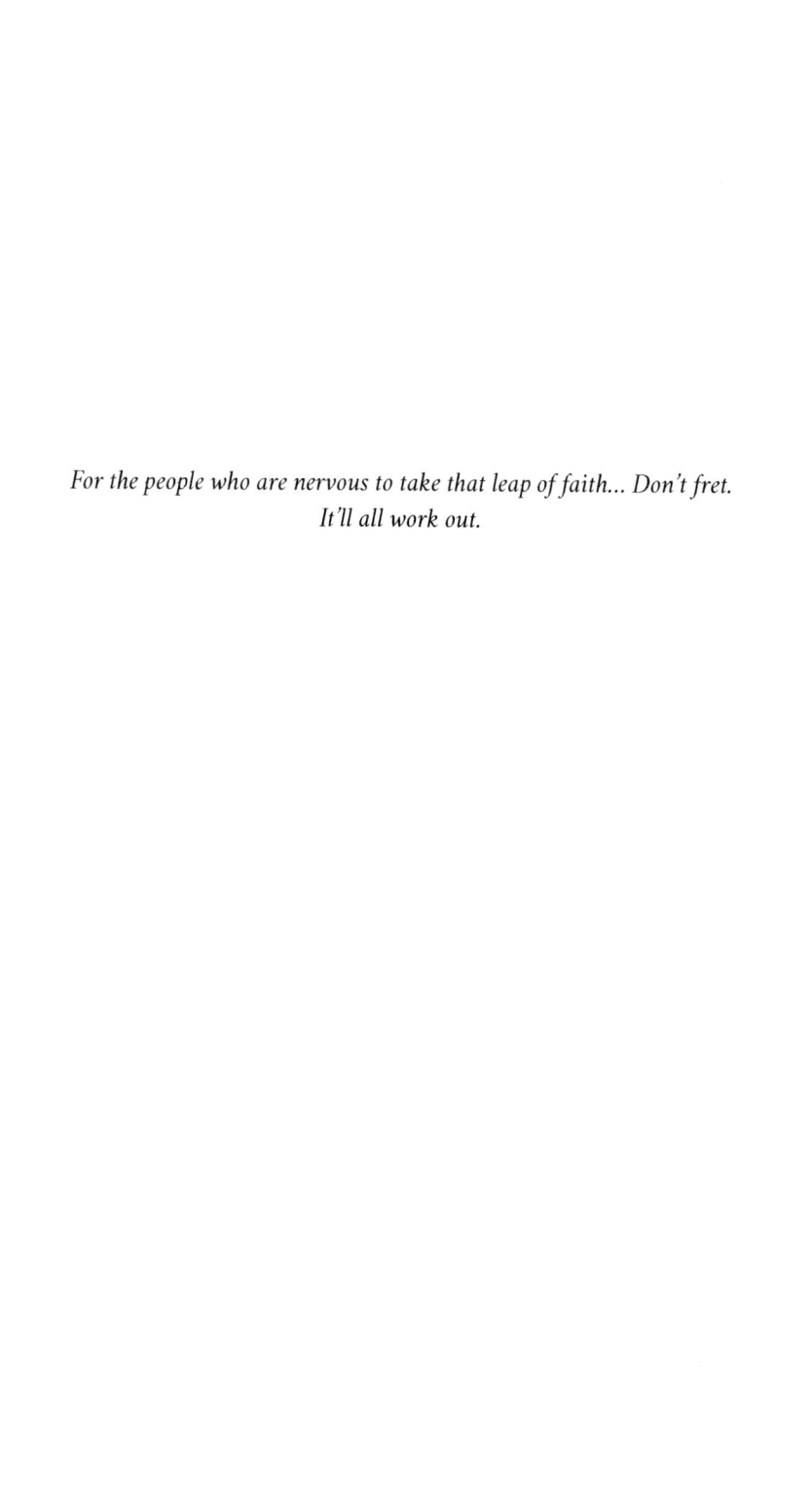

For the people who are nervous to take that leap of faith... Don't fret. It'll all work out.

PROLOGUE

"Finnley, I need to speak with you immediately."

I look up from the profit and loss report for my parents' business, O'Connell Landscaping. I have been poring over it for the past three days. I'm in the home stretch of dissecting numbers, and stopping now will derail my brain. Not a good thing. "Right now, Dad? I'm in the middle of something."

"Yes, right now."

I stare at him. He's not serious. He can't be. He knows how tedious this part of my job is. Or he *should* know. At the very least, he knows how important it is that I find the issues. Find where we are losing money. Figure out why their company isn't as profitable as it should be. I'm doing as he asked me to do. And, of course, as a Harvard Business grad, I am doing a phenomenal job. I'm sure I'm annoying my dad. He never likes when I outdo him in anything. Accounting may not be my passion, but I really am damn good at it. Math has always made sense to me. Not so much to my dad. And being better at running his business than he is has not gone over real well.

"Right *now*, Finn." He points at the floor in front of him. Everything about this moment transports me right back to being a child again, getting in trouble for spilling milk or not cleaning my room adequately. It's rare that I ever feel like the thirty-two-year-old I actually am. "I'm not joking around."

"Fine," I mumble under my breath. I pull my long, dark hair back in a no-nonsense ponytail, then take off across the small office space in our twenty-five-year-old trailer. I mention that it's twenty-five years old because, for a company that's been in business for over thirty years, it'd be lovely if we actually had a nice office *without* a leaky ceiling and *with* a nice, clean bathroom, where I can go to cry when I've had it up to here with this place. But no. It's a very dilapidated trailer. Describing it as a piece of shit would be going easy on it. Add it to the list of reasons why I should leave, but haven't.

What else is on that list? Well, my father's inability to manage money is number one. Cleaning up someone else's mess is not fun. Which actually has top billing on another list of mine: the reasons I will never want children.

Taking over the books for my parents' landscaping company and performing as the accountant I went to school to become has been far less glamorous than I pictured. Profits? What profits? Dad spends faster than we receive on most days. And I don't mean spending money to make money. I mean taking whatever is left and living the best life possible. Growing up, I didn't mind the lavish house, the in-ground pool, the trips to Spain and Italy. I had a new car when I was sixteen, more clothes and shoes than I could ever wear in a lifetime, and all the spending money I wanted. Although after I went to grad school and finally figured out why the business was failing, I realized it'd never be the multimillion-dollar company Dad has always dreamed of having, much less the one I grew up thinking would take care of me in my old age.

"What could possibly be so important?" I ask him as I reach his side.

"Close the door, please."

I do as he asks and close the hollow, wooden door behind me. "What is going on?"

His dark brown eyes, the ones I inherited instead of my mother's crystal blue, are boring holes into me. That's where our similarities die. He's short and stocky; I'm tall and lean. He has dirty blond hair; mine is dark. Neither of my parents has dark hair actually. If I had never seen pictures of my grandmother on my mother's side, I'd be convinced I was adopted. I started out with that O'Connell blond hair, but as I aged, it darkened to auburn. I have no idea how or why. I would have killed for blonde hair when I was sixteen. Now, I kind of like my dark locks.

"Have a seat," he says.

"Dad, seriously, you're freaking me out." I sit in the creaky chair and peer at him across his very cluttered desk. The clock at the edge died years ago, still stuck on the time 4:54. Maybe he thinks we can't even afford batteries. He's not wrong.

His heavy sigh accentuates the start of his sentence. "You know we've been in the red for quite some time." He intertwines his hands, folds them, and stares right at me. "I'm gonna have to let you go."

I let out a laugh. "Excuse me? I've only been back from school for two years. Are you just nervous that I'm going to unearth some strange skeleton from your closet with my superior forensic accounting skills?" I laugh again. "C'mon, Dad. What's going on?"

"I can't keep you on staff any longer." His wrinkled face twists, and I realize he's not joking.

I lean forward. "Dad, what are you talking about? I'm in charge of the books. How are you going to run your finances if I'm not here?"

"Your mother is going to step back in."

"Dad—"

"This isn't up for discussion, Finn."

I scoff at his stern voice, but his facial expression is enough to make me believe him. "Oh." I flop back in the chair. I can feel the threadbare hole on the side, barely patched with duct tape. "Wow."

"I'm sorry. I know this throws a wrench in your plans."

"*My* plans? You're kidding, right? I've been groomed for this job my entire life. I went to college to get an accounting degree. I went to fucking Harvard to get my MBA so I could take over this place. I did everything I was supposed to do. Everything you made me do. And now you're going to—what? Fire me? This is ridiculous. *You're* being ridiculous."

"Don't get upset with me." His elevated tone, his angry face, the sweat beading on his brow from the rising Florida temperatures *in a trailer*, the very old trailer with the failing air conditioning, are clear indicators that he's done being as nice as possible.

Years and years of dealing with his erratic temper have conditioned me to shrink, but something inside me snaps. "Don't get upset with *you*? Are you out of your goddamn mind?"

"Hey!" His voice pierces my frustration. "Don't take that tone with me, young lady." He jabs his big, burly finger at me. "I'm not happy I have to do this."

"Then don't! I don't mind taking a pay cut until things calm down."

"No, not possible."

"That doesn't even make sense. I know we're stretched thin, but me taking a pay cut would help things. I have money saved. I can handle it."

"Yes, it does make sense. Completely slashing your salary will help tremendously."

"Maybe slash your own salary," I toss back in his face. "Ever thought of that? It's not like you do anything when you're here except make dumb decisions that lead to the company failing miserably." I stand abruptly and glare at him. He does not like what I said, but for once in my life, I don't care. "What am I supposed to do, Dad?"

"You need to figure your life out. Outside of the company, I mean." His eyes soften, which is wildly unexpected. "You're not happy here. Your mother wants you to be happy."

My stomach bottoms out. "My mother, huh? Not you?"

"No, Finn, I do, too. And you aren't. At all."

Granted, I had to prod him to get there, but it's one of the first times he has ever seemed concerned over my well-being. I'm not sure how to handle it. "Dad, I'm fine," I assert. "You've never worried about my happiness before. Why start now?"

His cheeks puff out on his exhale. "Well, I do care about your happiness, contrary to what I've apparently led you to believe." He looks genuinely hurt by my dismissiveness. His eyes have started to well with tears, but, again, I truly do not care.

"And they say women are too emotional." My words, which were meant to be said under my breath, have a much higher volume than I expected.

"Finnley, that's it. You're done here."

"Dad," I say, hoping my laughter will diffuse the thick tension. "Come on. Seriously. Why don't you just take the day off and think about what you've done?"

"No," he shouts. And that's when I finally figure out that this isn't negotiable. His face has gone beet red, and the sweat that was only beading before has now started to slide down forehead. "You've put your entire life on hold since you got back from Boston. Your mother thought you'd stay up there, but you didn't. You came back, and for the past two years, you've been even more unhappy than you were before you left. I didn't see it. Your mother pointed it out to me. And, yeah, maybe it was my fault. I put a lot of pressure on you to take this job so I could hopefully retire. But, let's be real, I can't afford to fully retire. And you? You may love numbers, but fixing my mistakes is not what's going to bring you true happiness." He huffs. "This is not easy for me to admit. Any of it. You need to figure out what you want in this world. Because this job?" He motions to the crumbling trailer around us. "This isn't it. It never was. My only regret is not realizing it sooner."

"Is this because I've put you on a spending freeze?" It's a weak-ass attempt at humor, but I'm out of ideas.

He laughs. Whew. "I'd love to tell you yes, that's the reason, but it's not. At all." He shakes his head. "Honey, I don't want you to end up like me. Tied down to this sinking ship."

"I can fix it, though."

"It's not up for discussion."

"So that's it? I'm just… let go?"

"I'm giving you a month's severance. I want you to figure out what you want to do with your life."

"I *know* what I want to do. I want to work here with the MBA I spent a fucking fortune on."

"Your mouth. I swear to Christ Almighty." He stands and stalks over toward me, places his big hands on my arms, and jostles me gently. "I want you to be happy, for Christ's sake. I want you to figure out what you're passionate about. I want you to live your life and not worry about this place. Why is that such a crime?"

"Dad, I just—"

"Your mother has talked to her brother. She thinks you should go stay with him in Chicago. I don't agree because of his, y'know, *lifestyle* or whatever."

Why is my dad such a closed-minded idiot sometimes?

"The only good thing you have here is Steven."

I roll my eyes. "A man is not the only good thing in my life."

"Well, he's your fiancé. He will go with you if you want him to. And you should want him to." He removes his hands from my person, then rubs them over his sweaty face and receding hairline before he finishes with, "Your mother, in all her motherly wisdom," he says with a groan and it's his turn to roll his eyes, making me think he's not completely sold on the idea. "She thinks you should call your uncle and take advantage of this opportunity."

"Dad, this makes no sense. Chicago? I mean, I love Uncle Mark, but the Chicago winters are no joke."

He chuckles away my disgust for the cold. "Finnley, you're gonna land on your feet."

"No, Dad, that's not the point—"

"You're dismissed. Get your things and get out of here, Finn. Okay?"

I stand there, dumbfounded, trying so hard not to cry, not because I'm sad so much as I'm pissed off. Besides, crying now would make him think I am brokenhearted when, in reality, I am ready to punch him in the face.

"*Now.*" He turns so he isn't looking at me any longer.

"Fine," I say as I leave his office and slam the stupid hollow door behind me. I look around the trailer and the old furniture, the stacks of files Dad never got around to filing. The stained ceiling tiles from years of neglect stare back at me. Paperwork covers my desk. My last attempt at being angry has me swiping everything from my desk right into the trash can. I slam my half-full coffee cup into the trash on top of it. No way am I going to let him have the work I've done so far on that asinine report. As for the rest of the things on my desk… fuck it. I don't even have a photograph of Steven and me. Hell, I should call him right now and tell him about this bullshit. I should tell him how furious I am that I was canned by my own father. But, sadly, and it's not something I am proud to admit, Steven is the last person I want to talk to.

Honestly, I should be far angrier at that moment, but now, on the opposite side of the door from my father, I can't summon anything more than *disappointment*. My shoulders sag under the weight of it. I've spent the last ten years of my life being involved with this company. Even in Boston, I remotely did the accounting. And now I'm supposed to move on? To what? To Chicago? If anything, I should just go back to Boston. At least there I'd have some connections.

Fuck.

I slam my car door behind me. Oh, look. There's the anger. I pick up my phone and shoot off a text to Uncle Mark. *Looks like I might be making a move to the Windy City. Think you'd be okay with that?*

His response bubble appears immediately. *I already have your room ready, babycakes.* I snort, though not without appreciation. Apparently Mom has already talked to him. *You're never going to want to leave. It may not seem like it now, but your parents are actually doing you a favor. Trust me. And you know living in the big city with your even bigger gay uncle will be the time of your life.*

The smile on my face feels good in light of the reality I am currently facing. *I'm sure you're right.*

I am always right, Finnley. Love you, babe.

I swipe out of our conversation and click through my phone to Steven's name. Dread fills my body. I send him a simple text that says, *We need to talk.*

His response bubble appears even faster than Uncle Mark's. *Your dad already called me. Come over.*

My dad already called him? Jesus. Screw anger. I'm *annoyed* now.

The longer I sit with this recent development, the more I start to realize that maybe my dumb dad is right. Perhaps this job isn't the end-all, be-all for me. Maybe something else exists out there.

I just wish I hadn't wasted every single second leading up to this.

CHAPTER ONE

Two weeks have gone by since my dad fired me, and aside from a few miserable conversations with Steven, I've decided to be optimistic about this new journey. Don't get me wrong, I've had to have a couple of pep talks from my best friend, Jesse, who graciously drove me to the airport so we could say our sappy goodbyes in the departures lane at Tampa International. She's called twice already since I landed. In fact, she's the one I have to thank for the latest addition to my list of embarrassing moments.

Oh? Want to hear more? Well, okay then, let's talk about *embarrassing moments* and why I have more than the average person. You know the moments when you do something so ridiculous you cringe every time you remember them? Embarrassment like that happens far more frequently than I'd like to admit. And even though those horrifying times have done their fair share of scarring me, they have also helped me become who I am. They shaped me into someone who can take pretty much anything that's thrown at her, that's for sure. And they have taught me some invaluable lessons. Or, at least, I hope they have.

The slew of embarrassing moments littering my life… I swear, you'd think I was the main character in a really bad nineties movie or something. Not only am I a certified klutz, but I am also the last person to think before I speak. I laugh when I'm uncomfortable. I say the dumbest shit when I should literally shut the hell up. And I have zero chill when it comes to trying to make people laugh. I split my pants during my first year of high school as I ran up the stairs like an orangutan, trying to make my friends laugh. Sophomore year, I tripped up the stairs to accept an award for Most Improved Athlete. My junior year saw me flashing my bra to the entire audience during a drama club performance of *Into the Woods*. Senior year? Well, let's say I decided to profess my love to one of my teachers. Mr. Jackson, who, might I add, resembled a Muppet. It was not one of my finest hours. Days. Weeks. *Years* of embarrassment. Ugh.

Unfortunately, the embarrassing moments extended into college. They weren't as prevalent, but I still remember accidentally farting during a test in Western Civ. The whole class heard it, including the professor. Needless to say, I now have a fear of passing gas bordering compulsion.

As an adult, I try as hard as possible not to be distracted when walking up a flight of stairs. I don't eat foods that might irritate my gastrointestinal system. And typically, when I feel like I might actually like someone enough that it could be love, I abort the mission.

So when I fall down a flight of stairs on the Blue Line, on the way to Uncle Mark's Lincoln Park apartment, I'm not shocked. It's a new embarrassing moment to add to the string of moments that have helped form me into the neurotic mess I am today.

"Miss, are you okay?"

"Yes, yes, I'm fine." I groan as I peel myself from the dirty cement steps. "Just bruised my ego a bit."

The elderly Black man who rushed to my aid chuckles his amusement. "That was quite a fall."

"I have a knack for those." I brush off my clothing. "Thank

you so much for the help." I reach out, take my purse from his hand, and adjust my backpack, which somewhat broke my fall. "Where is my—" I turn, looking for my suitcase, and sigh when I see it. Still at the top of the stairs. Looking down at me. If inanimate objects could laugh, it'd be howling. "That's just *great*."

The man lets out another chuckle. "I'll watch your things. You can go grab that beast."

"You're too kind." I offer him a smile before climbing the steps as carefully as possible. My suitcase taunting me the entire time. "Shut up," I mutter as I grab the handle and wheel it down the steps behind me. It bangs onto the cement with each step. I hope it knows I am doing it on purpose. As if the suitcase has real feelings. I roll my eyes at myself. "Thank you so much for watching my things," I tell the man. "I think I can make it from here."

"I certainly hope so. I'm heading in the opposite direction." His sweet smile warms my heart. "You take care of yourself, miss."

"I will. You as well." I watch him lift his hand, a friendly wave offered as he walks away. I fix my stare onto my suitcase now. "Please behave," I say to it. "I promise I'll treat you more kindly if you don't trip me up again."

I somehow find my way onto the train, my purse, my backpack, and my suitcase at least *partially* unscathed. According to Uncle Mark, I should take the Blue Line to Clark/Lake, then transfer to the Brown Line. He was so worried about me even though I lived in Tallahassee during my undergrad; Cambridge, Mass., while getting my master's degree; and, because my parents moved to Florida to start the landscaping company I ran the books for up until two weeks ago, I have lived in Tampa for most of my life.

You know the company, right?

The one I was fired from?

Yeah, that's the one.

Anyway, big cities are not foreign to me. But I guess, in his eyes, I'll always be the same towheaded kid who was once afraid of her own shadow. I'm not afraid of my own shadow any longer, nor am I blond, much to my chagrin. If I'm being honest, those are about the only things that haven't changed.

I pull my phone from my pocket and see that I've missed a call from Steven. Dread. It's the only feeling that accompanies anything to do with him since we had our talk.

I should return his call right now before I succumb to the desire to let this relationship fizzle into oblivion. I bargain with myself and decide to simply send a text.

I made it to Chicago. On the train to Uncle Mark's.

As soon as the text is sent, the response bubble pops up. *Great news, baby. Please let me know when you get there. I'd love to hear your voice.*

The last two weeks have been filled with a lot of weird occurrences. Steven telling me that he won't let me break off our engagement holds top billing. Yes, even over my own father firing me. I just stood there with my mouth hanging open when Steven told me no. Just flat-out no. He wants to do long-distance, and I just went along with it. Like a fucking idiot. What the hell is wrong with me?

It's not that I don't *like* Steven. I said yes to his marriage proposal for a reason. At least, I think I did. How fucked up is that? I don't even know why I said yes! Other than not wanting to disappoint someone else, of course, which is sadly the basis for a lot of my decisions in life. My inability to stand up for myself has dissipated slightly, sure, but the part of me that won't take command when it comes to my happiness still needs work. Shit, my parents were right. I do need to find happiness. How irritating.

Sounds good. Talk to you soon. My response is short and simple.

His, on the other hand, is not. *I love you so much. I can't wait to come visit you.*

I do not respond.

As we approach downtown Chicago, the train car starts to fill. In an effort to take up as little space as possible, I situate my suitcase between my legs, holding on to it for dear life. The picture of it escaping, rolling down the aisle, and smashing into someone isn't hard to imagine. I swear, it has a mind of its own.

While I may not be afraid of my own shadow any longer, I have to admit I am nervous to be back in Chicago. And even though the cold weather has never been a favorite of mine, I am looking forward to the changing seasons. Especially now with the gloomy winter melting into the growth and opportunities of spring. I have taken the last two weeks to settle into the fact I will no longer be taking over the family business, I am still not sure what I want to do with my life. Over the past few days, I've had time to think. A lot of time. Thinking back to the numerous conversations I had with my mom and dad about the business, my dad retiring, and it becoming my business, it hit me that I was never super excited about it. It was just what I was supposed to do. I never thought it was an option not to go that route. And then my dad fired me.

I let out a puff of air when that memory pops into my mind. Talk about something coming out of left field. I never in a million years thought I'd get fired. By my dad. What a kick to the crotch.

I spent my entire adult life striving toward that one thing and one thing only, and then when I got it, I was told it wasn't what *I* wanted.

So here I am, moving to a new city with no job and a long-distance fiancé I only half love because I'm still too scared to fall entirely in love with anyone. Oh, and I have enough student loan debt to bury a small city.

I laugh and realize, only after the lady across the train car has glared at me, that I have actually laughed out loud.

Great. Now I look like a lunatic on top of everything else.

Three things are helping me stay grounded. The first is the idea of being able to fall in love with Chicago. It's one of my favorite cities in the States, and I want to know as much as possible about it. The second is I love Uncle Mark. He's my coolest and favorite relative. We talk and text all the time, so living with him is going to be amazing, I'm sure. The third thing helping me stay grounded is that maybe I'll actually find something to be passionate about and it will help me become the person I am supposed to be. I know I'll find a job. That isn't the part that has my nerves flared up. It's finding a job that will make me happy since, apparently, I was so unhappy working for my parents. Because the person I am right now, even though I don't hate her, is not as happy as I want her to be. She's worried about the future and terrified of being unsatisfied forever.

I hope to Christ I'm not a big, fat failure. Failure has always been my biggest fear. I have been a straight-A student my entire life. I have never done anything I didn't completely master.

Except, I guess, happiness.

Which makes me sad.

My dad was right. So was my mom. Now here I am, hoping against hope I don't fail at this too. The longer I sit with the facts, the sicker I am of just surviving. I want to *thrive*. I want to feel my heart beating for something again. Hell, for *everything*. Since, sadly, it's been way too long since it has beat for *anything*.

THE DOOR TO UNCLE MARK'S LINCOLN PARK TOWNHOME SWINGS open, and there he stands with a smile on his face and his arms open wide.

"Finnley!" He gathers me into his arms and hugs me like I haven't been hugged in years. We have kept in touch for forever, even if we haven't seen each other much. If a day or two goes by without hearing from him or me responding to his texts, it's a big deal. "It's so good to see you." He kisses the top of my head and musses my long, dark hair. "I'm so glad you decided to do this."

He gently pushes me away, still holding on to my arms, and squeezes them. "Are you okay? You obviously found the place without much trouble."

"I had no trouble whatsoever." I leave out the part where I almost died on the concrete stairs of the Blue Line and smile at him as I hand over the bouquet of flowers I purchased when I was walking toward his place. The little stand I stopped at was so perfect, with all sorts of different flowers. I found a gorgeous bouquet of sunflowers, chrysanthemums, and gerbera daisies. They all looked happy and free.

"Oh, these are gorgeous. You shouldn't have." He smiles at them, then me. His hair is shorter than the last time I saw him, and aside from a little more salt and pepper, he looks so dapper. His mustache suits him; his smile is still incredible. The way being near him affects me immediately is exactly what I was hoping for.

"You look great," I say. "Have you been working out?"

He flexes his biceps. "I have. I joined this gay gym about three blocks from here. Still haven't picked up many men, but whatever." He waves his hand through the air, then his hair, before he grabs my suitcase and yanks it into the house as if it weighs nothing. He eyes it, the dented corners, the years of wear and tear, and laughs. "This thing has seen better days." He wheels it into a corner. "Are you hungry?" He smacks his hands together. "I'm making roast chicken, prosciutto-wrapped asparagus, and a grilled pear salad with honey-glazed pecans for dinner. I hope that's okay."

"My God, Uncle Mark, it sounds divine."

"Oh, great! Before we do anything else, let me give you the grand tour." He spins around, and the floral caftan he is wearing spins with him. "This is the entryway into the living room. I don't have a typical TV out here, so I had a large projector and screen installed. I'll show you how to use it once we get you situated. There are TVs in each bedroom, too, with an Apple TV attached.

Feel free to create your own profiles on all my subscriptions. I have them all. Including, Netflix. I almost got rid of it, though, since, y'know, I have no one to *Netflix and chill* with, and it depressed me." He shrugs, a sadness layered beneath his comedic demeanor. "Anyway, the rest of the house is awesome... Come on."

He waves for me to follow him. The dark, hardwood ceiling makes the entire space feel warm and inviting. He motions toward the kitchen and living room. "You'll see those when we eat. I want to show you your room and the rooftop oasis." His movements are so much more flamboyant than I remember, and, for whatever reason, it makes me love him even more. Almost as if seeing him comfortable in his own skin makes him a better person. Or a better version of himself? I don't know, but it's super refreshing. His giggle is adorable. "I am just so thrilled with this space, Finnley." The wall at the top of the staircase is constructed out of river rock. He explains how each stone was gathered from his travels. "This one is from Banff. And this one, Lake McDonald in Montana. So beautiful. I have a story for each one."

"I love this, Uncle Mark. It's absolutely perfect."

"It is, isn't it?" He stares dreamily at the wall before he spins and heads into another room. "This is where the magic happens." He winks, laughs, and I join in the laughter with him. There's a spacious balcony off his dark turquoise bedroom. "For entertaining," he explains while wagging his eyebrows. He has chartreuse velvet curtains, which he buries his face in after he tells me how much he paid for them in Paris last year.

"Your room is up one more floor. The only bad thing about townhome living in Chicago is every single room is on a different floor. You'll definitely get your steps in for the day." I follow him up to a floor that has a sliding door with frosted glass to the right; to the left is the room where I'll be staying. In the middle of the three-hundred-square-foot room, there's a king-size bed. The gorgeous navy walls make the room feel even more deep and spacious, and they're accented by yellow trim, wooden beams along the ceiling, and a lovely Turkish rug. The pictures on the walls are of Chicago landmarks like the Wrigley Building, Tribune Tower, Sears Tower (I will never call it Willis Tower), and the John Hancock Building. "One of my great friends, who you'll meet, curated this art for me."

"This is, wow, it's so much more than I ever expected. The entire space is bigger than every apartment I've ever rented." I move across the room, over to the bay window with a built-in, padded bench. "I'm going to read every single book I can right here."

"The light, Finnley. It's spectacular. In the morning, the sun hits the building there and illuminates everything in the room. It's simply marvelous. And the best part?" He grabs a remote. "If you want to sleep in, this controls the blinds." He passes it over to me. "You're going to love it here."

"I already do." I look out the window and take a deep breath. "I feel so at peace right now."

"Well, I've worked my ass off to make sure this entire place brings me peace, so I'm super thrilled to learn you're feeling it." He wraps his arm around my shoulders and pulls me in tight. "I've never been happier that you wanted to stay with me."

"Thank you for being cool with it and not asking me a thousand questions," I say, smushed against his chest.

"Oh, I plan on asking a thousand questions. Don't you worry."

I chuckle as I shake my head. "Damn."

"Anyway, let's go see my pride and joy, The Oasis!" He takes me by the hand, and we breeze over to the sliding glass door we passed on the way into my room. When he opens it, he reveals a large area with couches, beanbag chairs, a giant television, a bar, and a small, propane fire pit.

"Holy shit." I walk out and look all around. The walls are painted with a mural of flowers and birds in all sorts of bright colors. The words "Welcome to The Oasis" are cut from wood and hanging on the wall.

"I love to sit out here and read at night. Even in the cooler months, it's beautiful. And around there is the view." He points, and I walk around to the other side of the balcony, where I can see the skyline of downtown Chicago in the distance.

"Wow." I can feel the emotion rising in my throat. I don't know why tears are forming in my eyes, but I'm completely bowled over. Is it the fact that I'm going to live in this wonderful house for the next however many months? Or is it because my entire life has changed in the last two weeks?

"Yeah, it's a nice view." He puts his arm around my shoulders again. "I want you to know this place is your place now, okay? I want you to feel completely at home. What's mine is yours."

I can only nod because if I speak, the stupid tears in my eyes are going to escape.

"You can thank my career for all of this."

"Who would have ever thought a middle-aged gay man was going to make so much money as a model?" I glance up at him, and he licks his lips. I've never been completely convinced he only models, so I definitely dropped that line to get a response. He didn't budge. I'm not an idiot. Unless he's working the runway in New York City on the weekends, he's not making the kind of money it would take to buy this place.

"Yeah. Modeling. Certainly not me." He sighed. "Let's head back down and eat before Lisa comes over."

"*Aunt* Lisa?"

"Oh, honey. I have so much to tell you. Let's go."

I laugh as I follow him out of The Oasis, into the house, and carefully down the stairs to the kitchen.

"Wait, wait, you're telling me you two divorced and still talk to each other?"

"I mean, we *just* started talking again," Aunt Lisa says softly. "I'm hoping it continues, though." She's smiling her megawatt smile, her dark eyes filled with so much happiness. Her hair is the same jet-black it has always been, still long, and still pulled back into a French braid. The only thing different about her in the ten years since I last saw her is she has probably put on a few pounds. Shit, who hasn't, though? Well, Uncle Mark hasn't.

"We'll see if I can trust you again." Uncle Mark points at her. "Either way, it does seem strange seeing us back together, doesn't it?"

"I mean, no? It makes sense. You two were always so great together. Some of my favorite moments as a kid were when I got to come visit the city and hang out with you both. Like the time you took me to Lincoln Park Zoo." I sip from my own glass of red wine. I don't usually drink red; my head cannot handle it the next day. But they both promised me it was a great blend and I'd be fine. So far, they aren't wrong. It's delicious.

Uncle Mark sighs. "It really was too bad I didn't like your vagina."

Aunt Lisa's gasp is perfectly timed. "Mark!"

"What? It's true." He glances at me and winks, a wry smile tugging at the corner of his wine-dyed lips.

"Aunt Lisa, Uncle Mark, I've missed you both so much," I say.

Aunt Lisa reaches across the dining room table and grabs my hand. "I'm so glad you're here. But, Finn, you're thirty-two. I don't think you really need to call us Uncle and Aunt any longer."

I blink and purse my lips. "Um, that seems like something I'm gonna need to ease into. I've been calling you both Uncle and Aunt since I was a child. It's a hard habit to break."

"Ahh, you might as well give it a whirl. I'd like to seem as young as possible, and Uncle just…" Uncle Mark—I mean, *Mark* —shudders. "Makes me sound so old."

"Okay, I'll try to get used to it."

"Lisa, babe, you're still in for tomorrow night's dinner party?"

"Dinner party?" My heartbeat starts to thud rapidly. "Here?"

"Oh, Finn, just you wait, my dear. Mark's dinner parties are —" Aunt Lisa holds her fingers together by her mouth and pantomimes a chef's kiss. "You will not be disappointed."

"And I want you to meet everyone," he says, a twinkle in his blue eyes. "I think it's a good idea for you to—"

"Put faces with names?"

"Exactly."

"Because, correct me if I'm wrong, Mark, but I guarantee you'll be hearing a lot about them." Aunt Lisa laughs. "We're both catty bitches, aren't we?"

Mark—ugh, I can't do it. *Uncle* Mark shrugs. "Once a bitch, always a bitch."

I'm not necessarily one for dinner parties. I'm not great when it comes to meeting new people or being the center of attention. It's probably the klutz in me. And my inability to act cool and not say something stupid. Of course, maybe making some friends would be a good idea. The last thing I want is to be stuck in the house the entire time I'm living in the city. "Any cute boys who could possibly persuade me into standing my ground with my long-distance fiancé?"

Uncle Mark's eyes widen. "I thought you said you were breaking it off with him?"

My heart sinks. "I know, I know. I tried to. But he said no."

"No? What the hell?" Aunt Lisa scoffs. "Fucking straight white men and their audacity."

I laugh. "Honestly. It's an epidemic."

"Finnley, you're allowed to tell him no right back. You know that right?" Uncle Mark pats my hand affectionately. The only other person in my life who uses touch as a love language is Jesse. Usually, I am not the biggest fan of it. But with him it feels natural. And I like that a lot. I take a bite of bread from the half-eaten piece still on my plate, and chew, chew, chew, as if chewing will give me the right thing to say. Because somehow, saying I was too afraid to be entirely alone seems so fucking pathetic. I swallow the bite finally. "I just didn't want to break his heart."

As if *that* makes me sound less pathetic?

"You're going to break his heart eventually." Aunt Lisa pulls a deep breath into her lungs and holds it for one beat, two, before she lets it out slowly through her nose. "Might as well break it off before you accidentally cheat on him or something."

"Accidentally?" I laugh. "Is it ever really an accident?"

Uncle Mark huffs. "Your aunt would know."

"Yikes. Walked right into that one, didn't I?" Aunt Lisa shakes her head, never taking her eyes off Uncle Mark. "I cheated way before I knew he was gay. Hell, way before *he* knew he was gay."

I let my eyes wander from Aunt Lisa to Uncle Mark. "Wow. I'm going to learn a lot while I'm here, aren't I?"

"You certainly are." Uncle Mark's eyes are sad when he lifts his glass of red wine and swallows the last sip. "As for cute boys? There will be a couple of cute boys here, but they're all gay. Sorry."

"Don't apologize. I've always wanted to be the straight girl who hangs out with gay men." I beam with pride. "I am an ally, after all."

"Atta girl," Uncle Mark says before he stands, his chair scraping against the hardwood as he does. "Lisa, will you help me, please?"

"I can, Uncle Mark," I say.

"Nope, Lisa will because she just brought the evening to a nice, mellow low I wasn't expecting." He smiles, but his poise has changed drastically. I wonder why he's so hurt after all these years when he obviously didn't want to be in a relationship with her anymore. I'm sure part of it is simply dealing with the lie, the dishonesty. And maybe it's rubbing salt in an old wound.

Either way, Aunt Lisa purses her lips and stands, both hands on the tabletop as she rises. "I should have kept my fat yap shut." She grabs my hand and squeezes. "You go relax. I'll help him. I love you, babycakes. It's so good seeing you."

"It's so good seeing you too." I squeeze her hand back before she retreats to the kitchen. I admire the bouquet of flowers Aunt Lisa brought in with her—pink and yellow roses which mean friendship and irises for being thankful, which makes so much sense now. Learning about flowers and their meanings became a hobby when I was younger. It was probably an effort to try and like the landscaping field since it was going to be my job one day. Once I learned all the names of the flowers, I wanted to know more. My desire to learn is probably why I decided to get that damn MBA in the first place.

Ugh.

I still my movements and try to decipher their hushed whispers over the sound of the running kitchen sink. I can't make out enough to know what's being discussed. I'm sure it's not great. And it makes me sad my first night is ending like this.

Steven has called twice, and I can't bring myself to call him back. So I do something even more ludicrous.

I FaceTime my parents.

"How was the flight? Did you experience much turbulence? And that landing at Midway, right? Geesh."

I roll my eyes. They really don't listen to me. "Mom, I flew into O'Hare."

"Are you sure?" My dad asks as he pulls the phone from my mom so he's in the picture. Of course, it's just the top of his head. I honestly can't with them.

"I think I know what airport I flew into."

"Oh wait, I remember now," my mom says with a wave of her hand. "And you found Mark's place?"

"Yes, Mom. I'm not at some random person's house right now."

"And? Is it nice?"

"It's amazing. Here." I turn the camera so they can see my room. "And all the art on the walls are pictures of the city."

"That's an awful lot of room for you," my dad shouts into the camera. "I'll never understand how Mark affords that place. He must be doing something illegal on the side."

"Hank, stop. You know those fancy male models." My mom laughs.

"Why does it matter what he does, Dad?" I don't even know what to say to appease them anymore. Smiling and nodding is so much easier, but I also can't stand letting my dad get away with his stupid remarks. Sure, my mom's relationship with Uncle Mark has always made me scratch my head, but he's her brother. She's allowed to be however she wants. My dad, on the other hand, is a jerk, while Uncle Mark is one of the most amazing people in my life. I swear, the only reason my mom doesn't feel the same about his presence in her life is because she's married to my far-right conspiracy-theory-loving father. And it pisses me off.

"Have you spoken to Steven yet? He's going to miss you so much. He's a great guy, Finn. You need to keep your claws in him." My dad gushing over Steven makes me want to jump out the window.

"Yes, I texted him, Dad. Don't worry."

"A text? You need to call him. It'd be a shame if he found someone else to occupy his time with. You'd have to give that ring back."

I fucking wish is all I can think as I glare at the engagement ring on my side table. "I have everything under control, Dad. Don't worry."

"He's a good guy. I think he's the right one for you."

"Hank, leave her alone about Steven. Geesh." My mom turns

the phone so it's back on her. She rolls her eyes at him. One of the only things we have in common is how easily he gets under our skin. "Okay, honey, go get some rest. We love you. Have some fun while you're there, ok—?" She disconnects and cuts herself off before I can even say goodbye.

My dad lecturing me on Steven was definitely too much, though, so I'm glad the convo is over. I'm not usually a horrible person, but recently, especially when it comes to Steven, I can't believe how despicable I have become. My relationship with him has been a whirlwind. From tutoring his daughter in math to literally tripping over him in line at Starbucks (told you, I'm a klutz) to dating him for three months to reluctantly saying yes when he asked me to marry him. I never moved in with him as he begged me to do. And now? Now I've moved across the continent and cringe every time I see his name on my phone. What the fuck is wrong with me?

After I unpack my suitcase, I start to go through the six boxes I had shipped to Uncle Mark's—I mean, Mark's. Nope, can't do it yet.

It's disheartening that I've only accumulated six boxes of stuff in the last ten years. Of course, if I had more random shit to pack up, leaving may have been a lot more complicated. I should be thankful I only have six boxes. Some people have *sixty* boxes and must move them from place to place. They have to go through it every time they move.

I don't dislike having items or holding on to things that mean a lot to me. I simply refuse to keep a lot of clutter around. It makes whatever space I'm in feel even smaller. But now, as I finish unpacking the last box in the largest room I've ever stayed in, I realize I barely have anything of importance. There's my diplomas, which are essentially super-expensive pieces of paper at this point; a small photo album that holds pictures of my friends, including a best friend from high school who sadly never made it to graduation; a few accounting textbooks I no longer need since most of them are in the cloud; and my wardrobe. Hands down, clothes, shoes, and jewelry are the most essential items I have, and I own more than enough. To be honest, fashion is the only thing about being a girl I genuinely enjoy.

My mind keeps wandering to the conversation at dinner. I want to ask Uncle Mark why he's still upset about Lisa's—nope, *Aunt* Lisa's—indiscretion. I have never cheated on any of my past boyfriends. Oh, sure, I've been tempted, especially in my first year of college. Florida State was the first time I was on my own, away from my overbearing ultra-religious parents. Needless to say, I let loose. I was decent looking, y'know, for a recent high school graduate who never really had much self-esteem, and I was in the best shape of my life. Playing volleyball every single day will do that to you. Funnily enough, on the volleyball court is the only time I am coordinated, so it became an obsession. I started dating Joe about halfway through that first year. He was cute and I was bored so I said sure. I stayed faithful to him because that's what I was taught. But something inside me snapped one day, so I broke it off with him. He wanted more and I wanted, well, significantly less, I guess. Being tied down to him made me feel suffocated, claustrophobic, everything awful and nothing good all at once.

Which is how I always think about relationships, I guess. Being tied down. Ugh.

At this point, I don't know if I even want to be in a relationship at all. Ever. It may seem inconsequential, but that embarrassing moment I referenced earlier with my high school teacher? The whole experience was traumatic—and ended with me having to apologize to my teacher and his wife.

His *wife*.

My entire body shudders from the memory.

Relationships, in general, are difficult for me. I don't trust easily. I have a lot of issues when it comes to intimacy. And the last thing I want to do is snuggle. Jesse says maybe I need a fuck buddy. It's an interesting concept. For a best friend, she gives questionable advice.

"Finnley?" Uncle Mark's voice interrupts my thoughts, followed by a gentle knock on the door. I didn't close it, but I like that he's being so considerate.

"Come on in," I say as I pat the spot next to me on the padded window seat. The city lights glow amber in the distance.

"I'm sorry about earlier." He rubs his hands on his sweatpant-covered knees as he sits. He smells fresh and clean, like laundry detergent and fancy soap.

"Don't be sorry. I had a superb time catching up with both of you. I have to say, there's a certain symmetry to the fact you and Aunt Lisa are back together, but only as friends."

He sighs as he leans forward and props his elbows on his knees. "This is a new development, our friendship. She's been trying and I…well…I can't help but love that woman." His admission doesn't need a response.

I can only imagine how it must feel to love her in whatever capacity he does. I have very few words of wisdom to offer since I, truthfully, have never been head-over-heels in love. The silence is nice, and the desire to let it continue because saying the wrong thing would ruin the moment is deep. I finally settle on, "I know nothing about love, really, but yours for her? It seems to make perfect sense."

"Does it?" He looks back at me, and I give him a resigned nod. "I wish it made sense to me."

"Maybe that's why it makes sense. Because love so often doesn't, and for some reason, regardless of orientation, your love for her, her love for you, simply *exists*. It's poetic."

The deep sigh he releases says more than any words could, as do his red-rimmed eyes. "You're too smart for your own good, you know?" He nudges my leg with his. "I'm delighted you're here."

"Ditto," I say. "You are so much more *you* than I have ever witnessed and it's so refreshing." We sink into a few beats of silence. The notes of my Stevie Nicks playlist are floating around us, and he starts humming along. "You know you're the reason I have such great taste in music."

He lets out a laugh. "I am, hmm?"

"Absolutely. My entire library is inspired by the music you used to have blaring whenever I was with you and Aunt Lisa. Damn bunch of hippies, you two."

"I am honored." He stands and starts to spin and dance to the music, his voice matching Stevie's almost perfectly. He reaches out, his hands grabbing mine, and he pulls me from the window seat, twirling me around with little effort. I allow myself to enjoy the impromptu dance party. I spin, flail, sing, and laugh as the songs move from "Gypsy" to "Dreams" to "Landslide." I'm so very blessed the most exceptional man in my life is a mustached, middle-aged gay man with a soft spot for one straight woman and a deep, burning love for Stevie Nicks.

Thankfully, my klutzy side never makes an appearance.

CHAPTER TWO

I was seventeen the last time I was at a dinner party, and it was, not surprisingly, at Aunt Lisa's and Uncle Mark's. They made the most delicious food together, moving in the kitchen like a choreographed dance. Their friends were some of the most extraordinary people my young self had met. Before the indiscretions and the secrets, Uncle Mark and Aunt Lisa were so in sync it was magical to be around them. It was almost as if they were meant to have found each other, meant to be together, and meant to, I guess, eventually fall apart. I'll never forget how in love they seemed. Learning of their impending divorce was not easy for me. Aside from my parents' dysfunctional marriage, Uncle Mark and Aunt Lisa's was my gauge for what I should strive for. As I age and learn more and more about how the head and the heart function in a relationship, I realize sometimes *being in love* and *loving someone* are two completely different emotions. Most of the time, though, they look and feel eerily similar. It's shocking, really, that love can have so many forms, yet the end of love always hurts just the same.

Uncle Mark is handling everything without Aunt Lisa tonight. His cooking is phenomenal, obviously, after the delicious dinner he made the night before, and he made sure to tell me how cooking for this crowd was something he had been looking forward to for weeks. He did hire someone to help out, though. "I know it seems weird, but I wanted it all to be easier. Not just for me, Finnley, my dear. I didn't want to have you do anything either, and I would have for sure needed assistance."

I'm grateful I don't have to help. Not because I don't enjoy helping but because I have a feeling my very low entry-level skills in the kitchen are not what Uncle Mark needs. He needs a Gordon Ramsay, and I'm not even a Rachael Ray. I can tell by the way he keeps saying to the catering person he hired *baste the bird* with a wild gleam in his eye.

What I do help with is setting the table and making it look dinner party–worthy.

"Like Ina Garten would set a table now, Finnley," Uncle Mark says. "You can handle that, right?"

"Don't you worry. I can set a table. I can handle this. I promise."

He finally relents and points out his impressive collection of place settings and silverware. I pair the burlap-colored tablecloth he has suggested with black plates, gold silverware, and maroon napkins. The floral arrangement consists of deep pink roses, eucalyptus, sunflowers, and purple hydrangeas, all flowers meaning friendship, welcome, and love. I arrange the three separate vases and set them along the center of the table. They're all low enough that people should be able to see over them without issue. Everything comes together beautifully.

The glasses he wants me to use are a blush pink. At first I thought they would clash with everything, but they end up looking classy.

"Those were your grandmother's," he says as he carefully hands them over. "I had to fight your mother for them."

"Why? She never entertains anyone."

"Oh, Finnley, who knows? Your mother is a weird one. I'm sure you've grown to understand that."

I laugh because he is so very right. As much as I love my mom, she is one of the few people I can barely handle. She knows exactly how to twist the knife she so delicately slips under my ribs.

"Is this okay?" I ask Uncle Mark from the dining room after I've lit candles and dimmed the lighting. He stops in the doorway and gasps.

"Honey, it's *beautiful*! It's perfect. I... wow. I'm so proud of you." He fans his eyes with a huge smile spread across his face. "I'm so glad you listened to your inner gay man."

I swat him away playfully. "If you don't need me to do anything else, I'm going to go clean up for the party."

"Nope, you're good. But before you go, take this with you." He passes me an old-fashioned in a highball glass and winks. "It'll help take the edge off."

"I'm not nervous."

"Yes, you are, my dear." He winks again, and I don't fight him. He's right. I am nervous. I take a sip, nod my approval, and head to my room.

Before I reach the stairs, Uncle Mark stops me. "Finnley?"

"Yeah?"

"I'm really glad you're here. I've always wanted to have a roommate. Makes all of this," he motions to his surroundings, "worth it, somehow, y'know?"

"I'm so glad I'm here, too."

"Go get ready." He winks and I do as he says.

The guest list isn't too extensive, thank goodness. Timothy and Walter, a couple who have been in Uncle Mark's life since he divorced Aunt Lisa. Cecily and Francesca, a cute couple Uncle Mark said he stumbled upon, whatever that means. Aunt Lisa and a friend she's bringing, whose name is Emerson. And

Rebecca and Chaz, whom I know already. They were friends with Uncle Mark and Aunt Lisa when they were married.

I hope I'll be okay. I don't want to get too tipsy before people arrive because I don't want to be an annoying asshole, which can happen when I drink too much. I have the ability to be personable and fun. I just rarely let those parts of me really shine.

Ugh, what if I'm not fun?

I pull a pair of black velour leggings on over a black bodysuit and throw on a black-and-white houndstooth blazer. My long, wavy hair, which is usually very unruly, is behaving, and my natural auburn color is on point. I don't know what it is. Maybe the Chicago water? The fact I feel genuinely at peace for once? I don't know, but I'm digging it.

I throw on some powder, blush, and a slightly shimmery eyeshadow. I accomplish a perfect cat-eye with my eyeliner before applying mascara. I've been blessed with great eyebrows, so I barely have to touch them. I take a pair of tweezers to them every now and then, but otherwise, they behave.

I look in the full-length mirror. My gaze keeps focusing on the simple gold chain around my neck. Steven got it for me before I left. It feels heavy, and I find myself hating it more and more. "Take it off then, you asshole," I whisper as I reach around and unclasp it. The weight lifting from around my neck is intense. I breathe in deeply as I set it on the dresser. How can something so simple make me feel a thousand pounds lighter? I put on a new necklace, gold hoop earrings, and the watch my grandmother left me. It's an old Seiko she wore all the time. I used to love it when I was a kid, and of all the things she left to me, it's my most cherished. I slip on my gold-framed glasses and take a final look at myself. I turn, examine my leggings, my dark-red Doc Marten Chelsea boots I've had since college, and I nod my approval. "You look good."

The party starts in fifteen minutes. I'd better get down there before I hear Uncle Mark asking me if I decided—

"Did you decide to bail, Finnley? The party starts soon."

I chuckle as I head out of the room and downstairs, carrying my freshly emptied highball glass with me.

∽

AUNT LISA IS THE FIRST TO SHOW, AND SHE ARRIVES SLIGHTLY inebriated. She keeps apologizing about how her friend Emerson will be late. Uncle Mark seems annoyed that she has clearly been drinking already, but he gets over it as soon as Timothy and Walter show up.

They are so fun. I instantly enjoy their company. Timothy is an editor for a small publishing house and Walter sells Mercedes-Benzes. They brought their dog, a small cocker spaniel named Farrah. "After Farrah Fawcett, of course." When I sit next to them, she crawls into my lap and promptly falls asleep. Needless to say, I fell in love with her.

"If you ever need a dog sitter, I'm your girl," I say as we chat in the living room. Uncle Mark has the fireplace going even though it's May and not nearly cold enough. The front door has been propped wide open, and the windows are all cracked now to let in some cooler air. About fifteen minutes in, he waves me over to tell me to put on some music. I am under pressure, so I pull up my Taylor Swift playlist. So far, no one has complained. Thank God.

"Have you met Cecily and Francesca yet?" Timothy asks me when I re-join them. "They're perfect. You'll really like them."

"Oh, their story is so adorable." Walter shakes his head slightly, a smile on his face. "They were both dating the same woman, at the same time, and the woman broke both of their hearts. And then—"

"They found each other in Vegas," Timothy says, finishing Walter's sentence. His dark brown skin is flawless. And his teeth!

He has the most beautiful smile ever. Now, *he* could be a model. "It's so beautiful. I love it."

"Holy cow, that's intense." I lean closer to them. "How extraordinary their relationship survived at all."

"I met them through Marky. He's such a good person to meet people through. I feel like he's just like, y'know, a friend collector. He surrounds himself with all these wonderful people, and if you're lucky enough, you get to be included. I'm super thankful for him."

"Yeah, same here. And what a great way to put it, Timothy. A friend collector. I love it." Walter smiles again. He's gorgeous, with the bluest eyes I've ever seen and sandy blond hair. He and Timothy are so cute together. While I'm listening to them tell me stories about Uncle Mark, I realize again just how good I feel. How *not good* was I before all of this?

"Oh, there they are." Timothy stands as two women walk in. One has long, blond hair, and the other has long, dark hair. "Fran, Cecily, come here! You have to meet Finnley, Marky's niece."

"Oh my goodness, we have heard so much about you." The blonde leans in and hugs me tight. "I'm Cecily. This is my wife, Francesca."

"It is so great to finally meet you." Francesca hugs me next. She smells like honeysuckle. "Your uncle has not stopped talking about you since you said you were moving in."

"Oh, great," I say with a forced laugh. "All good things, I hope."

"Yes, Miss Harvard, all good things."

I feel my cheeks heat up.

"I'm glad you decided to give Chicago a shot," Cecily says before she answers Timothy's question about what they want to drink. "Tito's, rocks. She'll do Tito's and soda."

I smile. One day, I want someone to order *my* drink for *me*. I thought it was what I was getting with Steven, but after telling him seventy-five times I don't like rum, I realized wanting that in another person wasn't in the cards for me. "I'm glad too," I respond to Cecily. "I've always loved Chicago, so I'm excited to really sink my teeth into her, y'know?"

"You have your MBA, right?" Francesca wraps her arm around Cecily's waist. It's hard not to notice the way Cecily melts into her. I'm enamored with both of them instantly. "I think that's what Marky said."

"Oh, yeah, my parents own a landscaping business in Florida. They wanted me to get my MBA, so I did as they asked, then went back to work for them. Then, out of nowhere, my dad canned me." I shrug. No use in trying to sugarcoat it. They chuckle at my exasperation. "So here I am. I have an interview on Monday to be a small company's accountant."

"Anything sounds better than working for family," Cecily says, her face pulling the exact look mine probably has taken on now that I'm free of it.

"Seriously. And landscaping? It's so not my passion."

"What is your passion?"

Francesca's question slams into me. I open my mouth to answer, but nothing comes out.

"I have no fucking idea. God, how pathetic." I laugh, and they do as well, which helps me find my bearings. "Truthfully, I like numbers, but I'm not in love with accounting, y'know?"

"I can relate," Francesca says, followed by a sigh. "I was a bartender in Vegas for years. About a year ago, I finally finished my nursing degree. I like the nursing field, but… I don't love it."

Cecily smiles as she stares at Francesca. "You can do whatever you want to do, baby."

The love these two have for each other is palpable. I almost feel like an intruder in this conversation.

"Thank you, my love," Francesca says as she leans forward and kisses Cecily quickly on the lips. "Whatever path you choose," she says to me, "you let us know if there is anything we can do for you, okay?"

"Absolutely," Cecily agrees. "I have a lot of connections. You say the word, and we'll brainstorm with you."

"Thank you. That's, wow, super nice of you both." My heart has warmed from their sincerity. I feel better about my indecisiveness already.

"Cecily, Fran, I'm so happy you both could make it," Uncle Mark says as he glides over. His fitted black trousers and dark gray sweater look great on him. He's carrying their drinks on a small tray, but before he hands them over, he gives them both a side hug. "You both look ten years younger than the last time I saw you. Must be all the sex you have."

I feel my eyes widen, and Francesca and Cecily laugh heartily.

"He's not wrong," Francesca whispers with a wink.

I am in such a different world right now. My parents would never air their dirty laundry in public... And neither would Steven. Yikes.

"Did you get to see Rebecca and Chaz? They're so excited to see you." Uncle Mark puts a comforting arm around my shoulders. "You look lovely, by the way. I'm glad to see I don't have to help you with your makeup any longer."

"I love you, Uncle Mark."

"Just call me Mark, for Pete's sake! And call your aunt by her name. We love you. We know you respect us, okay?"

I nod. "Old habits die hard."

"I know, beautiful; I know. Go see Beck and Chaz. I need to steal Cecily and Fran for a bit."

I do as I'm told and take off in the direction of the kitchen. Timothy and Walter are in conversation with Aunt—*err, I mean*—Lisa, who says to me, "Chaz and Beck are upstairs on the roof."

I head up, nerves taking over. Maybe it's seeing people from my past? I'm so different from the person I was when I was seventeen. Back then, I was a dork who had no idea who she was or what she wanted. Well—wait. Maybe I'm not that different. I'm still unsure of who I am and what I want. Oh God. Either way, I'm literally the same person. This realization brings a whole new set of nerves to the forefront.

When I step into The Oasis, though, I hear Rebecca gasp and Chaz let out an excited squeal. "Holy shit, you grew up!" Chaz stands and pulls Rebecca up with him. "I can't believe this! Look at you."

Rebecca hugs me first, burying her face into my neck. "You are so beautiful and tall, and you just—wow! You look fantastic." She pulls away to study me fondly. "Just fantastic."

I am all smiles, too, both out of relief and because they look exactly the same as I remember. Rebecca's dark hair, maybe with a thread or two of gray, is pulled into a bun on top of her head. She's dressed in a trendy tweed blazer, black jeans, and Sarah McLachlan T-shirt, which makes me chuckle. And Chaz is in a tie-dyed Grateful Dead T-shirt with ripped jeans and lime green Adidas running shoes. He's always been a little on the stoner side, and I love it. I had no reason at all to be nervous. "You two haven't changed a bit. It's like I've traveled back in time."

Chaz gives my shoulders a squeeze. "Tell us about Cambridge. About college. About everything! Goddamn, we have missed you. You were by far our favorite of Mark's nieces and nephews."

"Well, that's great to hear," I say as I choose a non-beanbag seat.

Chaz passes me a vape pen. "Do you partake? It's the devil's lettuce."

I laugh. "Sure, what the hell?" I take a puff.

Why not? It'll relax me, that's for sure. Not that I'm not relaxed. I am. I totally am. Wait... am I? Oh, fuck. Who knows? All I know for sure is that I'm thrilled I'm here in Chicago. I'm delighted I get to meet all these terrific people. I'm ecstatic I get to see Beck and Chaz because it's been too fucking long. And I'm so very happy there is a vape pen in my hand because this is a party, and I haven't had this much fun in years.

∽

EVERYTHING UNCLE MARK HAS DECIDED TO SERVE TONIGHT HAS been phenomenal. The turkey is out of this world. The roast potatoes are delicious with this crispy outside that is to die for. The goat cheese and roasted beet salad is the best I have ever had. And the leeks are dressed to creamy parmesan perfection. I'm sure all of my tastebuds are on high alert because of the THC I inhaled, but who cares? I'm enjoying every last bite.

So far, the evening has been shaping up to be one of my favorites. By the time dinner was ready, everyone had shown up except for Lisa's friend Emerson. At dessert she checks her phone and announces they'll be coming in the next ten minutes. I'm intrigued as to who this mystery guest could be when, all of a sudden, the front door opens, and a female voice says, "Hey, hey! I'm here! *Finally!*" The voice continues to chatter as it approaches down the front hall. "I'm so sorry I'm late. I was held up at the gallery. You won't believe the new artist we've signed. They're mind-blowing. Seriously. And I had to do some finishing touches on the piece I've been working on."

And in rushes... this *woman*. Her honey-blonde hair, which is hanging in large, loose beach waves around her face, moves with her, almost in slow motion, as she glides into the dining room. Everything about her is flawless. Her skin, her makeup, her outfit, which is a very chic black suit. I can't take my eyes off of her. Even her hand movements as she waves her hellos to the people around the table. I am speechless.

"I was sure you weren't going to make it," Uncle Mark says as he stands and gathers her into his arms. "You had me worried sick."

"Emerson, babe, you had us all worried. I thought you'd been in an accident or something." Aunt Lisa is hugging her now, hand lightly patting her back. "You need to get a cell phone."

"I refuse to get a cell, you *know* that," Emerson says with a sardonic tone. "Everyone, hello, hello. I'm so sorry I'm late. Duty called. Pedaling art to the masses is not a job for the weak-minded. I'll hug you all when dinner is over." She sits next to Aunt Lisa with an exaggerated sigh. I wait patiently for her eyes to land on mine. I'm a new person at the table, after all. She's going to notice me, right? I'd notice me if I were her. But her eyes never land on me, and I can't decide if it annoys me or debilitates me.

"Here, I put this to the side for you, Emerson," Uncle Mark says. He places a plate in front of her. She grins at him, and I have to remind myself to breathe. "What would you like to drink?"

"Water, please. I got pretty stoned on the walk over, so I need to, y'know"—she moves her hands around her head—"re-center or whatever."

Everyone laughs, especially Chaz, who elbows me. "Same here, am I right?" His voice is probably whisper-soft, but I am so zeroed in on Emerson that I swear it sounds like he shouted it at me. I feel myself nod in agreement.

"Have you all been watching the latest season of *The Essence of Time*?" Emerson picks a piece of turkey up with her fork, pulls it off with her fingers, and places it in her mouth. She grabs a roll from Aunt Lisa's plate as well. Her jaw muscles flex as she chews. She licks her full lips before she takes another bite. I cannot stop watching her. It's the strangest sensation I've ever felt. "It's been such a fucking mind-trip."

"Oh my God, what a great show, though, right? Like, the writer is so spot-on when it comes to highlighting the struggle between classes." Cecily leans forward. "I saved two episodes to watch back-to-back last night and was just blown away."

"And the sex scenes are so fucking hot," Francesca adds with a laugh.

Emerson wags her eyebrows and points at Francesca. "Right? I mean, come on. The actresses they have put together have the best chemistry. Like, it's perfection. I'm so into it." She forks a piece of potato and places it into her mouth. She chews, chews, chews, and, sweet Jesus, the line of her jaw... I just... *holy shit*. She moans her approval, then swallows, slaps the table, and says, "Mark, oh my fucking God! These potatoes."

"I'm good, right?" He beams.

"They're orgasmic."

"Oh, Emerson, this is my niece, Finnley." I think he points at me, but I can't stop looking at Emerson long enough to make sure.

She makes the most intense eye contact I have ever experienced. *Finally.* "Hey there, nice to meet you."

I blink once, twice, three times before I realize I haven't responded. "Same. Yeah. To you, I mean. Nice to, uh, yeah, meet you, um, too." I choke the words out.

The rest of the table either senses I have completely lost the ability to function or they don't give a fuck because they decide to steer the conversation away from anything having to do with me. Either way, I'm grateful because I can't seem to string more than a couple of words together to form a comprehensible sentence.

Because *this woman...*

Emerson.

Her blond hair is a perfect complement to her fair skin tone. She's watching Lisa talk now, and when she licks her lips again, I notice how perfect their shape is. The peaks, the fullness, the mauve lipstick she's wearing, everything. She has the best lips I have ever seen on another human being. And, to make matters worse, she has a tiny mole between her nose and top lip. Like, how is that something I'm noticing? And why, oh why, that would make anything about this current situation *worse*, I have no fucking idea, but for some reason, it fucking does.

Cecily starts to speak now. She's sitting beside me, and Emerson has to shift her gaze across me to get from Lisa to Cecily.

Her eye contact is so powerful it's making my body temperature rise, and she's not even looking at me. As she listens to Cecily speak, I notice that her eyebrows are impeccably shaped. And her nose is adorable: the slope, her nostrils, the tiny, gold stud she has in the left one. Everything about this woman is fucking *perfect*.

For someone who has spent most of her life comparing herself to women, all I can do is admire everything about her. My attention to her details is bordering on obsessive.

Emerson reaches up with her right hand and threads her fingers through her hair near her temple, then tosses it lightly over her shoulder, exposing part of her neck, the part that can be seen over the collar of her white button-down. She's paired it with a loosely knotted black tie. She looks like she belongs in a goddamn magazine.

If *gawking* were an Olympic sport, I'd be at the top of the podium, for sure.

Suddenly it hits me. The idea that I'm being a fucking creep makes me stand abruptly, pushing my chair so hard it falls backward. Thankfully, Chaz catches it before it hits the ground. "Whoa, Nelly, you okay?"

"Uh, yeah, I gotta, um," I say, placing my hand on the chair to steady myself. I'm high as a kite and dizzy as fuck. "I have to, yeah, so BRB."

BRB? Oh my God. Please tell me I didn't really say BRB. What a fucking idiot.

I rush to the powder room, close the door behind me, and collapse onto it with my back. The flat surface beneath me. It's what I try to focus on because I need to bring myself down from the rafters, *stat*. I can hear them all laughing about something. Probably about me. About me saying BRB as if I'm a total child. What is going on with me? Is this the weed? It's gotta be. Right? Like, I'm *just* stoned, and things are weird. Every single thing is *weird*. It's making me hyper-aware of everything.

The loud knock on the door startles me so badly I let out a yelp and slap my hand over my mouth.

"Um, someone is in here," I mumble.

"Obviously," the voice from the other side says. I'm staring at myself in the mirror, and my eyes widen upon the realization that it's Emerson's voice.

"I'll be just one more second," I finally say. After adjusting my jacket, taking what feels like fifteen deep breaths, and running the water for good measure, I unlock the door and open it. Emerson is leaning against the wall. She is so fucking sexy. What the fuck? Why am I thinking that? Am I allowed to think that? What is happening to me? Her eyes connect with mine. I feel myself grip the door handle to steady whatever is happening to my legs. "Sorry about that."

"Sorry about using the bathroom?" Her tone sounds flippant, almost irritated, and my heart clenches.

"Um, no. I don't know." I want to crawl into a hole and die. "Anyway, here you go." As I step past her, my wobbly legs almost run me right into her, and I use the wall to keep me upright. She doesn't budge, doesn't immediately head into the powder room, doesn't do anything. When I glance back at her, she's staring at me, and I, being the klutz I am, and apparently, *the collector of embarrassing moments* that I am, run right into the wall next to the doorway I need to go through. "Jesus *Christ*." If I could evaporate into thin air right this second, I wouldn't hesitate to do so. "Watch out for this wall on your way back," I say, trying to make a joke out of it. "It'll jump right out at you."

"Thanks for the advice," she says, and the low lilt of her voice causes my entire body to flush with heat. I take one step to the left and rush through the doorway, making it a point not to look back. *Don't ever look back again, Finnley, you dumbass.* I know better. I know I'm a klutz. I know I have no coordination. Yet...

I find my spot at the table and lean into Chaz's space. "What the hell was in that pen?"

"Pot."

"And what else?"

"Nothing else, Finn." He laughs. "I mean, it's medical grade, but that's it."

"Florida doesn't have pot like that," I whisper. It's only after I am leaning back in my chair chuckling that I realize the entire table has quieted down and been listening to me. "I'm an idiot."

Chaz pats my knee. "No, you're adorable. Don't worry about it. We all smoke."

"Except me," Francesca says.

"Yes, you do." Cecily huffs. "Don't make her feel bad."

Francesca winks at me before she stands and holds her hand out to Cecily. "Let's go *not smoke* on the roof." Cecily is pulled up by Francesca, and they both follow Chaz upstairs. Timothy and Walter look at each other, shrug, and also follow them. Aunt Lisa is next. And before I know it, Uncle Mark is leaving me as well.

He pats my shoulder on the way out of the dining room. "Come on, slugger. Don't let the high leave too soon."

"I think I'm gonna take a breather for a second."

"Okay, well, come up soon. You gotta see The Oasis at night. You won't be disappointed." He squeezes my shoulder when I don't respond right away. "Are you okay?" He squats next to me, moving his hand from my shoulder to my hands, which, until he touched me, I didn't even realize were balled into fists in my lap. "What happened?"

"Nothing." My answer is quick, sharp, to the point. Because nothing is wrong.

"Finnley, your entire mood changed." He smiles. He's so *handsome*, so kind, so loving. God, I have missed being around him way more than I thought. "You can tell me."

"Have you ever—" My words catch in my throat. I stare up at the ceiling as tears start to form in my eyes. "I swear to God something else was in that pen," I say softly, and his lighthearted laugh brings me an ounce of peace. "I am having a midlife crisis at thirty-two, I think."

"Man, maybe something else *was* in that pen." He squeezes my hands, then takes one in each of his, unclenching them as he does so. "You are allowed to have break*downs*, break*throughs*, break*ups*, whatever you want, while you are here with me. I've got you, okay? And believe me, I have been through enough in my life to be able to help you through anything."

"Thank you, Mark," I whisper.

He gasps. "Oh, yeah, I like how that sounds. Mark. No more 'Uncle.' I feel younger already." The twinkle in his eyes is adorable. "Get yourself another drink, okay? Have some cake. Then come up and relax. I'll be spinning Florence + The Machine for the remainder of the evening."

"I wouldn't miss it for the world."

"Atta girl." He stands, leans forward, and kisses me on the forehead. "I got you, okay?"

All I can do is nod my response. I am torn between wanting to bawl like a baby and wanting to dance around free as a bird. It's the strangest feeling. I pull my phone from my jacket pocket. Seven missed calls from Steven. *Seven.* I haven't called him once since I've been here. I'm more than positive now isn't the time, but before I know it, I'm clicking through the lock screen to his contact info. It rings and rings. Am I getting lucky enough to get his voicemail? That would be fucking amaz—

He picks up. Dammit.

"Holy shit, Finn. I thought I was going to have to call the police or something. I thought you'd been kidnapped."

I regret calling him immediately. "No, just busy getting settled."

"How is it? Are you happy to be there?"

"It's wonderful. I'm so happy." I smile as I glance around the dining room, at the plates on the table, the used wine glasses, the empty bottles of red and white scattered on the credenza behind the table. "Super glad I'm here."

"Well, I miss you."

"It's been two days."

"I'm sure I'll miss you even more after three days. And four."

"Maybe by the fifth, you'll realize it's not me you miss." I hear what I've said, and I breathe in sharply. "I didn't mean that."

The pause from his end of the phone is unlike him. I can only imagine him, his messy red hair, his unshaven reddish-blond scruff, at the kitchen table in his khaki chinos and University of Tampa button-down, summer school lesson plans spread out in front of him. "What's going on, Finn?"

"Nothing, Steven. Nothing." My leg is bobbing frantically. Not a good sign. "I just wanted to touch base and let you know I'm alive."

"Wow, thanks." He huffs.

"Steven, seriously? Don't."

"I guess I should have listened to you when you said long distance wouldn't work."

"I gotta go," I say into the phone. "And yes, you probably should have listened to me." And I disconnect the call. Within seconds, he's calling back. I silence it. He calls again. I silence it again. And again. And again. I hold the power button down until the phone turns off. "What the hell am I doing?" My question is so loud, and not just because it's completely quiet in the lower level of the house. It's loud because it needs to be answered.

Who knows why I am doing this, though? If I don't know, no one else is going to. I need to let the answer come to me. The last twenty-four hours haven't shown me much, but I am slowly but surely coming to the understanding I wasn't happy in Tampa. I needed to leave, and the only way I would have was if my parents fired me. They both knew that, and, sadly, so did I. Now I need to figure myself out. How do I do that, though? I don't even know the questions to ask myself. Thirty-two years old, a shit ton of student loan debt, and not one fucking clue. Awesome.

Whatever the case may be, I one hundred percent should not be worrying about existential crises while I'm stoned. I stand abruptly, spin back to the kitchen so I can make myself another drink, and stop dead in my tracks when I see Emerson standing there, leaning against the countertop as if she's in some sort of photo shoot and the only direction she was given was "be sexy *and* mysterious," which, of course, she's nailed.

"Boyfriend?" She nods as if motioning to my phone call she obviously overheard. Her right eyebrow is arched, and I find myself wanting to know: Is it always like that? Or is she arching it on purpose right this very second? Whatever the answer is, my mouth has gone completely dry.

"Fiancé," I manage to rasp.

Her eyes widen the tiniest of amounts. I wonder if she meant for me to notice it. She pushes the rolled sleeves of her blazer up, revealing an anatomically correct heart tattoo on her left arm. "Sounds like a good guy."

Her tone is dripping with sarcasm and it has me feeling suddenly territorial. "He's not bad."

"Sure."

"He's not. You don't know him." Why is she assuming she knows anything about him? "He's actually very sweet." Ugh. No, he's not. Why am I lying now?

"Sure."

"Okay." I roll my eyes. "Why are you lurking around in here? Shouldn't you be upstairs with your friends?"

"Looks like they're your friends now too." She picks up a fork, slices it through the chocolate cake, and takes a bite. There's a spot of icing near the corner of her mouth. She chews, licks her lips, and still, the icing remains.

"You have a, um…" I motion to my own mouth. "A bit of icing…"

She takes a step toward me. I hadn't realized how far into the kitchen I'd gotten until she took that step. She's so close to me I can smell the chocolate on her breath mixed with the lavender-lemon scent of her perfume. "I do?"

I nod. It's all I can do. I'm too taken aback by the fact I can smell her. I can see the pores in her skin, the tiny hair follicles, and the slight shimmer of her makeup. Her skin is *flawless*.

She licks the corner of her mouth. I'd love to say my eyes are drawn to it again, but I'd be lying because I can't stop looking into her green eyes. A lump has formed in my throat. I try to swallow around it with not a lick of luck. "Did I get it?"

I haven't the foggiest. I can't look down. I'm frozen in place. "Probably." It comes out as a whisper.

"At least we can say with one hundred percent certainty you have great eye contact," she says, oh so softly.

I can feel the smile starting to form on my lips. The way my irritation is veering straight into captivation is only slightly annoying.

She raises both of her brows. "He's not bad, hmm?" I swallow again and try to answer, but nothing comes out. "That's good to know," she says as she moves past, leaving me standing there dumbfounded.

CHAPTER THREE

When I peel my eyes open in the morning, I'm immediately reminded why I don't drink more than one old-fashioned. My head is pounding, my stomach is queasy, and my extremities are trembling. Being hungover is not something I enjoy. Is there anyone who loves a good hangover, though? Probably not.

After I go to the bathroom, brush the bourbon fur from my teeth, and wash the rest of the makeup I didn't get the night before from my face, I creep back into my bedroom.

"Uncle Mark, what are you doing?" He's lying face down on my bed on the left side. He looks like he came in and passed out.

"*Mark*," he corrects me, his voice muffled by the comforter. "I am so hungover I could die."

I slide back under the covers. I've never been more thankful for the ultra-room-darkening shades. "I'm not in the best shape either."

"We need food."

"Yes."

"Do we want to go get it?"

"No."

He laughs, his face still buried in the comforter. "I think if we both get moving, we'll feel better."

"Is that usually how hangovers work for you?" I eye him warily as he rolls onto his back. Thankfully, he's fully clothed. I don't know why, but I assumed he slept in the nude. Gross.

"No. But we're gonna give it a go." He doesn't move. "As soon as I get up and get dressed." He still doesn't move. "In one second."

"Take your time."

"Jesus, what did I drink last night?"

"What didn't you drink?" My stomach churns at the thought of all the different shots we started doing. "No one in this group is twenty-one, so why were we acting like it?"

"The Oasis, man. It'll fuck you up."

I let out a very small laugh as I continue to rub my head. "We gotta make a decision. Are we going or not?"

"We are going. There's a cafe within walking distance. The fresh air will be good for us." He slowly starts to sit up, then stand. When he is on his feet, he groans. "And then we nap before dinner tonight."

"Dinner tonight?" I whine.

"Don't worry. It's pizza. No biggie. Just you and me."

"Oh, thank God." I roll off the bed onto my feet. "Can I wear yoga pants now?"

"I'm going to wear sweats, so yes." He turns, points at me. "This will be the one and only time I wear sweatpants out of this house, though. You hear me?"

I give him a very half-hearted salute. "Yes, sir."

"Be downstairs in fifteen."

∾

The cafe is exactly what I need, a little Greek-owned place where they have ninety things on the menu, all of them delicious.

When the server comes over to our table, Mark orders pancakes and bacon. "Extra crispy, please. Coffee, orange juice, and all the water you can bring."

The server, whose name is Joanne, laughs. "Mark, you feeling rough today?"

"I don't even want to talk about it, JoJo." He shakes his head. "This is my niece, Finnley, by the way. I think I told you about her."

"Yes, you did. How you doin', sweetheart? You hungover too?" She smiles, and all I can do is groan my response. "What'll you have, dear?"

"Eggs, bacon, hash browns, one pancake, and a cup of the chicken lemon rice soup. Please. And coffee."

"My lord." She chuckles. "Anything else?"

"Oh! A cup of the sausage gravy." I scrunch my face. "I like it on my hashbrowns."

"You're going to love this gravy too. It's delicious. Nico's specialty." Joanne whisks back to the kitchen and shouts, "Order," before hurrying back with our drinks. She even brings me water, bless her soul.

After my first sip of coffee, I start to feel slightly better. As Mark had said, the fresh air did help, but hydrating myself will help even more. At least, I hope so.

"Everyone loved you last night. I've had, like, fifteen texts about you." Mark sips his coffee, then takes a gigantic drink of his orange juice and smacks his lips together. "You were a hit, for sure."

"That's great news."

"Yeah, even Emerson sent a message. Not a text, of course, but she sent me an email. It's hard to get her to like anyone new."

"Oh?" My heartbeat quickens.

He waves his hand through the air. "She's just a hard sell."

I want to ask him to explain himself, but why? It's not like it will matter, and I have no idea why I want to know anyway.

Everything about last night is a blur. The few moments I can remember clearly are the ones with her in them, which makes no sense to me, of course. Like the time on the roof when she joined me as I looked at the downtown skyline and the gorgeous city lights and we stood there in complete silence the entire time. The only thing I could hear was her breathing. And I could smell the lavender-lemon scent surrounding her. And I could feel the heat from her body. And I could taste the bourbon from my drink even though I'd finished it a half hour earlier.

There has been exactly one person who made me question everything about myself. And now I can add Emerson to that list.

"What's her deal?" I hear my question before I have a chance to stop myself.

"Artists, y'know? She's on another level." He breathes in deeply. "And personally, I think she is super fucking bored. Not that there's anything wrong with being bored. I think a lot of us are bored with things in our lives."

"Oh?"

"She's been stuck in the same spot for a while." He leans forward and makes meaningful eye contact. "By the way, I'd tell her all this to her face, so it's not like I'm talking about her behind her back. I love her so much, and all I want is for her to be happy. She's one of those people who makes you want to pay attention, y'know?"

Yes, yes, I know. I know exactly what you mean. "Yeah, I guess I can see that."

He narrows his eyes as if he's unlocking some sort of combination lock. "Mmhmm."

"What?"

"You seemed pretty taken by her presence." His small smile is very telling. I just have no idea *what* it's telling.

"Oh, no, I was high as a kite." I force a laugh.

"Mmhmm." His eyes flit over to the door, and his smile spreads from small to large in an instant. "Well, well, well," he says before he raises his hand and waves to whoever has arrived. "Hello there"—he pauses for dramatic effect—"Emerson."

I practically choke to death on my sip of water.

"Mark, baby, I had a feeling you'd be here," Emerson says. "Care if I join you two?"

I turn to look at her as she approaches our table. She looks so much more laid-back today. Her hair is pulled into a low ponytail, with loose curls framing her face. The oversize cream sweater with black leggings and black combat boots is a far cry from the suit she was wearing last night. Even the black, puffy North Face vest she is wearing is laid-back.

The desire to get to know her that is overtaking my subconscious *and* my conscious? It's anything but laid-back, which is downright unnerving.

"Please," Mark says with a giggle. "You know I love our time together without Lisa hovering over the two of us."

"Yeah, she can be a little overwhelming, can't she?" Emerson slides into the booth next to me. "This okay?" She is looking at me now, her lips curling into a smirk as if she knows her presence has affected me in a way that I will spend the rest of the afternoon, evening, and entire next day trying to comprehend.

"Absolutely." My response is too soft, but repeating myself will only make me sound like an even bigger dork.

"Last night was fun," she says to Mark. "So fun. Thank you so much for hosting." She grabs my water and moves the straw so she can drink from the rim. My eyes are drawn to her lips, to the way the red, plastic diner cup is pressed against them. The amount of heat in my body at the moment, I have no doubt, would burn an entire mountainside to the ground. "Did you have fun, Finnley?"

I jerk my gaze away from her and focus on the straw wrapper I was fidgeting with earlier. "I did, yes."

"You hungover?" Emerson nudges me. "Or did the crossfading help you out?"

Her gentle nudge is unexpected. "I'm very excited about food," I say, followed by a small laugh. "So, yeah, I fear I'm hungover, unfortunately."

"Damn, I feel great this morning. You two are rookies."

Mark gasps. "Hey now! What do you mean 'you two'?"

"C'mon, buddy, I could tell from the second I saw you that not only are you riding the struggle bus, but you're also the driver." She reaches over and pats his hand. "You're getting old. It's okay, babe."

"Oh, shut up," he says. "I am not."

"What's on the rest of your agenda today?" She drums her fingers on the Formica tabletop, and I notice a ring on her left ring finger that wasn't there last night. I'm instantly filled with questions. Well, one question in particular: *Is she married?*

"I don't know what's on Finnley's agenda," Mark says, "but there is absolutely a nap on mine. And a shower. Then dinner. What about you?"

"Heading to the studio for a few. I'm putting together an exhibit. You should come to the show next month." She looks at me. "Unless you want to come see the studio with me after breakfast?"

I freeze. What? Did she just ask me to come with her? I've opened my mouth to answer when Joanne rushes over with a tray filled with food. As soon as she sets the four plates containing my meal in front of me, I am instantly self-conscious. My face fills with heat as I berate myself for ordering so much. Could I look any more like a pig?

"Emerson, baby doll, how are you?" Joanne asks, and Emerson stands to hug her. "It's been far too long. You're finally back in town!"

"Yeah, the Big Apple was fun, but you know Chicago has my heart."

"You want the usual?"

Emerson's smile is gorgeous. "You know it. And can I get a

hot chocolate?"

"You bet, baby doll."

Emerson sits down again, then turns toward me. "So? You wanna come with?"

I have no idea how to answer. Last night was so weird, and today she's being really cool. Maybe I should just go and get to know her. Everyone seems completely enamored with her, so I'd be jumping on the bandwagon, apparently. So, yeah, just go, right? Then again, lounging around and taking a post-hangover nap does sound tempting…

"I promise I don't bite."

"Hard," Mark adds under his breath.

I snap my eyes to his "What? I didn't say anything" face and finally reply, "Uh, yeah. Yeah, I'll go with you. Sure. Why not?"

Her soft snort makes me wonder if my thoughts were a lot louder than they sounded in my head. "Great. I promise not to wear you out."

It's Mark's turn to snort.

I am so confused now. "What?"

"Nothing," Mark says, low and from around a piece of wheat toast he's snuck from my plate. "Nothing at all."

~

THE REST OF BREAKFAST IS FINE, EXCEPT FOR THE MOMENTS I spend worrying myself sick about being alone with Emerson, which, let's be real, is *the rest of breakfast.*

As we walk down Halsted together, I will myself to stop obsessing. There is no reason to be this in my head about hanging out with this woman. She's *just* a person, for Christ's sake. That's all. A very intriguing, very beautiful person.

A shudder runs through my body. I take a deep breath, hope she didn't notice, and shove my hands into the pockets of my Harvard hoodie.

"It's a lot cooler today than yesterday. You okay?"

Shit. She did notice. "Yeah, I'm good. Thank you."

"Probably a lot colder than Tampa, right?"

"Absolutely. I think it's, like, eighty-five degrees there today." We've resorted to talking about the weather. Great. Real fucking cool, Finnley.

A minute passes, our shoes on the concrete the only sound I can focus on. I've been looking down the entire time, which is so not like me. I love walking around the city, taking it all in. I am so unnerved by her, though. By Emerson. What the fuck kind of name is Emerson, anyway? Pfft.

She looks over at me. "You okay?"

Shit, did I *pfft* out loud? Oh, Lord. "Nothing."

"What?"

"I mean, yeah, I'm good. Sorry."

"You're a ball of nerves right now," she says, her tone a mixture of warmth and playfulness, as if she's slightly amused by the fact I'm a nervous wreck. "Talk to me. What's going on?"

"Honestly, I'm fine."

I lie because I hardly know her. Why does she think I'll talk to her and share whatever is going on with me? I would *never* open up to a new person like that, and not just because it has to do with her. I'm also not the most trusting person in the world.

"Interesting."

I finally look over at her, at the way she's studying me, and aside from the heat filling my abdomen, I find myself irritated by her tone. "What?"

"You think you aren't transparent."

"Excuse me?" I stop dead in my tracks. It takes her two and a half steps before she realizes, turns, and moseys back to me.

"What?" She smiles, her right eyebrow quirks upward, and my question from last night is answered. She simply does that. *Goddamn.* "Don't get upset with me. I'm only trying to get to know you."

"Oh."

"Here's a thought, Finnley." She has her hands in the pockets of her puffy vest, so when she moves them, her vest opens. "Maybe don't assume everyone is out to get you."

"I don't assume that."

"You don't?"

"No," I say defiantly. "I barely know you. I just…" My voice has trailed off, and my defiance goes with it. "I don't know why… I'm nervous. I'm sorry."

"Don't apologize." She reaches up and tucks my hair behind my ear. Her fingers are warm against my skin. "You apologized last night, too, and you hadn't done a thing wrong."

"I'm sorry," I whisper. I smile when she does because she understood my joke. My very stupid joke.

"Come on." She takes a step in the direction we were headed and motions for me to join her. When we're both walking again, I hear her take a deep breath, hear the way the air passes through her nostrils, and, I swear to God, I can even hear the way the breath fills her lungs. "Tell me about your fiancé."

Ugh. I'd rather talk about literally anything else. "His name is Steven. He's a professor at the University of Tampa." I search my brain for details I know were present two days ago. "He's thirty-eight. A dad." She looks at me. "Not mine. Obviously." I laugh. "I mean, not my kid, not that he's not my dad. Jesus. I just mean—" I run both of my hands through my hair. It's a nervous habit I have been trying to break, but here it is, rearing its ugly head. "Her name is Rory. She's sixteen. Her mom, his wife, passed away when she was five." I don't have the heart to tell Emerson how I have never wanted to be a mom.

"And he's not bad," she says, quoting me from last night. Her small smile on her perfect, pink lips has my heart in a vice.

"Yeah, he's not bad."

"Is he *good*, though?" The quick breath she pulls in after her question is doused in *something*, but what? She waves her hand through the air. "That's not cool. Don't answer that. I'm glad he's not bad. When's the wedding?"

I want her to explain herself, but I wouldn't even know what to ask in order to get what I want. "We haven't set a date." I shrug. "He's *not* good." I confirm what she somehow already knew. "Not for me, anyway. I tried to break it off with him, and he wouldn't let me."

She lets out a solitary laugh. "He wouldn't let you? What does that even mean?"

"I know, it's insane. I told him I was leaving and maybe we should reconsider marriage, and he promised he'd move to Chicago, and I didn't want to fight with him, so..."

She shakes her head. "Finnley, my dear, you're going to have to do something about him before he's standing on Mark's doorstep."

I groan. "Believe me, I know. He's called me, like, fifteen times since last night." I hold up my phone. "Strike that. Eighteen times."

"Jesus."

"Yeah, I'm a coward. I'm hoping he just, like, gets the hint or whatever."

"Yes, you're a coward." Her laugh is so lovely. "But"—she glances at me—"I get it."

"Thanks." My voice is so quiet I barely hear it. I hope she did.

As we're approaching a large, colorful brick building, she smacks her hands together. "This is it." The sign out front reads *The Living Room, An Eclectic Art Gallery*. She pulls out a keyring, unlocks the large, wooden door, and slides it open. "It's open air, even in the winter. I had heat fans installed, so it pushes the cold air out and allows us to keep the doors open. It gets a little chilly sometimes, but now that we're in the warmer months, it's been awesome. Here, come with me."

I follow her through a maze of white walls, around empty pedestals and blank canvases hanging from the ceiling. She did say they were getting ready for a show, so I'm assuming this place will be transformed in the coming days. We are approaching a door toward the back, similar to the entryway. She slides it open to reveal a huge warehouse. It has about fifty small areas with each artist's work displayed, and there are people everywhere inside it. There is a row of sculptors with their sculptures, clay wheels with all sorts of creations, canvases upon canvases, photographs of all shapes and sizes.

My entire body is covered with chills. "Emerson, this is outstanding."

"This is what I always wanted." She waves a hand across the warehouse. "I give each artist a place to do their art if they want to, but mostly they house whatever they'd like to put in the show here. I give each one a chance to showcase five pieces." She points to a young girl in the corner. "Beth Weber is in from Italy for two months to show her paintings. And over there is Hans Steidler; he's a sculptor from Germany. And at the back, there is this new photographer, Tania. I just signed her. I'm very pumped about her work."

"I love it. Everything about it."

"Thank you," she says, still beaming. "The area we walked through will be completely transformed by the exhibit night."

"Will they sell their work?"

"At the last ten shows, every single piece sold, and not a single piece went for less than five thousand dollars."

I gasp. "Holy shit."

"I know." She places her hand on the small of my back. I look at her, at the softness of her features in this moment. The awareness slams into me that I will remember everything about this second for the rest of my life. "Do you want to see my work?"

My voice has abandoned me. I can only nod. As I'm following her to another part of the warehouse, I brace myself for whatever is about to happen. We turn into a well-lit office space. "Emerson," is all I can say as I'm standing there looking at the paintings in front of me. There's a large skeleton painted onto a huge, black canvas with all sorts of flora and fauna growing from the bones. There are flowers of all shapes and sizes, moss covering some of the bones, grass in areas where organs would be. It's so weirdly beautiful that I can't stop staring at it. The expression on the skeleton's face... It sounds so crazy, but he looks *happy*. How is that possible?

"I call it *deComposition Paper*." She turns and points at another large black canvas with a painting of lungs filled with flowers and leaves. "*A Breath of Life*." She walks to the other side of the office and motions to one that has a human heart on it, similar to the tattoo on her arm. "I haven't decided what else to put on this one, though. I have a few weeks to figure it out."

"I love them." I look at her, at her face, at the joy in her eyes, at the pride in her smile. "You're so talented."

"No, I'm not." She nods toward the warehouse. "They are the real talents. I'm a hack compared to them."

"Don't do that." I haven't stopped looking at her. "Don't belittle yourself."

Her face twists, and then a grin spreads across her lips. "Wow. Look at you, taking a stand."

"Well, don't. You are talented. I wouldn't say it if I didn't mean it." I place a hand on her arm and push her gently. "I'd buy one if I wasn't poor."

"Noted." She backs away from me, a look on her face that makes me think she's working something out in her head. I want to know what. I need to know. But it's too soon to ask. "I'll walk you back to Mark's."

"Oh." I don't mean to sound so defeated. "No, you don't have to. I can make it on my own."

"I don't mind, though. My place is right around the corner from his." She flips the light switch off, leaving me standing in the dark. "Take advantage of my offer," she shouts while walking away.

Confusion courses through me as I rush after her. We walk in silence through the warehouse, back through the maze of the showroom, and out the front door. After about two minutes, I can't handle it any longer. "Emerson?"

"Hmm?"

"How old are you?" Really? That's what I want to know?

"Forty-three."

"You don't look a day over thirty-five."

"Oh my God. You need new glasses."

I adjust the pair of tortoise-shell framed glasses I have on. "These are actually a brand new prescription," I say as I nudge her, trying to lighten the mood that has somehow become heavier in the last fifteen minutes.

"You need a new doctor then."

"Well, either way, you're gorgeous."

Her cheeks have turned a lovely shade of pink, and she looks down as if she's trying to hide her sly smile. "Thank you."

"No, thank *you*. Seriously. For getting me out of the house and taking me to your studio. It's been amazing."

"You're welcome."

"Did you always want to be an artist?"

"That's better," she says softly. "I mean, my age? Really?"

"I know, I know. I told you, I'm nervous."

"Still?"

I shrug. "The nerves are fading. Slowly."

"Good." She slows her pace a tiny amount before she answers with, "I guess technically, no, I didn't always want to be an artist. I was a high school art teacher for about ten years. That's how I met Mark. We taught at the same high school together. Then I started teaching at Columbia College downtown. I loved teaching about art, sure, but my real passion is curating it. Finding the talent is a drug for me. I swear, when I stumble across a new artist with a new style, it's a high I cannot replicate." I am so enthralled by every word she's saying, by the passion behind her tone, I don't even realize we are now standing in front of Uncle Mark's townhouse until she leans against the wrought iron fence surrounding his tiny front yard. "You're very easy to talk to."

I blink as if I'm trying to break out of the trance she has put me in. "Ditto."

She laughs, low and smooth. "Do you think you could talk to your nerves and settle them down so we could hang out again?"

"Ha!" I shake my head. "If only it were that easy. But yes, I would love to hang out again."

"Are you busy tomorrow?"

"I have an interview tomorrow morning. But after, I'm free as a bird." I cringe. "I swear I don't always sound like an old man with my weird sayings."

"You're adorable." Her eyes are sparkling, and her words hit me square in the chest.

"Well," I start, pushing down the nerves begging for me to let them run rampant. "I'll try to be adorable tomorrow too."

"I'm sure you will be. Good luck." She pushes away from the fence and heads down the street. "I'll meet you at The Bean at noon. Come hungry." I watch her until she turns down the next street, wondering the entire time what the hell just happened and why I'm feeling the happiest I've felt in quite some time.

∽

My phone buzzes to life on my side table. I grab it, hoping that it's Jesse because I have so much to talk to her about. I feel my face fall when I read the name on the screen.

Steven.

My thumb hovers over the "Decline" button. He is the last person I want to speak to right now. But eventually I decide I've left him dangling long enough, bite the bullet, and answer it.

"Hey," I say, trying to sound happy to speak to him. It doesn't work. I sound irritated. Which isn't far from the truth.

"Wow, you answered. That's amazing," he says with a laugh. "You still mad at me?"

I search my memory bank. Oh, yeah, last night. "I'm tired, Steven. That's all." I lie back on my bed, secretly hoping my phone dies. Not the battery. The entire phone. Just dead.

"Hungover today? You were pretty tipsy last night."

I sigh. "I was earlier. Feeling better now."

"Did you have a good night then?"

My mind flashes back to Emerson, to her face and hair and outfit and the way she held my attention without realizing how taken by her I was. "It was good, yeah."

"You're not super talkative. Everything okay?"

Ugh. No. I don't want to do this anymore. "Yeah, everything's fine."

"You sure?"

"Actually, no, Steven, I'm not sure. I really don't think we should try to do this long-distance thing. I'm just not feeling good about it." *Whoa.* I shocked myself with those words.

He laughs. "Finn, you're freaking out because of the big changes in your life. That's all. You love me. I love you."

"You sure about that?"

"I am sure. I know you love me. It's okay."

Aunt Lisa's words from the other night come back to me. Straight white men and their audacity. "You're pretty cocky for someone who has no right to be that way."

"Ahh, there you are. The Finn I know and love." His laughter makes my skin crawl. "You're okay. You'll be back one day, and we'll finally get married. Everything will work out."

"Do you actually hear yourself? What about me not feeling comfortable about this means I'm going to just move home and marry you?" I'm trying to maintain my composure, but he's not listening to me, as usual.

"Listen, Finn, I know you. You don't like change—"

"Yes, I do! I've never hated change."

"I don't think that's true."

"What in the world are you talking about?" I sit up. I can't handle him any longer. "You don't know me at all."

This sets him back on his heels, but only for a moment. Finally, he rebuts, "I think you're picking a fight with me to make yourself feel better about missing me."

"Oh, my God!" I yelp. "Steven, I am hanging up. I try to talk to you, and you don't listen. Have a good night."

I disconnect the call before he gets a chance to say another word. I toss my phone away from me when it starts vibrating again with yet another call from him. My blood is boiling. I just can't with him. Not tonight.

⁓

THERE ARE THREE THINGS CHICAGO CAN DO UNEQUIVOCALLY better than anywhere else: hot dogs, popcorn, and pizza. I'm sure some people would fight me over the pizza, but I'm going to stand firm on it because not only can they do *typical-crust* pizza well, but they also do deep-dish pizza. And Pequod's is the best deep-dish pizza I have ever had. The first time my parents took me to Chicago to visit Uncle Mark, we went to Pequod's, and I remember thinking I wouldn't like it. I was a picky child and disliked anything that wasn't Kraft Mac & Cheese or Pizza Hut personal pan pizzas. I grew up, thankfully. Either way, that was the day I became a fan of deep-dish pizza.

The memory of the deliciousness is causing my mouth to water. As Uncle Mark and I sit at the small booth in the bar area of the Lincoln Park Pequod's, my eagerness to get the cheese pizza we've ordered is palpable—and very drooly. I've barely had anything to eat since breakfast because, truth be told, once I came upstairs after my afternoon with Emerson and had that awful conversation with Steven, I sprawled out on my bed and passed out.

"You are very quiet tonight," Uncle Mark says as he lifts his beer to take a sip. We're seated in the bar area. My eyes keep wandering to the TV where the Bulls are playing the Knicks. I've never been a huge basketball fan, but I do enjoy the Bulls. "Penny for your thoughts?"

"I think the events of the last two days have finally caught up with me." It's not a lie, just not the whole truth. "Maybe I'm getting too old for all-night drink-a-thons."

The laugh that pops from him is adorable. "Oh, babycakes, you have no idea what this summer is going to have in store for you. I should have warned you so you could start conditioning."

"Probably would have been a good idea." I drink my own beer and hope the ol' *hair of the dog* saying is true because it's way past the time when a hangover should still be hanging on, and yet here we are. The breakfast food extravaganza didn't help; the copious amounts of water I drank didn't help; the fresh air didn't help; Emerson didn't help. At this point, beer is my last-ditch effort. Well, beer and pizza.

"How was your afternoon with Emerson?" The way his eyebrows wag makes my stomach bottom out. "Did you like the studio?"

"What's that?" I point. "Why are you moving your brows like that?"

He lets slip a small gasp. "Whatever do you mean?" Hand to his chest, he smiles at me. "I'm simply asking how your afternoon was."

He's lying, but I have no idea why. "It was fine," I answer, narrowing my eyes at him. "You're being weird."

"Nope, I just want to make sure you enjoy your time here. That's all." He smooths out the paper from the straw. "Speaking of enjoying your time, how's Steven?"

I glare at him. "Uncle Mark, please."

"Mark," he corrects me. "And I think it's important you and I have open lines of communication at all times. Sure, there may be moments when you want to be left alone, and vice versa, but we have to be able to tell each other things. And this is a pretty big thing in your life you sort of, *pfft*..." He waves his hand through the air. "Like, you peaced out on your fiancé. That's a monumental moment we should discuss before you continue to ignore all of his phone calls and he winds up on my front porch at two in the morning while you're in bed with someone else."

I can feel my jaw drop open as I stare at him. "What in the world? Do you really think I would do that?"

"Do I think you'll cheat because you're a horrible person? No."

I breathe a sigh of relief.

"Do I think you'll cheat because you are so not happy with him? Abso-*fucking*-lutely." He shrugs. "Finnley, baby, I know you. Not only have I known you since birth, but I'd like to think we've gotten fairly close over the years. And you, my dear, do not like to be unhappy. You may think you're happy, but everything in your movements, your carriage, your demeanor, says otherwise. You would have fought with your parents for your job if you were happy. You would have never moved here if you were happy."

He's not wrong, but damn. "And to think I thought this was going to be a drama-free night."

"I love drama, and you know it." The way he reaches across the table and smothers my hand with his is calming. My entire body relaxes.

"I sort of hate how right you are."

"I know." He squeezes my hand again. "It helps to go ahead and admit I'm always right."

I chuckle, suddenly uncomfortable with the emotion bubbling into my esophagus. I move my hand away and rake my fingers through my hair, breathing in deeply as I do. "I should have broken it off with him. Why didn't I? Live and learn, I guess?" I can't bring myself to make eye contact with my uncle because I'm on the verge of tears. If there's one thing I hate, it's crying in front of people.

"Maybe that's a conversation you should have with him in the next couple of days? Just, y'know, like, 'Hey, Steven, I think maybe I don't love you and don't want to marry you and be a mom.' Short, sweet, to the point."

"How did you even know I don't want to be a mom?"

He tilts his head. "You're joking, right?"

"What?"

"You have never been a kid person. Even when *you* were a kid, you didn't like kids. Every other child I know runs up to the babies they see, all interested, wanting to hold the baby, feed the baby." His imitation of a child's voice is hilarious. "You were always standing at the back of the room, a disgusted look on your face."

I snort. "You're so right."

"I know. I'm always right, remember?" He drinks from his beer, rubs his hand over his mustache, then leans over the table. "You are allowed to be *who you want to be*." He accentuates his words by tapping his index finger on the tabletop. "Stop thinking you have to fit into a mold you don't want to fit into." He scoffs. "Would you have really wanted your parents' lawn care business? I mean, come on. Is that even what you want to do? Can you honestly, in your heart of hearts, tell me you want to run your father's failing, holding-on-by-a-thread business? For the rest of your *life*?" The groan he lets out causes me to smile. "You know, I was trapped in a job I was told I wanted. Sure, I was a great high school teacher, but once I decided to get out of it? Man, the sky's the limit."

I blink a couple of times. Now's the time to ask him what he actually does because I'm even more sure that he's not really a male model. I knew he left teaching. And I knew he was super happy and fulfilled. But... "Um, so, weird question."

He raises his eyebrows, a sly smile on his lips. "Yeah?"

"What *do* you actually do? Because I think I'm starting to realize you don't actually model…"

He comes right out with it. "I'm a high-end escort."

And there goes my jaw again. "Excuse me?"

"You heard me right."

"Holy shit. I thought you were going to say drug dealer or maybe you got rich in the last crypto-currency rush."

He laughs. "No. I'm an escort. And get this…" He leans forward again. "For women." When he leans back, he nods, his blue eyes twinkling. He can see the shock on my face; I'm sure of it. A fucking satellite orbiting the earth can see the shock on my face, and I'm not even standing outside. "Mmhmm. I know. It's crazy, but I honestly love it."

"Mark," I say, and I hear the way my voice is strained. Why is this knocking the wind out of me? "Like, *escort* escort?" He nods. "Wait, like, you have sex *with* women?" He nods again. "But you're gay."

"As the day is long."

"And you enjoy it?"

"I still find women attractive; I just am more attracted to men. And, I mean, I enjoy making women feel good." He shrugs. "I do whatever they want."

"Like, what do you mean?"

He puffs his cheeks, blows the air out between us, and then shakes his head. "Sexually, whatever they want. But…" His face softens as he swipes his fingers along his forehead. "A lot of them? They simply want to be *held*. Isn't that sad? Or they want to go to dinner, be taken care of, have the door held open for them, hold hands with someone. It's…" The sound of his voice as it trails off hits me square in the chest. "It's changed my life. Everything about it. It's made me happier, more open to new things, and it's made me a fan-fucking-tastic listener."

I let out a chuckle. "Holy shit, Mark." He smiles because I once again left off *uncle*. "You aren't kidding."

"I am not kidding."

"Does everyone know?"

"My closest friends, yes."

"Does—"

"No, your mother does not know. Your father does not know. And I do not want them to, okay?"

"I would *never* tell them. Honestly, I would never tell them anything we talk about anyway. These conversations are too special to share."

"Aww, Finnley, I agree." He grips his Chicago Bulls T-shirt over his heart. "I'm just so glad you came to stay with me."

"I am too."

An easy silence falls between us as the restaurant starts to fill. The Bulls are winning, but only by a couple shots. Every time the ball goes into the air, the whole restaurant takes a breath. Boston, Tampa, Chicago, it doesn't matter—all sports fans are rabid, but Chicago fans seem as if they have had to fight tooth and nail to get every win. Tonight, I find myself so much more invested in all the Chicago games than I have been in the past. Probably because I need to focus on something else at the moment. Take my mind off the truths falling like bombs. The idea of needing to break it off with my fiancé, and that conversation's inevitable fallout, makes me want to combust.

In spite of all that, I haven't felt this light in years. I learned some pretty intense information about my uncle, I admitted to myself that I need to break it off with Steven, and I was told point-blank that I am not happy. Yet here I am, feeling good, feeling calm, feeling every feeling.

The gasps as Zach LaVine shoots a three-pointer, the "awws" when the Knicks' center, Hartenstein, pulls down the rebound, the crowd going wild...

Is this what happiness feels like?

At eleven that night, I hear Uncle Mark's alarm from his bedroom. I lie in bed, my nightstand light on, listening to him getting ready. At least, I assume that's what is happening. The shock has worn off from finding out he's an escort. A *high-end* escort. I feel myself smiling. *Uncle Mark is a prostitute.* A laugh bubbles from me, and I rub my hands over my face. *And he sleeps with women.* What a twist!

Before long, there's a gentle knock at my door.

"Come in," I say.

The door swings open, revealing him standing there in a tailored, navy blue suit, a white button-down with the top button undone, and brown wingtips. His salt-and-pepper hair is styled, but it still looks a little messy, as if he meant to leave it like that. He's also freshly shaven, except for his mustache, and damn, he looks really good.

"Wow."

"I look okay?"

"You look handsome as fuck. Especially for eleven on a school night."

He laughs. "I wanted to ask you before I leave: How do you want to do this? Like, do you want me to tell you when I leave? Or do you want me to just disappear into the night?"

It's actually very sweet of him to ask. "You can tell me. That way, I'm not worried. Not that I would be. Or…" I purse my lips. "Yeah, tell me."

"Okay. I will. I'll see you tomorrow, kiddo." He does a two-finger salute and disappears.

I'm so happy for him, but suddenly, I feel this immense loneliness.

It's late. I should go to sleep, and it'll fade. Right?

My mind wanders to Steven. To him, lying in bed, all by himself… I should call him now. I can start the week off right, as a brand-new woman. Newly single. Ready to mingle. I have a job interview and—

Emerson.

I'm meeting Emerson tomorrow at The Bean. One of my favorite spots in the whole city, and I'm meeting *her* there.

What is it about her that makes me so nervous? There has to be a reason. Yeah, sure, she's beautiful, but I've seen beautiful women in my life, though I have never looked at a woman before like I look at her. It's unnerving, the attention I have paid to her details. The tiny smile lines next to her eyes. The perfect shape of her lips. The mauve color of them. The way her green eyes seem to always be searching for some deeper meaning. Her hands. The dark blue of the veins running along the back. The ring on her left ring finger. Is she married? If she is, why didn't she have it on last night? Who is she married to? What is he like? Is he as magnetic as Emerson?

Emerson.

The very thought of her name has my heart racing.

The possibility of making another friend is making me feel so strange. I've made friends as an adult before. In fact, I met Jesse after college. And she's the Thelma to my Louise, the yin to my yang. Leaving her was almost harder than leaving Steven.

Oh, who am I trying to kid? Leaving Jesse was absolutely harder than leaving Steven.

God, I am so fucking stupid.

Just as those words pass through my head, I hear the doorbell ring. The noise startles me, causing my heart to shoot into my throat. "What the hell?" I say aloud. Do I answer it? Do I ignore it?

It rings again.

I rush over to my bedroom door and fly down the stairs as if my life depends on it, all the while hoping and praying it's not Steven. The front porch's light is on, so I stand on my tippy-toes to see through the peephole who's standing there.

Emerson.

My mouth goes completely dry.

The bell rings again, and this time I yelp. "Shit," I whisper.

"Mark? It's Emerson."

I slowly unlock the deadbolt, my hand trembling. As I pull the door open, I remember I am not wearing pants.

Emerson's eyes widen, and she blinks once, twice, before saying, "You have no pants on."

I close my eyes and sigh. "I know. I literally just realized it."

"Is Mark… home?"

"No."

"Okay."

"Can you come in so I can put some pants on?" I am pulling at the hem of my sleep shirt. Not my normal one that's longer and covers my ass. Oh, no, I had to put on the one that's almost too small on me and is showing off my underpants. "Please?"

She steps in and closes the door behind her while I rush up the steps and into my bedroom.

"Jesus Christ, you dumbass," I curse at myself, at my stupidity. Why am I such an idiot? I pull on my pajama bottoms with so much haste my stupid foot gets caught in them, and I tumble over onto the bed, then slide off onto my knees. I glance at my reflection in the full-length mirror so I can chastise myself as I realize: "Oh, my God, my nipples could cut glass right now." I pull myself from the floor and search frantically for an oversize sweater.

"Finnley, I can leave. It's really okay." I hear Emerson shout up the steps.

"No, no, just, y'know, putting on clothes…" I groan. "So my motherfucking nipples don't poke your eyes out," I finish under my breath. Once I find a sweater and pull it over my head, I take a few deep breaths and head back downstairs.

But I don't have my contacts in, and since my glasses still give me issues with my depth perception, I slip on the steps and slide down the last few on my sock-covered feet. *Calm the fuck down, Finnley. You're gonna kill yourself.*

"Are you okay?" Emerson asks after she rushes over to me. Her left hand is on my arm, and her right is on my hip.

I wave her off. "Yeah, I'm good. I'm a total klutz. I should come with a warning label."

Her soft giggle is accentuated by her smoothing her left hand over my arm. "I'm sorry about this, by the way." She bounces on her toes. She's wearing a pair of Adidas running shoes. "I, um, I run at night. It's not safe. I know. But it's when I get the best thinking done." She breathes in a sharp breath. "Not that you asked."

"No, it's absolutely not safe. Especially if you don't have a cell phone." I'm shocked her husband is okay with night running. I smile. "But coming down any sort of stairs isn't safe for me, yet I still do it. Stupidly."

"That could have been a horrible fall, by the way."

"That? That was nothing. Friday, on my way here, I fell down the stairs that go from the airport to the Blue Line."

"Is that what that bruise is from?" Emerson's eyes are locked onto mine when she asks.

I swallow. *Hard.* "Which bruise?" my words croak out.

"On the back of your thigh." She licks her lips.

My stomach has fallen into my ass. "Um... probably." The self-conscious part of me, which, let's be real, makes up ninety percent of me, is wondering why she was looking at my half-naked body, let alone taking inventory of bruises. I take a step toward the kitchen. "Would you like something to drink? I'm going to make myself a hot tea, if you'd like one."

"Sure, that'd be nice."

I hear her following me in, her soft footfalls weirdly loud in the quiet of the night. "I'm sorry Uncle Mark's not here," I say.

"Oh, it's okay. I was having a breakdown—" Her abrupt stop is denoted by a shake of her head as she leans against the doorframe. "I can catch him tomorrow."

"A breakdown, hmm?" I toss her a look over my shoulder as I'm filling the tea kettle. "Interesting."

Her arched brow rises the tiniest of amounts. "Oh, you want me to share? You think we're at that level?"

"You did see me in my underpants."

She laughs, soft, light, *lovely*. "True. I guess we're a lot closer than I realized."

"Easy to understand. I think we've only known each other for—"

"Twenty-six hours."

The fact she knows the exact number of hours sends chills through my entire body. Thank Christ I put a sweater on because I can feel a tightening sensation in my nipples. "Entire relationships have happened in less time," I manage to say as we wait for the kettle to whistle. I am leaning against the countertop, she's still leaning against the doorframe, and I wonder how quickly this would all come tumbling down if we weren't holding it up. "I'm listening."

She sighs. It's deep and deliberate. "I got into an argument with someone, and it has thrown me for a loop."

"'With someone,'" I say, adding air quotes. "Who's the someone?"

"My wife."

My breath catches. A *wife*? Not a husband. A wife. *Oh.*

"We're in the middle of a separation." She is looking at me, and the intensity of her gaze has my armpits sweating. And the underside of my breasts.

"Oh."

"Yeah, so," she says. The quietness of her admission isn't lost on me. "I'm done. And she's just… not."

"Why are you done?"

"Because she cheated on me."

"I'm sorry, what?" I furrow my brow as if it will help me hear her correctly. "Did you say she cheated on you? And she wants to stay married?"

She shrugs. "It's a modern-day predicament, that's for sure."

"Oh, I don't know." The stress from earlier has begun to melt away. I have no idea why, but to question it too much would be stupid. "People have screwed up for years and thought the grass was greener on the other side. Turns out, it rarely is."

"She fucking shredded me."

"Emerson," I whisper. "I'm really sorry."

She wipes at her eyes, swipes at her nose, then clears her throat. "So, anyway. I came over to get emotional support from Mark, not you. I don't have to unload any of this onto you."

"It's okay. I promise. It's not like I was doing anything. I didn't even have pants on."

Her laughter, once again, has my body responding. The tea kettle begins to whistle, giving me a reprieve I desperately need, so I pour the water over the tea bags in the two cups I've prepared. I pass a mug on a saucer over to her. Miraculously, this entire conversation hasn't caused me to be a nervous wreck, so the ceramic isn't rattling against itself.

"We can sit in the living room if you'd like. After the excitement of the last ten minutes or so, I'm not going to be able to get to sleep for quite some time." She doesn't respond, simply follows me back to the living room. When I sit, she picks a spot close to me but far enough away at the same time, as if she doesn't want to overstep a boundary neither of us has established. Little does she know, that right this second, I feel more at peace than I have in years.

We sip our tea in unison before she finally says, "How was dinner?"

"It was delicious." I sigh dreamily. "Pequod's is my favorite pizza. And I ate more than my share. My hangover has finally subsided."

"Good lord, your hangover lasted the entire day?" She groans. "Another reason I stopped drinking."

"You don't drink?"

"I haven't had a drop in almost five years. Health decision. I have a bad heart." She sips her tea, and then her eyes are on mine. "It is what it is."

"Are you okay?"

"Do I look okay?"

You look fucking incredible. I clear my throat. "Um, yeah, you look fantas—*okay*. You look okay."

That damn eyebrow of hers arches before she sips her tea, sets the mug back on the saucer, and then slides it onto the coffee table. The noises are so intense, as if someone turned the treble up and the bass down. "Mmhmm."

"Is that what this is for?" I reach out and touch her arm, where her heart tattoo resides.

"Yes and..." She shrugs and a wave of something seems to wash over her. Is that embarrassment? "Someone once told me I wear my heart on my sleeve, so..."

I can't fight the grin on my lips. "I love that."

"Thanks," she whispers. A second or two passes. I can't take my eyes off of her. I wonder if she feels weird being studied. "So, I'm assuming since he's not here that Mark told you about his gig?"

I nod.

"You're cool with it?"

"I literally couldn't care less. As long as he's happy? I'm happy."

"Good." She repositions herself on the couch so she's sitting cross-legged. "He was very worried you'd be squicked out by it."

"Squicked out? That's a new one." I laugh when she shrugs. "I am not squicked out. At all. In fact, I'm hoping I can figure out my life in the same way." I stop and put my hand in the air. "I don't mean I want to be an escort too. I just mean, like, y'know, be happy and all that jazz."

"I think my favorite part about you is how nervous you get when you say something you don't want taken the wrong way." The green of her eyes excites me in a way I've never experienced. I can feel it in my toes. "We'll get you to a happy place. I promise."

"You promise? You barely know me. It's not your job to help me get to a happy place." I hope my words came across as kindly as I meant them. "But thank you for caring."

"What if I told you I really want to help?" She leans her head slightly to the side. The line of her jaw down to her neck is mesmerizing. "Would it freak you out?"

"Don't you mean 'squick'?" I ask, and her entire facial expression lightens. "No, it wouldn't. Quite the opposite, actually. And that"—I take a breath, hear the faint clatter of the ceramic tea cup —"*that* freaks me out."

"You have no idea what's going on, do you?"

I want to be upset with her candor, but she's so spot-on. A couple ideas have come to mind. Maybe she thinks I have some artistic streak I'd like to explore at her studio. Or maybe she knows a guy she'd like to hook me up with. "Not a goddamn clue."

"Well..." She uncrosses her long legs, stands, and places her hands on her hips. "When you get to the place where you finally freak out—because, I can assure you, you one hundred percent will—please let me know, okay?"

I can't tear my eyes from her. Her white spandex tank, her fluorescent orange running shorts, the definition of her quadriceps, the scar on her knee. "If I don't have a clue as to what's happening, how will I ever freak out?"

Her arched eyebrow. *Goddamn.* "Thanks for the tea," she says softly before she takes the few strides to the door. "Lock this behind me." And she leaves.

I notice only after she's gone that my hand is still trembling.

CHAPTER FOUR

Welp, I didn't sleep a wink. Not a solitary wink. I tossed and turned the entire night. As the minutes passed, I got more and more upset with Emerson. For coming over uninvited, for being all beautiful and cool, for everything she said—for all of it. By the time I got myself out of bed and got ready for the interview, I wasn't even sure I wanted to go anymore; I was livid.

First of all, how dare she tell me my uncle was afraid I'd be squicked out by his choices? He's my uncle. I love him no matter what.

Second, what on earth was she thinking just popping over like that?

And third, why the hell did she say anything about me freaking out? She has no idea who I am or what would freak me out. She has a lot of nerve.

And then the way she stood and left! No explanation, no goodbye, just *poof!* Not that I need a formal goodbye, but damn. She barges in, then vanishes into the night, leaving me so confused, irritated, and weirdly turned on.

Squicked out? Squicked *out*? Ugh.

And why the *fuck* would I be freaked out about anything going on with *her*? Nothing is going on with her. At all!

This woman is going to drive me nuts simply by existing. I can feel it.

~

Uncle Mark isn't up when I head downstairs to grab a banana and a cup of coffee to go, which is a relief. Last night was weird enough without having to actually talk about it with someone. When has talking about something ever actually helped anyone?

I chuckle to myself as I head east on Grand toward Michigan Avenue. I've followed Uncle Mark's directions, and I haven't gotten lost yet. The weather is gorgeous too. Maybe it's going to shape up to be a good day? I could get hired, bail on meeting Emerson, and head back to the house to obsess over everything in peace and quiet. It sounds like a spectacular idea, except for the fact I have no way to contact her to say I'm not going to meet her. How does someone survive in this day and age without a cell phone? Especially her. She runs an art studio. Doesn't she need to be available for phone calls?

I guess it's a good way not to have people bail on you by sending a cowardly text like I was planning to do.

I'm super early for my interview, so when I reach the DuSable Bridge crossing the Chicago River, I pause and look east. The sun's rays are peeking through the smattering of clouds in a way that feels just right.

My phone starts buzzing, and my first thought is that it's Steven. I almost don't look at it but am thankful I do when I see

Jesse's name across the screen. I answer the FaceTime call to see her smiling face in front of me.

"What is up, girl?" she shouts. She's on the beach because of course she is. She is the only person I know in my life that will never have to work. Her parents are wealthy, so, by association, she is as well. She's thirty-two and will never move out of her parents' guesthouse. I don't blame her. They're steps from Pass-a-Grille Beach near Saint Petersburg, Florida. The house is immaculate, as is the guesthouse. I used to be very jealous of Jesse. As I've aged, I've learned that I'm no longer jealous. I'm grateful to have her as a friend. She's the most loyal person I know.

"I'm literally on my way to my interview. And I'm freaking out."

"Oh, please, you got this. Don't let your nerves feed your inner critic. You are so prepared to do whatever it is you are going to be doing." She tilts her head. "What is it that you'll be doing?"

I laugh. "Bookkeeping, accounting, y'know, massaging numbers."

"Ugh, again? Barf."

"I know, Jess. Seriously. I feel like I'm a boat lost at sea. It's been a real roller coaster the last two weeks."

Jesse pushes her sunglasses up to her black hair and brings the phone closer to her.

"What are you doing?" I ask. "Are you looking at yourself?"

"Duh. You don't look at the other person when you're on FaceTime, do you?"

"You are an asshole. You know that, right?"

"Whatever," she says while placing her sunglasses back on her face. "When are you coming home? I miss the shit out of you."

I groan. "Jess, I told you I may never be back home. This is my life for now."

"Boo, you whore."

"Why don't you come visit?"

She shrugs. "I mean, I guess I could make that happen. Tell me, though, what else have you been doing?"

"Nothing. I've been here for like three days. I unpacked, Uncle Mark threw a dinner party, I met his friends."

She grins. "Any cute guys?"

"Yes, but they're gay."

"Damn."

"Although…" My voice trails off as I try to decide if I want to mention Emerson or not. "I may have met someone who is… intriguing."

"Whoa, whoa, whoa, do tell." She is fully engaged now, leaning forward and everything. "Does this mean you might actually break up with Steven? He's such a drag."

"I mean, he is my fiancé."

"Jesus, I know. It's so sad. You are way too good for him."

"Well, thank you, I guess." I shake my head and chuckle. "So… it's a good thing you're sitting down for this."

"Why? Is it a chick?"

I don't respond, just twist my lips and stare into the phone. Her mouth drops open.

"Shut the fuck up! I knew it!"

"Wait a second—knew what?"

Jesse pulls her glasses down her nose and tilts her head again. "Girl, you queer. I've always thought it."

"I am not queer." I semi-shout at her, then realize everyone on Wacker Drive can hear me. At a lower volume, I add, "I think I'm just, like, super intrigued or whatever."

"Riiight, super intrigued. Not gay. Got it."

"Whatever, you're supposed to be supportive."

Jesse gasps. "Are you kidding? I am always supportive."

"Yeah, you are. I'm sorry."

"And besides, you've never actually wondered if you might be maybe just a little into women? You seem to get pretty wrapped up with the most random chicks. Like that chick from your intro to accounting class? Or that one older woman barista who you thought was like the most beautiful person you'd ever seen at the Starbucks so you'd only go to that one to get coffee and then you even had her schedule memorized?"

I laugh. "Jess, none of that means I like women."

"No? What about that lady bartender at 3 Daughters? She was all hot and looking like Elisabeth Shue? Remember her?"

I do remember her, but this line of questioning is irritating me considering I've already said I'm not into women. I roll my eyes at her.

"C'mon, like, just a smidge into women?" She holds her forefinger and thumb a tiny bit apart. "A skosh?"

I shake my head. "Not even in the slightest. You're really reaching here." I check my watch. "Jess, I gotta go."

"Call me tomorrow. I want to hear more about this intriguing person."

"I love you," I say before I hang up. Her voice and inability to focus have been the perfect distractions. Now that our call is over, I'm nauseated yet again.

~

I'VE ARRIVED EARLY, SO I'M WAITING. AND I'VE NEVER BEEN REALLY great when it comes to having patience. I get irritated, antsy, and full of anxiety. My impatience typically comes out in the form of fidgeting while holding a perfect resting bitch face, which isn't great in this setting, so I'm working on containing it. And, honestly, having that awful look on my face is so not normal for me. I'm very approachable, and I like people, for the most part. And instead of fidgeting, I'm worrying myself sick. My mentor and favorite professor, Dr. Padburg, set me up with this last-minute interview, so I don't want to let her down.

And yet.

How is it that I've spent most of my life immersed in this field, and now that I'm old enough to take over the family business and finally do what I want with it, I'm being forced to leave it? The business would have been mine. All mine. I'd have been able to do whatever I wanted and needed to bring it into the twenty-first century. I could have made changes to the marketing plan, the communication plan, literally every single step. But nope…

Don't get me wrong, I was exceptional at managing it. I am great with numbers and money, two skills my dad had to make up for with charm and lies. I was able to pay off astronomical amounts of debt that he had racked up while trying to make ends meet by spending every ounce of profit the business made. He was the one who should have taken a class in running a business, not me.

"Miss O'Connell?"

My attention jerks to the sound of my name being called across the small lobby. "Present." I cringe. "I mean, yes?"

The slender woman chuckles and waves for me to follow her. "Justine will see you now."

"Wonderful. I look forward to meeting her."

She's wearing jeans and a sweatshirt. I'm instantly worried I'm overdressed in my black blazer and pencil skirt. What is a person supposed to wear to an interview for a job they know nothing about? Aside from some brief conversations I had with Dr. Padburg, I have had no idea what I'm getting myself into.

I'm taken aback by the cleanliness of the office space as we breeze through it. Every item appears to have a specific place. The crisp air smells brand new. All the furniture is mismatched, seemingly intentionally, in bold colors. The walls are lined with very beautiful oil paintings, photographs, and watercolor paintings of hydrangeas, lilacs, amaryllis, azaleas, and hyacinths. I'm proud of myself for knowing all their names right off the top of my head.

The woman knocks on a door that stands ajar. After a moment, she pushes it open. "Justine? I have Miss O'Connell."

"Great, send her in."

"Good luck," she says as she motions for me to enter the office.

I'm now so nervous that I feel lightheaded. Even more so than I was earlier.

"Finnley? Hi, I'm Justine." She stands and holds both hands out in a defensive position. "I'm sorry, but I stopped shaking hands after COVID. I hope that's okay?"

If only she knew the true extent of how people in Florida treated COVID. She'd be horrified. "Completely understand. And not offended at all."

She gives me two thumbs-up and a giant grin. "Great. Have a seat." She moves around the desk and sits in the chair across from the one I've chosen. She reaches across her desk and pulls a piece of paper from a manila folder. "Sasha had some really great things to say about you."

It takes me half a second to realize she's talking about Dr. Padburg. I let a small laugh slip past my lips. "I'm so sorry, I was like, 'Who is she talking about?' I've never called her by her first name."

"Oh, yes, Dr. Padburg," Justine says as she leans back in her chair and crosses her left leg over her right. She seems so comfortable in her skin. It's refreshing. And I love her dark, curly hair. She's absolutely adorable. "Did she tell you anything about the position?"

"Um..." Should I lie? "No," I admit. "Just that it'll be an accounting position. I should have asked more questions obviously. I was, well, I was fired by my dad. Long story." I am a mess. What the hell? "It wasn't because I was bad at the job. I was great. In fact, way better than him. Oh my goodness, I'm rambling. Anyway, I was eager to get out of Florida, so I jumped at the opportunity when she said she'd talk to you." I'm sweating. Great. "I'm sorry. I should have asked more."

"No worries." She seems slightly irritated about my lack of knowledge regarding the job. "She told me in this email that you're one of the best accounting students she's ever had in her entire teaching career. That's impressive." Justine pulls the black-framed glasses from her face and lifts her chin as she studies me. "You want the job?"

I let out a puff of air. "What? Just like that?"

"Listen, I need to hire someone to do this while I'm busy opening the sister store in Wrigleyville."

"Okay..." My brain is racing. "I'll take it, but can you tell me at least what I'm getting myself into?"

A laugh flies out of her mouth. "Jesus, I'm so unprofessional. I apologize. I'm not a very good HR person. Essentially, it's a bookkeeping position for my company, Petals for Days. I don't want to toot my own horn, but it's one of the most successful flower shops in the Chicagoland area."

"Wow, that's so cool."

"I can't even begin to tell you how busy we are. I've blown up on TikTok and Instagram. I think we have close to a million followers on each. I have weddings booked every single weekend this summer through the end of *next* year."

"Well, I'm your girl then. I will be more than happy to manage the finances. I'm a professional, for sure."

The look of joy on her face makes me feel slightly better. "We're a match made in heaven then."

"We really are."

"So, you're in?"

"Absolutely."

"Great, I'm going to email you all the details. You can DocuSign everything. Can you start tomorrow?"

I gulp. "Sure."

"Don't worry." She leans forward, fully engaging with me. "If you're as good as Sasha says you are, I feel like you'll have this place whipped up in no time. All I need is for you to do the job. That's it. I don't need you to marry this place. I don't need you to be here for forty hours a week. I need the books to be squeaky clean. I do not want to worry about the money. I want to do what I'm passionate about."

I feel my shoulders fall the tiniest of amounts when a wave of sadness coupled with jealousy washes over me. That's the exact reason I was forced out of my family's business, to find what I'm passionate about. Now I'm going to do the same thing for a different business and not follow my own dreams? Cultivate my own passion? Maybe I shouldn't do it… I have some money saved up. I can make that last. But then what? When I'm broke as a joke, what am I going to do then? Ask Uncle Mark for an allowance? The very thought makes me want to jump out the window. "I'd love to be involved in any way possible."

Justine's eyes widen, her eyebrows rise, and she dips her head. "Seriously? Don't joke with me like that. If you want to learn, and I mean really learn, I'll teach you everything I know about flowers and floral arrangements. Obviously, not the books. You don't need me to teach you how I do them wrong."

I laugh and respond with, "That is wonderful. I love to learn." I feel as if I'm on a date or something. I'm trying to tell my entire life story without saying too much, so I don't freak her out. I gather my thoughts after I sit up straighter and stop myself from carrying on like an idiot. "I want to do this. I want to learn. And I swear, I will not let you down. You won't have to worry about anything. I'm a whiz with numbers and budgets. I'm also damn near perfect when it comes to managing money." I realize I've cursed. "I'm sorry. I mean, darn near perfect."

"Don't fucking worry about it." After she winks, she finishes with, "Finnley, this is so, so great. I told you, we're a match made in heaven. You're going to love all my other staff too. I've got a great group of people helping me out. You'll get to meet them all tomorrow morning. Meet me here at ten." She pushes a brochure toward me. "That address is my downtown location. Not only will I get to show you the space, but you'll also see why I need to expand and why my office is here, six blocks away, and not in the store." She stands, so I follow her lead. She's quite a bit shorter than me, with a stocky build. Everything about her screams *friendly*. The brown color of her eyes is the deepest I've ever seen before, as are the dimples in her cheeks that her wide smile makes. "I'm excited about this. I'll let Sasha know she's a lifesaver."

"Thank you so much for this, Justine. I won't let you down."

Once I've made it outside the building, I take a deep, cleansing breath and let it out. This isn't exactly what I thought I'd be doing. That's for sure. Managing my parents' books to managing these books? Not exactly something to be passionate about. But this could be a jumping-off point, right? Maybe this will lead to what I am supposed to be doing with my life. The whole point of coming here was to find happiness.

And I am doing that. I am so much happier. And learning this business may be exactly what I'm supposed to do. Who knows? I have to stop framing everything in my life so negatively.

This city is awesome. It's going to change my entire life. I need to be glad I decided to take this leap of faith. Not only do I get to live with Uncle Mark, but I also get to learn about a new business in my most favorite city.

"Hey, lady! Stop daydreaming and get out of the way!"

I jump out of the way as a man on a bicycle speeds past me. "Jesus Christ! Watch it, mister."

He flips me off. Yeah, so that part of the city sucks.

∼

LAST NIGHT, WHILE I COULDN'T SLEEP, I DECIDED TO CRAM AS much knowledge as possible in my head about The Bean. I've been to Millennium Park before. About five years ago, I came and visited Uncle Mark for a night when I was interviewing for the MBA program at the University of Chicago. I got into the program, by the way, but for whatever reason, I decided to leave Florida and go to Cambridge for Harvard. The MBA program is the same wherever you go. I learned the same things I would have in Chicago, including the fact that, unless you really care for what you're learning about, it doesn't matter what prestigious university's name is printed on your diploma.

Loved Harvard. Don't get me wrong.

Ultimately, what ruined the entire experience was the impending doom of having to go back to Florida.

So, anyway... *The Bean.*

Cloud Gate, actually, is the official title. The artist, Anish Kapoor, named it that because of the reflective surface, which resembles liquid mercury. It looks like a bean, though, hence the nickname. Aside from being weirdly beautiful, it's one of my favorite places in the city. Kind of interesting that Emerson picked it out of the millions of places we could have met. Like, of all the gin joints...

Approaching The Bean is one of the best parts of the entire experience. When you arrive from Michigan Avenue, you can see the skyline reflected in its surface. But as you move around it, the shiny metal reflects everything—not just the skyline, but the sky, the trees, the people surrounding it. Seeing it for the first time was so much fun.

Seeing it now is a different experience. I live here now. I am not leaving. I don't have to be the tourist who snaps a thousand pictures. I can simply take in its beauty.

"She's gorgeous, isn't she?"

Is The Bean a she? I start to think, but my head jerks toward the side when I realize the voice those words belong to is Emerson's. I swallow around the immediate lump that forms in my throat. "She really is."

"I come here once a week. Normally on Mondays." She shrugs. "Thanks for meeting me and coming with."

"Any time." My voice sounds far away, and I have to stand there for a full three-count to make sure I responded out loud.

Her hair is down, loose waves surrounding her face. Her sunglasses are pushed up above her forehead. She's squinting without them, but she seems like the type of person who doesn't want the color of the lenses to ruin a single frame of memory. She's wearing a short-sleeved, black button-down with lemons all over it. Her dark blue jeans are ripped at the knees, and she's wearing brown, wingtip oxfords.

"How was your interview?" she asks.

She isn't looking at me, just staring straight ahead at The Bean.

"It was great. I took the job."

Finally, she turns, her green eyes locking onto mine. "Finnley, that's great news. Congratulations." She touches my arm, wrapping her fingers around my bicep. Her touch is much more familiar than it has a right to be, considering we barely know each other. Who am I to protest a touch, though?

"Thank you. I'm trying to remain optimistic."

"And?" she prompts. "What will you be doing?"

"Bookkeeping." I sigh. "Sounds exciting, right?"

She laughs. The sound causes my entire body to stutter. "No, it sounds awful." She laughs again when I let my face fall, defeated. "Wait, wait—no, I think it's great you found a job. But..." She nudges me, and we start walking toward The Bean. "Isn't that what you were doing at your parents' company?"

This is exactly the point I made to myself earlier. "Good memory."

"I'm a great listener. Especially when you're speaking." Her words... Yeah, I'm lost in them, the meaning behind them, the tone of her voice as she said them. I can feel myself looking at her as she waits for me to respond. I'm studying her again. For the fifteenth time. Or the millionth, honestly. But I can't stop because everything about what she just said has my brain asking a thousand questions. "I'm only asking now to make sure you're really excited and not simply talking yourself into excitement."

"Thank you for caring enough to make sure I'm not making a mistake. That, um, that means a lot to me."

"You're worth it," she responds, softly but with conviction. "Listening to, I mean. You're worth listening to."

I couldn't restrain the smile that's spreading across my lips even if I wanted to. "Thank you, Emerson."

She's looking at The Bean now, the gentle breeze blowing through her hair and casting her scent onto the air. She smells delicious—I mean, incredible. What the hell? How can someone smell delicious? I'm losing my mind. I swear to God.

The silence falling between us has gotten progressively less nerve-racking, and I wonder what she's thinking. I wonder what I'm thinking, honestly. There's something going on with me. I'd love to say it's just the beauty of rebirth and that I'll get my head on straight eventually. I'll call Steven and fix things, and he'll move to Chicago. I'll remind myself that, at one point in time, I was happy with him. Except that's not true, is it? I wasn't ever truly happy with him. I was flatlining with him.

I feel a tear roll down my cheek, and within half a second, I am swiping at it. I turn so I'm looking at anything other than Emerson. I don't want her to see me crying. What am I even crying for? I need to start my period. Clearly.

I hear a gentle sigh and feel her slip her hand into the crook of my arm. "What's going on?" she asks in a way that makes it seem as if she's seen me cry a thousand times and has cataloged each tear type and cause.

"Nothing. Just happy for the first time in a long time."

"Oh? Being near me is making you happy?" She places her hand on her chest and grins. "I'm honored." She nudges my arm, then adds, "I actually am honored. You being happy is really gorgeous."

I'm instantly filled with heat, from my cheeks all the way to my toes.

"And now you're blushing, which is also really gorgeous," she says. My first instinct is to cover my face, but as my hands shoot up, she stops us and catches them halfway. She's standing in front of me now, her eyes searching mine. "You still have no idea, do you?"

An idea has started to form in my head like a small seedling that has been given the perfect environment to thrive. Water, sunlight, warmth, and it starts to germinate until it's a full-fledged thought. "Would you think less of me if I said no, I don't? But that I'm really just enjoying you? And your company?"

A flash of something passes in her expression. I want to ask what it means, that tiny crack that is showing the beginning stages of... *fear*? Is that what it is? "Finnley," she starts. She's still holding my hands, her thumbs stroking the backs of them. Determination floods her face, but it leaves as quickly as it arrived. "You know what? I'll take that answer."

I wonder what else she was going to say. Was there a *but* at the end? *I'll take that answer, but...*? Or something more final, like, *I'll take that answer for now*?

"Can we go eat something?" I need to break the tension, and food is always my go-to for that.

"Yes, please. I'm starving." She drops my hands.

I miss the sensation almost immediately.

∽

"Okay, I've introduced you to my favorite sushi spot, my favorite sculpture in the city, and my favorite cup of coffee. What else do you want to do?"

I'm leaning against the railing of the Riverwalk, sipping on my cappuccino from Intelligentsia, enjoying every single second of the caffeinated goodness. I was skeptical at first. When she said it was her favorite cup of coffee, it worried me. What happened if I didn't like it as much? But after one sip, I was completely hooked. I'm not much of a coffee connoisseur. I drink it black. I always have. I've tried it a million different ways, and I'm always disappointed it's not *just black*. Intelligentsia, though? I'm now convinced other types of coffee can be good.

"I'm at a loss," I finally respond. "I'm content right now. Maybe the most content I've been since... well..." The only memory I have of the last time I was truly filled with joy floods my mind. I was eight years old, exploring the city with Uncle Mark and Aunt Lisa, bopping around from spot to spot, enjoying the sights and sounds. It was one of the best long weekends of my young life. Lincoln Park Zoo, the art museum, the Field Museum, and Shedd Aquarium. We hit all the great spots. I didn't realize until a lot later in life I was left with them for the weekend because my parents were going through a rough patch and took time away from their kid so they could figure out what they were going to do.

"Well, what?"

"Nothing."

"No," Emerson says. She is facing the river, her elbows propped on the railing, the right one so close to mine it's all I can focus on. "Tell me. When was the last time you felt content?"

"I'm going to keep that one to myself for now, okay?" I glance at her and am stunned, instantly, by how the sun's rays are striking her features. The light is bringing out the golden color of her hair, the green of her eyes, the pink of her lips. "God, you are so pretty." Her eyes go wide, and I realize what I've said and *how* I've said it and that I've said it out loud, for Christ's sake. Me flinging myself over the railing right into the river is the only thought in my head. *Geronimo!* "I'm sorry. I don't know why I said that like that, just blurting it out like that." I shake my head, hoping the movement rids my voice of the nervous tremble it has suddenly taken on.

She breathes out a small puff of air that almost sounds like a laugh. *Almost.* "You think telling me I'm pretty is something you need to apologize for?"

"Yeah, but only because I am not, like, gay or whatever."

Her face shifts. It's tiny, really, the shift, and if I hadn't spent the last however many hours memorizing every single detail of her, I probably wouldn't have noticed. Yet I did. And the shift gives me pause. Did I overstep? Should I just shut up?

"I know you're straight." Melancholy hangs from her words. She seems disappointed. She purses her lips before finishing with, "Well aware of it, actually."

Yeah, I should have just shut up. "Oh." Now it's my turn to *seem* disappointed. Except I know that feeling bubbling right beneath my surface. That *is* disappointment. I *am* disappointed. And yet again, I have no idea why. "Did I do something wrong?"

Her shoulders fall as she turns her body toward me. "No. You have been perfect. Almost *too* perfect."

"I've never been perfect before, so that's kind of nice."

"You've been perfect since the second I laid eyes on you." She reaches forward, and everything around us freezes in time. She runs two fingers down the side of my face, along my jawline to my chin, where she gently presses her thumb into the dimple that resides there. "And I'm trying so hard to stop myself from liking you."

"So, you're not hoping I become a new artist at your studio?"

She lets out a small laugh. "Not in the slightest."

My previous guesses were wildly incorrect. My words snag on the shock that has lodged itself in my throat. I open my mouth to speak, but nothing comes out. A fish gasping for oxygen would look less ridiculous.

"You don't have to say a word. I'm perfectly happy being your friend. And besides." She holds her left hand up, motions to her wedding ring, and shrugs. "It's not like I'm free yet to explore."

I'm still so stuck on Emerson saying she's trying *not* to like me that it barely registers she's talking about her soon-to-be-over marriage. All I can think to say is, "Wait… you don't want to like me? Like, at all?"

"Oh, Finnley," she says softly. She's smiling, though, and—

Holy shit. Electricity zips through me. "*Oh.* You mean *like* like. *More than friends* like."

"Finnley—"

"Emerson, I'm straight. I like guys. I'm just oblivious, I guess." Cutting her off was not my finest move, but this has taken a turn toward uncomfortable, and suddenly, I'm not as okay with it as I thought I was. "I don't mean to be rude. But this isn't me." When I finally make eye contact with her, the expression on her face makes my stomach hurt. The speed and poise with which she gathers all the pieces of whatever I've just shattered are remarkable, though.

"You do not need to explain." Her voice is suddenly much lighter, airier, as if she hadn't moments earlier told me she was liking me more than she should. "I didn't think you would be interested or anything. I shouldn't have mentioned it or pushed the issue. Forget the fact you're in a relationship with a guy, but I'm also a lot older than you. That was really stupid of me. Please, I apologize."

"No!" The word flies out of my mouth, and my hands grab hers. "Don't apologize. You didn't *push.* I've never had this happen to me before. I am the one who should apologize. I am not handling this right at all." She's the one trembling now, and my heart aches in my chest at the realization that this, saying what she said and now taking it back, was probably so hard for her to do. After all, I've been rejected before. It's not fun at all.

"It's really okay." She pulls her hands away, instantly shoving them into the pockets of her jeans. "Thank you for being honest with me."

Ugh. My heart is being squeezed to death by the walls of my chest. "Of course. I'll always be honest with you, Emerson. And… you didn't make me uncomfortable before." Looking into her eyes is too much for me to handle, and the ground has captured all my attention. "I think you took me by surprise. Truthfully, you've taken me by surprise since the second you walked into the dining room the other night." My feet are tingling, my hands are aching, and my knees are shaking. I pull a deep breath into my lungs and will myself to look at her again. "Something about you makes me want to get to know you. No ounce of me is freaked out or doesn't want to see you again. Okay?"

She nods. It's small, but it's enough for now. When she takes off toward the stairs to Upper Wacker Drive, a feeling deep in the pit of my stomach begins to take root. It's a feeling I've never felt before, one that has me instantly questioning myself.

I have always been sure of my sexuality. There's never been a moment when I wasn't sure. I mean, *right*? Has there been? My mind is racing, opening up the cabinets of my memory bank, thumbing through the different files, looking for moments when maybe I felt this same feeling. I keep coming up empty-handed. Nothing is shouting at me that maybe, just maybe, I'm not as straight as I thought I was.

Until I get to the memory of my high school teacher.

And his wife.

His wife.

I glance at Emerson as we walk up the steps together, at her profile, at the slope of her nose, the sharp curve of her cheekbones, the fullness of her lips, and my heart starts to race.

Shit.

CHAPTER FIVE

Nerves? What nerves? I am cool as a cucumber as I make my way to the downtown location of Petals for Days. Yeah, right. Only if cool as a cucumber means shitting bricks. Then? Sure. I'm a cucumber of coolness. But in the real world, where I unfortunately live, I'm freaking out.

Starting a new job is something I've never experienced. I never had to have a job in high school. I was an athlete, so the free time I had, I spent working out because I wanted to get a scholarship. Then I went to Florida State on that scholarship. Those were the best years of my life so far. After, I started working for my father. I didn't have to interview, and I knew every single person who worked there. So, no nerves. After a few years, I left and went to Boston. I was a teacher's assistant while I was getting my master's, which wasn't nerve-racking at all. I was handed the job by Dr. Padburg.

Wow. I've been insanely lucky throughout the course of my life. Suddenly, I am not nearly as impressed with myself as I was when I finished school. I've never had to fight for anything in my entire life. How fucking sad.

My reflection in the window of the store I've stopped in front of catches my eye. I look presentable and professional. I know what I'm doing. I'm smart and creative. I can handle this. So, why am I freaking out?

"Pull yourself together," I whisper to my reflection. It's a weak pep talk, but it's going to have to do for now. I don't want to be late on my first day.

Aside from being nervous, I'm about five percent excited. Having a mentor like Justine could be just the thing I'm looking for. And I'll get to meet some new people who may one day become friends. It would be lovely to have friends who are all mine, not Uncle Mark's first. Not that I mind being friends with his friends. They're really nice. I enjoy them all. Walter and Timothy, Cecily and Francesca, and Chaz and Rebecca…and Emerson…

I haven't spoken to her since yesterday. Our conversation after I put my foot in my mouth was light. I'm sure I was more thrown by everything than she was. After all, I stumbled upon a treasure trove of memories where I might have possibly had feelings for a woman, an older woman. An older, unobtainable woman. Like her. Christ.

While I wanted to talk to Emerson about my discovery, I was way too afraid to even get into it with her because I wasn't *absolutely positively sure*. I was only suspicious. Of myself, which is such a weird place to be in. Questioning my every thought has been exhausting. And intrigue is not enough to base anything off of… I could have talked to Uncle Mark, but how do I say to him that I want to see if maybe I like women? Just blurt it out? Or do I sit him down and go over every single second I've spent with Emerson? It would be enlightening for me, I'm sure, but probably very boring for him.

That's enough, Finnley. It's time to focus.

I arrive at the address Justine gave me and push through the revolving door of Petals for Days, taking in all the trinkets, knickknacks, and cards that adorn the shelves lining the entryway. I finally get to a long countertop, where there is a cash register and what I'm assuming is a flower wrap station. I glance around at the natural light the store gets and find myself quite impressed with the space.

The shop is very inviting. Its exposed ceilings have been painted white, I'm assuming to help brighten the area during Chicago's doom-and-gloom winter months. There are hundreds of different kinds of plants, succulents, and floral arrangements. It smells like spring, fresh and clean, and I know if I lived nearby, I'd get all of my flowers from here. Music is softly playing on the overhead speakers. I think it's country, which is not my jam, but whatever. I won't be at this store every day. There's a note near the cash register that reads: *Finnley, go to the back of the store.*

I do as the note says. As I head farther in, there's a wall of flowers on my right side, and I stop to admire them. There are all types of irises, roses of all colors, hydrangeas large and small, sunflowers in all shades of yellow, daisies for days, and ten different colors of alstroemerias. I am amazed by their beauty and bowled over by their heady scent. There are flower arrangements strewn all over the back countertops too. I am in love with the way the bouquets are put together. The arrangements are gigantic, with large flowers at the center, bordered by pops of greenery.

"Finnley, you made it!" Justine says as she pokes her head out of a door. "Come on in. Everyone is back here."

"I'm sorry, I was just admiring all the flowers."

"Don't be sorry." She smiles. "You say sorry a lot, don't you?"

All I can do is grimace.

"Yeah, we're gonna work on that." Justine throws her arm around my shoulder and ushers me to the very back of the building. We squeeze through a small opening into what I can only assume is an employee breakroom. There are three people already crammed into the space. "Everyone, this is Finnley. She's going to save me a lot of stress."

"Oh, the new bookkeeper, hmm? I'm Lydia," an older woman says with a grin. "I'm the grandma of the place."

"She's not lying. She's *actually* my grandma," Justine explains. She introduces me to an older Black woman named Vivian next, who has worked there for ten years and is her right-hand woman. There's also Blake, a student at Columbia College, majoring in theater and radio broadcasting. I was nervous that none of them would like me, but they seem okay. Before I know it, I've been invited to join them after work for Taco Tuesday—though this is a development Blake doesn't seem too excited about.

I sit back and prepare for the meeting.

Blake is the first to speak. "We have at least fifteen arrangements to do today and tomorrow. I've already started four of them, but Vivian, I'm going to need you to help me with the rest. Lydia, too."

"Fifteen arrangements isn't bad," Justine muses. "We have two weddings this weekend as well: one at the Harold Washington Library in the Winter Garden and one in City View Loft. I'll need all hands on deck for those events."

"Lucky for you, this place is my life," Lydia says. "Finnley, you're more than welcome to come to the events to learn the ropes if you'd like."

"Oh, wow," I say. I'm torn between being happy to be involved and not wanting to give up my weekend freedom. "I'll definitely help out," I decide. "I'd love to learn."

Blake scoffs, but as I turn toward them, Justine cuts off any further conversation. "As far as the day-to-day for the next week, we need to tighten our belts," she says. "The checking account is low. I may have to hold payroll if we aren't careful."

When I say I *literally* feel my eyes widen, I mean it. What the hell is she talking about? She just hired me and now I may not get paid? What the actual fuck?

She must sense my worry because she leans over and winks at me. "I'm kidding. I've only had to hold payroll a couple times."

A *couple* times? That isn't any better. Even at the struggling family business we never had to hold our paychecks. I'm floored. So floored, in fact, that I am having a hard time paying attention now. What have I gotten myself into?

"What about the contractors for the new store? Who's going to be taking care of them? Is that where you'll be more involved?" Vivian's question pulls me back, though only slightly.

Justine's smile is more of an irritated smirk than anything else. "More involved? I'm *very* involved, Vivian. And no, they'll be handling themselves."

Vivian hums, but that's as far as her protest goes before I notice Lydia give her a pointed nudge.

This whole meeting is its own kind of interesting. This is the first time I've seen this side of Justine. To say it has made me more nervous would be an understatement. Regret is starting to fill my stomach.

Justine wraps the meeting up quickly after Vivian's contribution, saying, "Let's just remember we have to get through the next three months. Please? I know it's going to be rough, but we can do it. We have to, okay?" She doesn't wait for a response before she disappears from the room.

I'm left sitting there, bewildered and worried. Wasn't I supposed to go with her back to the office? I shake the confusion from my head and decide to make my way to the office on my own. Hopefully the nice version of Justine, who helped me before the interview, will be there and can let me in. I'll be the amazing new employee and figure Petals for Days' accounting issues out on my own. It sounds like a stupid plan, if I'm being honest, but like everything recently, I'm hoping it'll all just magically work.

"She's lost her goddamn mind," I hear Vivian's hushed whisper from the hallway. "If she thinks we'll be able to do all of this without her help, she's got another thing coming."

"Viv, you know she's been going through a really rough time the last few months," Blake says softly. "Don't forget that, okay?"

Have they forgotten that I'm here? Do they think I left with Justine?

"Don't you think we all have?" Vivian's hushed whisper is coated with frustration. "Ever since her life fell apart, we've been picking up the pieces of this place. It's not fair."

"Blake, I know Justine is my granddaughter, but I'm gonna side with Viv on this. She needs to get her head on straight or we might not even need to open another storefront. Do you think you could talk to her?"

"Yeah, Blake, can you talk to her? She loves you, obviously," Vivian says sarcastically.

Oh? I'm fully engaged in eavesdropping, leaning closer and closer to the door to hear what's been said.

"*Love*? Please." Blake scoffs. If I knew them better, I'd bet that was embarrassment in their tone. "Besides, we had to stop all that when... y'know... Never mind."

"Blake, come on." Vivian is pleading.

"Fine," Blake relents. "I'll talk to her. But you have to remember, what I say to her about the business isn't always received well. And honestly? Between you and me, I think she's making a huge mistake with that new girl. Hiring her is not a good idea. We all know what happens. People see the books and they run. She's gonna run, too. I just know it."

Whoa, whoa, whoa. I'm irritated now. Sure, they might be slightly right, but who cares? They don't know anything about me.

Lydia has my back, though. "I have a good feeling about this one," she says. "If anything, Justine will let her go because she tries to tighten the ropes too much." She laughs. "We all know she has no idea how to manage money."

"And she doesn't take direction on it well either," Vivian adds with a chuckle.

Great. This would have all been great to know before I accepted the role. Why is it that only candidates are expected to be candid during job interviews?

"I'll talk to her," Blake says. "And can we not have that new girl come with us for tacos, please? I am not in the mood to be kind."

"Are you ever?" Lydia asks.

Blake gasps. "Lydia, what the hell?"

Once their voices and laughter fade, indicating they've moved their gossipy hen session to the front of the store, I take my chance and head for the exit, hoping they don't notice me when I sneak through. My hopes are dashed when Vivian says, "Oh! Finnley, we thought you left with Justine."

"Yeah, I sort of figured." I force a smile instead of glaring at Blake like I want to. "I'm going to head to the office now. It was really lovely meeting you all." I am so thrilled I won't have to deal with them on an everyday basis. Actually, I take that back. Vivian and Lydia seem like awesome older women with great backgrounds and even better stories. Blake, on the other hand, seems like a real jerk.

"Don't forget to meet us around five at Mercadito for tacos, you hear?" Lydia's reminder is delivered with a lot of sincerity. Don't think I don't notice Blake shooting daggers at her with their eyes, though.

"Yes, please, don't forget. You need to make some friends, my dear," Vivian says, a concerned look on her face. She pushes her glasses to the top of her head, so they're propped on her salt-and-pepper hair. "How are you going to make friends with us if you're not here?"

"We may look old, but we are a damn good time," Lydia says, a wide smile on her lips. "So it's settled. You'll come with us for tacos tonight."

Blake hasn't made eye contact with me since the invite was extended. I wonder if they'll come now that I'm going. Being disliked drives me nuts. I'm hoping I can win them over so my work life doesn't have to be half this weird. There's something peculiar in the way Blake looks at me, though. I want to ask what their problem is, but I think it might be a little too soon to be confrontational. Of course, if they keep it up, it's going to push me to say something.

∼

When I arrive back at the office, Justine is sitting at her desk, door closed, which I'm assuming means I shouldn't bother her. But what am I supposed to do? Sit there on my first day, twiddling my thumbs? I mean, I guess that wouldn't be horrible. As long as I got paid. Except, after the team huddle, I'm not even sure if I *will* be getting paid. I really picked a winner, didn't I?

I knock on the door and wait for her to respond. She doesn't, which is doing nothing but ratcheting up my regret factor, so I swing open the door. "So, should I just go home or…?" I ask, trying to contain my anger at the blatant waste of both of our time. She doesn't look up. "I don't know what exactly happened back there, but I really just want to sit down and start to work. I don't have a computer or access—"

She finally looks up. "I'm sorry," she says softly. "I'm just at the end of my rope."

"I get it." And I do. I don't agree with how she's handled everything, but at this point, I'll say anything to get the awkward tension out of the air.

"Your computer and office are all set up." She motions to the office next to hers. "Why don't you go in and get settled? I'll be right there." She's only slightly dismissive. That makes me feel a tiny bit better.

I head into my new office. There's a MacBook Pro on the desk with a stack of papers beside it. I start to flip through them before I even set my bag down. They're bank statements and receipts dating back at least three months. Man, I've been here before.

I let my bag slide off my shoulder and fall onto the floor as I sit and start separating the papers into organized piles. Bank statements, receipts, check stubs, invoices.

"Okay," Justine says as she enters my office and sits across the desk from me. "So, yeah. Entering things is not my favorite part of the job."

"Do you have any accounting experience at all?" I ask, and she shakes her head. "Not even a class in high school?"

"I mean, I can balance a checkbook."

"Do you balance yours?"

She groans.

"Jesus," I whisper. "So talk to me. What is the problem with your money?"

She leans back in the chair. "We have a lot of money that is on its way to us. But... it doesn't get here quick enough." She shrugs. "And I don't ever know exactly what we have in the account." She adds that sentence under her breath. Unlucky for her, I have excellent hearing.

"That's literally the dumbest thing you can do," I point out.

"Hey, I'm your boss, y'know. I wouldn't speak to my boss like that." Her shoulders fall after she reprimands me. "But yeah, it's dumb. I had someone doing that for me, but she quit. I had someone before her, too. She also quit."

"I don't plan on quitting." At least not right now. "I'm going to start entering these. I'm assuming you have QuickBooks or something?"

Her face lightens, her dark eyes holding a gleam of happiness. "Yes, we do. You mean I don't have to train you?"

I laugh. "No, I think I can handle it."

She stands, gives me a huge smile, and leaves. It's one of the most off-the-wall interactions I've ever had in my entire professional life. There is definitely something going on with Justine. I don't know if I'll ever get to the bottom of it. Hell, I don't know if I want to get to the bottom of it. All I know for sure is that this day is shaping up to be a pretty crappy first day.

∼

Mercadito is hip and trendy and, according to Vivian, one of the best Mexican restaurants in the city. At this point, it won't take much to convince me. I left Uncle Mark's that morning and forgot to pack a lunch, so by the time we head over, I am starving. After the day I've had, being talked about behind my back, trying to figure out Justine's moods (which only got worse as the day progressed), and dealing with data entry hell, I'm ready to chow down on some Mexican food. I'm actually salivating in anticipation of the salsa and chips. And guacamole. And queso. *Sweet Jesus*, I think, *please let their queso be as heavenly as The Green Lemon's in Tampa.*

After the margaritas are delivered, Lydia excuses herself and pulls Vivian along with her. I have no idea where they're going, but I'm irritated because now I have to be by myself with Blake, who hasn't warmed up to me at all. The high-top we're seated at in the bar area isn't large enough for them to act like I don't exist or for me to fade into non-existence, either. Blake not looking at me or acknowledging me in this small space is only making it more awkward. Honestly, I'd leave it alone except I barely know this person, so I'd like to know why I'm being treated this way.

"How long have you worked for Justine?" I ask in an attempt to start a conversation.

"Six years."

"Ahh." Ask open-ended questions, Finnley, you dumbass. "And what is it about working there you like?"

Blake still doesn't look at me when they answer. "It's fun." They swipe their hand through their short blond hair. It's buzzed on the sides and aside from their horrible attitude, they're really adorable. The blue of Blake's eyes is the most intense blue I've seen in quite some time.

"Okay..."

"You don't have to try and befriend me, Finnley," they bluster. "I don't want more friends."

"Wow. Okay."

"I'm not in the market for all this small talk either."

"Message received."

Blake rolls their eyes. There's not much that will set me off. But that? The rolling of the eyes? That will absolutely do it. I didn't want to be confrontational, but fuck this. I slam my hand on the table and glare at them. "What the hell is your problem with me?" I've caught them with a chip piled with salsa halfway to their mouth.

"Why do you think I have a problem with you?" Blake shoves the chip into their mouth and chews, the sound of the chip crunching loudly even with the Ranchero music playing over the speakers.

"I don't know," I end up answering. It's not a great answer, but as I sit there and think about it, I realize I don't have a reason to think they have a problem with me. "I guess I just assumed... since you don't want to talk to me."

"Look," Blake says, leaning forward and grabbing another chip and a heaping pile of salsa. "I spend most of my days being outgoing and exciting. I'm a theater major and I have to be that way."

"Theater? How awesome. Do you like it?"

Blake sighs. "it's great. I love it. That's not the point. I'm not sharing myself with you."

"Whoa, *okay*."

"When I come to work, I turn that part off. Otherwise, I'll die. Okay? And..." They glare at me. "I have a sixth sense about people. I talk when I think they're worth my time. You? You're not worth my time right now. I work there because I care about Justine and it's a paycheck. That's it. I don't go out of my way to be friends with anyone new she hires."

"Okay. I'm sorry."

"Don't be sorry. Just don't expect me to talk to you. It's not like you'll last long." This last part is said under their breath, and it takes me half a second to realize what's been said.

"What's that supposed to mean?"

"It means we all know this is just a rest area for you. You'll be moving on soon enough, and Justine will have to scramble to find someone to replace you. Just like the last accountant. And the accountant before that. It's not worth cultivating some long-lasting relationship."

"Oh?" I clench my hands into fists to stop myself from launching across the table and slugging Blake. How dare they think they know anything about me.

"Yeah." Blake's eyes are finally locked onto mine. They nod, then smile. "What? You think I'm not right? Prove me wrong then." They stand and push their chair in before heading in the direction of the bathroom. I'm fuming. My face feels like it's on fire.

The worst part? Blake isn't wrong. I don't plan on staying forever. But I certainly don't plan on leaving anyone in a bind. I don't do that.

"Where's Blake, sweetie?" Vivian's voice breaks through my anger. "They go to the bathroom?"

"Yeah." My answer is soft. "I think I'm gonna head home, actually. I'm beat."

"Oh, dear." Lydia groans when she sits on the stool next to mine. "Was Blake a jerk? I keep telling them to stop being like that to new people. I swear it scares them away."

"No! Goodness. Not at all." Lying is the easiest option. "I'm seriously just tired. It's been a whirlwind of a day."

"If you're sure…"

"I am. Thank you so much." I leave thirty dollars on the table. "For my drink and tip."

"Get your money out of here." Vivian shoves the cash back into my hand. "We will see you tomorrow, okay?"

I thank her and Lydia before weaving through the restaurant to the exit. I pass Blake on the way. They smirk, almost as if they're saying, "Told you so."

All I can think as I take off toward Grand Avenue is that I am going to make this work. Numbers and managing a budget may not be my passion, but I'm going to work my ass off regardless. I'll show Blake. Not that I should even care what they think. But dammit, I do. I care what everyone thinks. It's an unfortunate curse I can't seem to shake.

∽

Hearing the music coming from The Oasis the second I step into the house deflates my mood even further. All I want to do is get something to eat and go to bed. Not sleeping the night before is wreaking havoc on my mind and body. The whole conversation with Blake has depressed me, too, so at this point I'm ready to hole up and not see another human being tonight. Maybe I can get a snack and sneak into my room without being caught.

After grabbing a granola bar and a bottle of water, I take one cautious step onto the stairs, but Aunt Lisa appears at the top, heading down. When she sees me, her face lights up. "Finn! Babycakes, you're home. Come on up and hang out. We just ordered takeout and are having a couple of beverages."

My shoulders sag under the realization that I'm not going to be able to get out of this.

"Take this bottle of wine up," she says as she passes me a bottle from the reusable Trader Joe's bag sitting on the kitchen table. "And this." She hands me a package of cookies. "And this." Next is a bag of cashews. "Actually, just take the whole bag." She dumps the items back in the bag, pulls my arm through the straps, and secures it onto my shoulder. "You okay?"

"Yeah, Lisa, I'm good. Just tired."

"Go get some food. And drink. You'll feel better." She places a hand on my cheek and lightly caresses it. "Mark will be happy you're home."

I am so not in the mood for any of this, but I head upstairs and try to remember that withdrawing has always been a flaw of mine. Here's a perfect opportunity to overcome something I need to work on. When I slide the glass door open, Uncle Mark lets out an excited "whoop!" and rushes over to me.

"How was your first day?" He takes the bag from my shoulder and leads me to the couch. Tears form in my eyes when I see they've ordered Mexican takeout. "Oh no! Finn," he clucks as we sit. "What's wrong? Why are you crying?"

"Low blood sugar," I say before I grab a chip, dip it into the queso, and shove it into my mouth. After chewing, I mumble, "Oh, God, I needed this."

He sits next to me, his hand on my back, rubbing light circles. "First day was that good, hmm?"

I chuckle as I grab another chip and nod.

"I feel like I haven't seen you in days." He grabs a few chips and gobbles them up. "How was your date with Emerson?"

I choke. *Literally.* I start coughing, and he jumps up and grabs my water bottle for me, opens it, and shoves it at me. I can't drink because I'm still dying from inhaling the piece of tortilla chip into the wrong pipe.

"Jesus Christ," he whispers once I've calmed down, which takes forever, it feels. "Are you okay?"

I'm crying from coughing, so I wipe my eyes. "I'm falling apart," I manage to answer before finally taking a drink of my water. "Also, it was not a date."

He lets out a *pfft* just as Aunt Lisa walks out. "She said it wasn't a date."

Aunt Lisa's lips curl into a smile. "Sure it wasn't."

"What the hell? It wasn't a date. I'm straight. I don't date women." I grab Uncle Mark's margarita and take a drink. It's delicious, so I take another drink. And another. Until, "Whoops, it's all gone." I hand it back and wipe my mouth. "I'll take another, please."

He grins at Aunt Lisa. "*She* loves my margs. I can't believe you don't."

"It's because you try to kill me with the tequila, you asshole." Aunt Lisa sits cross-legged on one of the Turkish pillows dotted around the coffee table. "Also, yes, it was *so* a date."

"Who said it was a date? Did Emerson? Because I literally told her I don't date women."

"Actually, that's exactly why I think it was a date. Because you said it wasn't. And so did she. So, it was a date." She shrugs before drinking from the freshly opened bottle of wine, right from the neck. "It's okay, Finn. You're allowed to see if this is what you'd like."

"Are either of you listening to me?" I look at both of them. Actually, I glare at both of them. "I am not gay."

"Neither am I." Aunt Lisa takes another drink from the bottle. "But I've dated women. Why do you have to have a label at all, Finn? Come on. Your generation is all about being fluid and loving people for who they are, not for what genitalia they possess."

"Well, shit." She's right. I relax my shoulders and my spine and take the drink Uncle Mark hands me. "I guess you have a point."

"Do you love Steven?" Lisa asks.

"Nope." I take a drink of the margarita. "Not at all."

"Break it off with him."

"And date Emerson," Mark says with a smile as he hands me a taco he just finished assembling. "She hasn't stopped talking about you."

I point at Aunt Lisa. "I'm going to break it off with Steven. I will. And"—I point at Uncle Mark now—"even if I were interested in Emerson, I wouldn't want her to be my rebound. Besides, I wouldn't know the first thing about dating a woman."

"She's a human being. It's not that different."

"She's fucking flawless, though. And one of the most beautiful women I've ever seen in my entire life." I take a huge bite of the street taco. I'm instantly transported to heaven. "Goddamn, this is good."

Uncle Mark hands me another taco, then passes one on to Aunt Lisa. "As far as Emerson goes, she's a wonderful person."

"And she is recovering from heartbreak," Aunt Lisa says. "So you two could sort of help each other out."

"I'm not heartbroken, though."

"No, but you're super confused, aren't you?" She raises her eyebrows and tilts her head. I can't argue, so I nod my agreement. "There is not one single thing wrong with hanging out with her and keeping your options open."

"I don't want to lead her on, though."

"You mean to tell me you wouldn't make out with her if she tried?" Aunt Lisa lets out a small laugh. "If you say no, I'll know you're lying."

"I haven't thought about it." My lie tastes awful in my mouth. I have thought about it. I've imagined every single second of it and how it would feel for her to touch my face, my neck, my lips. And I make myself stop because thinking like that means… "My mom would have a stroke if I told her I'm dating a woman."

Uncle Mark lets out a loud laugh. "Are you fucking kidding me?" He shakes his head as he loads up another chip with salsa. "She's been fairly positive you're queer for most of your life. Why do you think she pushed you to actually go to college and live in the dorms and not stay at home and go? Why do you think she pushed you to move here? With me? Your big gay uncle?"

"Whoa, whoa, *whoa*. You mean to tell me she's been pushing me to take these leaps of faith because she wants me to be gay?"

He clenches his jaw, the muscles flexing under the skin. "No, God. That's not what I'm saying. I'm saying she keeps nudging you gently because, Finn, honey, you have got to figure out who you are."

"What do you think I'm *trying* to do?"

"You're doing what you've always done. You're not making any waves. You're using your degree you didn't even *want*. You went to school so you could run the family business you don't even care about. Everything you've done in your life has been to appease your parents. And now that your dad, in all his fucking wisdom, fired your ass, you have the perfect opportunity to stop doing things for them and start doing things for yourself. You are so much more than this empty shell of a person." His tone and delivery have me considering every single aspect of my life in the span of a few seconds. As I look out toward the skyline, he continues. "I love you, and you're amazing. But you have got to decide what you're passionate about. And you need to decide who you're passionate about. Because bookkeeping and Steven are not the answers."

"Y'know, all I wanted was to come home and eat a granola bar and go to sleep, and here you both are, lecturing me on how awful I am for not following my heart."

"Hey now, I am not telling you you're awful. I'm telling you you're unhappy. It's painfully obvious." He gently turns my face so that I'm looking at him. "I'll be your fairy godfather if you need me to be."

I pull him into a hug. "I love you, Uncle Mark." I let out a laugh, which strangles into crying more abruptly than I thought it would. "Oh God, you're so right. I'm not happy. How the hell do I fix this?"

"Honey?" Aunt Lisa's voice is closer now, and I feel her sitting next to me. I let go of Uncle Mark and look at her. "I have to tell you this because I think people think because your uncle and I divorced that we weren't happy. It's the farthest thing from the truth." Her eyes move from mine to Uncle Mark's. "I loved your uncle more than I have ever loved another person. I still love him. He's the brightest light in my life. And even though I cheated and it was stupid, I think I can say with one hundred percent certainty we have always been happy together."

"She's not wrong," he says softly. "I was hurt, yes, but I've always been happy with her."

"When we divorced, we did so because we wanted to continue to love each other. We didn't want to hate each other. And honestly? I love him more now than I did then. And I think he feels the same way about me."

"I do," he says, and Aunt Lisa's smile, the smile she seems to reserve just for Uncle Mark, is gorgeous.

"Being happy sometimes means sacrificing things in your life that seem to make sense. You're allowed to do whatever you need to do in order to sink your teeth into a life that will bring you joy. You're a remarkable person, and you deserve every ounce of happiness available to you. My advice for now? Keep your job. At the very least it'll get you out of the house. But remember, this is a time for rebirth. You have the opportunity to create a life you are thrilled to live." She lets out a giddy laugh. "And that's so exciting, isn't it?"

I wrap my arms around her and hug her tightly. "Thank you so much," I whisper. I had no idea this was the route I would be heading down when I picked up my entire life and moved here. I figured I'd find a job and life would be better simply because I wasn't working for my parents. Little did I know I was going to embark on a journey to find happiness, and on that road, I was going to have two of the best tour guides ever.

∽

Halfway through my fourth margarita, Uncle Mark and Aunt Lisa disappear into the house. I'm left by myself, mesmerized by the crisp, cool air, the beauty of the evening. The evening sky is free of clouds, and the playlist Uncle Mark has put on is exactly what I need. Florence, Phoebe Bridgers, Taylor Swift, a little dash of Leon Bridges, and a sprinkle of Tedeschi Trucks Band. I've made my way to the other side of The Oasis, where I'm taking in the sights of the city, thinking about everything that has unfolded today. What else can happen? Hopefully not much else; I don't think my inebriated brain can handle it.

"Whatcha thinking about?"

The voice startles me. I let out a gasp as I swing around to see none other than Emerson standing there. I spoke entirely too soon. She's wearing faded jeans and a black sweater she's clearly worn a few hundred times because it has a hole near the shoulder. "Hi," I shout at a volume that is way too loud, considering the minuscule distance between us. I am so not smooth. "Hey," I amend. "Sorry. You scared me."

The smile on her face is... *wow*... "No need to apologize." She takes a step closer so she's next to me. I can smell her scent as it envelops me. I want to bury my face in her neck. *Jesus, is that the tequila talking?* "We need to work on you apologizing all the time." She leans against the railing with her hip and crosses her left leg over her right. "How are you?"

I'm still so taken by her standing there in front of me that I have to remind myself I do, in fact, know how to speak, to respond, to answer her fucking question. "Uh, peachy," I blurt out. "I'm good. Yeah. Good."

Her eyes are sparkling from the Edison bulbs Uncle Mark has strung up around The Oasis. I was so drunk and high the last time I was up here with her that I don't recall the lights, but I'm sure they were on. "How was your first day?"

"Awful," I say after I let out the breath I didn't even realize I was holding.

She lets out a chuckle, low and smooth. Now that I've been told it's okay to want this, to want her, to want to fall into whatever this is with her, I can't take my eyes off of her. All I can imagine is kissing her. "Day one is never a good gauge, right?"

"I hope not."

She licks her lips before she breaks our intense eye contact. "Listen, Finnley, I wanted to tell you how sorry I am about everything I said yesterday. I don't know why I thought it was a good idea." She looks up from the artificial turf to the sky. The line of her neck… What would it be like to kiss her there? To run my tongue from the hollow where her neck meets her chest up to her chin? "I think I'm struggling, trying to figure things out since my divorce should be final soon. And feeling like a failure on top of it all. Y'know what I mean?" She glances at me, and our eyes lock for one beat, two, three, before she looks away again. "And you… You've made me feel like myself again instead of an empty shell."

I don't know how it happens except to say I am tipsy, but without even thinking about it, I close the distance between us, take her face in my hands, and kiss her. Her lips, *her perfect lips*, taste like peppermint ChapStick. The warmth of her breath when she breathes out her nose makes my hands ache. Our mouths fit together, and everything sort of clicks into place, like finding a missing puzzle piece under the couch and finally being able to complete the masterpiece I've worked on for most of my life. So many times, I almost put the puzzle back in the box because I thought the piece didn't exist, but lo and behold, it does. It has been standing in front of me with icing on her lip, a chip on her shoulder, and sexiness seeping from her pores.

I hear Uncle Mark shout, "Ladies, we're back up here now if you want to join us," and I pull away from the kiss. Her eyes are still closed, her right hand gripping the railing, her left clenched into a fist.

"I'm sorry—"

"Shh." She hasn't opened her eyes yet. Regret begins to fill my stomach. "Don't apologize, please."

"Okay." My voice is whisper-soft as I observe her take a deep breath, unclench her left hand, and slide her eyes open. "Are you okay?"

She nods.

"Okay."

"What..." She pauses. It's clear she's fighting a smile as it tugs at the corner of her lips. "What was that?"

I shrug. "I knew you wouldn't make the first move after our conversation yesterday. And I haven't been able to stop thinking about it. Kissing you, I mean. So I figured, what the hell? YOLO."

She lets out a laugh. "YOLO, huh?"

"Yeah, YOLO. Come on," I say as I take her left hand in mine and pull gently. "Let's go hang out with Mark and Lisa."

She doesn't allow me to pull her away yet. She hasn't taken her eyes off me, though, and the look of wonder on her face is one I'm not ever going to forget. When she finally pushes away from the railing and follows me, she intertwines her fingers with mine. The only thing I can think, aside from how perfectly our hands fit together, is how I have never wanted to hold anyone else's hand. And now? Now it's all I want to do...

∼

AT TEN, AUNT LISA ANNOUNCES SHE HAS TO LEAVE. "MY BED calls," she says, a drunk lilt to her voice. Uncle Mark ends up talking her into staying the night, though. Even though she was going to take a Lyft, it was still a load off, knowing she wasn't going to be drunk in the back of someone else's car.

Emerson helps me clean up The Oasis. I didn't ask her to and was shocked when she loaded her arms with the miscellaneous items our night of takeout decadence has littered across the space. It warms my heart for some dumb reason. I tell Siri to turn the lights off, and once we're both inside, I turn to look at her.

Her eyes are full of questions, and I haven't been able to give her a single answer. "Will you stay with me?"

She takes a full three seconds before she nods. It's insane how long three seconds actually last when you're standing there waiting for an answer to a question you never thought you'd ask. After I reach forward and slide my hand down to hers, she lightly links our fingers. The softness of her skin is intoxicating.

I don't know what I plan on happening when I lead her into my bedroom. I do know I want to talk to her. I want to ask her questions, laugh with her, get to know her and all her eccentricities. And I weirdly want her to get to know me, which is not normal. I hate being the object of anyone's research. I have this desire now, though. It started out so tiny I didn't even realize what it was, but it has blossomed into a full-grown monstrosity. I want us both to feel like this isn't me only wanting to experiment. Because that's what it could easily feel like, I'm sure.

I look over at her, she's still facing the door. She is struggling with all of this. "Emerson?"

"Hmm?"

"I don't want you to take this wrong, but I am only looking to get to know each other at this point."

She looks over her shoulder at me. "Oh, thank God."

A puff of air pushes out of my mouth. "I'm not sure how to take that sigh of relief."

She rushes over to me. "No, no, that's not—*no*. That's not what I meant. I just mean I don't think you're ready for this. I'm not ready for this. But I like you, Finnley. You don't have to worry about that."

I sit on the bed, my legs hanging over the edge, and she does the same. "I have no idea what is happening to me."

"I know." She is so beautiful in the dim ambiance of my bedroom. Whatever I've said up to this point, the confidence I had in myself to be an adult and get to know her is starting to dwindle. Wouldn't it be so much more fun to make out with her for the rest of the night? "You're still with Steven."

Oh yeah. *Steven.* Welp, that puts a damper on things. "I am going to break it off with him. I need to."

"Okay."

"I promise."

"Don't promise me. You need to do what you want to do."

"I know."

"But," she starts, and I notice how she is gripping the edge of the mattress. "Why didn't you before you left? Not that it's any of my business. I'm simply curious."

"Truthfully? Because I'm an idiot."

Her laugh is so lovely. "You're not an idiot. But you're not happy with him, right?"

I shake my head, hold back the tears forming in my eyes, and answer with a simple, "Not at all."

"I almost feel bad for him."

I let out a laugh. "Oh God, why?"

"I'm sure it'll be a shock."

Another laugh pours from me. "No, it won't be. I already told him he should have let me break it off with him."

"You're brutal," she teased.

"And to think I'm normally not very good at hurting people."

"Why did you say yes when he asked you to marry him?" She repositions herself so she's facing me, her right leg bent on the bed, her left still hanging off the edge. I'm envious of her ability to be comfortable right now. This amount of sharing has me on edge, like a loud noise would make me jump.

"There has always been a part of me that thought a relationship was *supposed* to be the way it felt with him. Comfortable, boring, bland."

Her snort is adorable. "Please never write my obituary."

"I know, right?"

"Have you really never thought you might like women?"

The memories of high school, my teacher, and his wife punch me in the gut. "Funny story, one I should have told you yesterday. I was way too shaken to come up with the right words..." I gather all the courage I can muster. "I'm pretty sure I had a crush on my high school teacher's wife."

"Oh?" Emerson's eyes widen. "Do tell."

The details are as vivid as always when I launch into one of the most embarrassing moments of my entire life. The letter I wrote to my teacher, the janitor finding it, the meeting with my parents and the teacher and his *wife*, the way I felt like a complete fucking buffoon for the rest of high school. "The pièce de résistance? She was my drama coach, and her initials before she was married to him were the same as mine. I thought one of my castmates was playing a prank on me when I saw 'FO loves MJ' on the back of one of the set trees. I freaked out, and the wife had to say, casually on the side where no one could hear, 'Finnley, my last name used to start with an O.'"

Emerson's grin is almost too much to handle. "What was her first name?"

"Fiona."

"You had a crush on a *Fiona*?"

I can feel the heat in my cheeks. "Until about two nights ago, I would have said no. But now? Yeah, I'm pretty sure I had a crush on Fiona Jackson, who used to be Fiona Olsen."

"You must have been so embarrassed."

"I was mortified. Hell, I still am. I didn't go to my ten-year high school reunion because of it."

"Finnley," she says as she leans her head back and laughs. "You are too much."

"It was awful. My parents were so upset with me. My mom especially."

"Oh, boy, moms. They always seem to have issues..." Her eyes fill with sadness, and I can't stop watching the way the story has moved her. She is so beautiful when she smiles and laughs, but right now, sitting in the middle of whatever memory she's pulled out of the archives, she's breathtaking. Emotions look stunning on her.

"How did you know?"

"Know I'm into women?" She shrugs, a nonchalant air surrounding her as if she's told this story a thousand times. "I guess I sort of always knew something about me was different. I had my share of boyfriends, but it always felt—"

"Forced? Not fun? Awkward? Nauseating?"

She laughs. "Yeah, honestly, all of that. Finnley, you felt that way about your relationships with men and never wondered why?"

"Oh, I wondered all the time." I laugh when she does again. I could so get used to hearing her happiness for the rest of my life. "I just figured once I found the right guy, all of those feelings would fade."

The look on her face, the sadness in her eyes, as if she feels so bad for me that I went through all of that. "I'm sorry," she whispers. "That had to be frustrating."

It's in that moment that I feel every ounce of my inability to acknowledge this part of myself dissipate. "I never thought about it like that before but, yeah, it really was frustrating."

"Coming to terms with why things don't feel the way you've grown up thinking they should is really freeing."

I want to kiss her. I want to capture her lips and feel her against me. I want everything about her. And she's right. It's really fucking freeing. "Tell me more about you." It's the only thing I can think to say because if she doesn't keep talking, I'm going to act on my desires. And it's entirely too soon to spend the rest of the night making out when I explicitly said I wanted to get to know her. I do. I just happen to also want to get to know her lips and tongue.

"It's been forever since I've been the one under a microscope." The way she pushes her blond hair over her shoulder makes my stomach bottom out. How is such a simple move so fucking sexy when she does it? "I figured out pretty early on that the last thing I wanted was to end up like my parents, who were wonderful parents but horrible together. They stayed together because it was the right thing to do, not because they loved each other. To this day, they can't stand each other." She pauses, glances down at her hands, and rubs the dark spot on her thumb where the charcoal she must have used to draw something stained her skin. She's not wearing her wedding ring, but she does have a thick silver band on the middle finger of her right hand. "I started hanging out with this group of young artists in college, which, man, feels like a lifetime ago. They were free and exciting, and I was young. God, so very young and impressionable. But I was also eager, unafraid, which caught the eye of this student, Renee." Emerson has moved her hand to her neck, where her fingers, with their short, black-painted, manicured nails, are touching the side of it, the back of it, the length of it, and I cannot stop staring. Her voice is dreamy, and the sigh she releases is enough to make me melt into a giant puddle. "She was a writer. Boy, did she know how to string words and sentences together to make me think I was the most important person in the entire world…" She pauses, her voice dropping away, her gaze falling once again to her hands, which are now clasped in her lap. Sadness swaddles her demeanor like a blanket. I wonder if she even realizes it. "And that was it. I knew. I knew what I wanted and why and how often and with who." She still hasn't looked up, but her voice no longer sounds strained.

"What did it feel like?"

"What do you think it felt like?"

"Like this." It comes out as a whisper. I can only hope she heard it because I can't repeat it.

She places her fingers under my chin and turns my head to face her. "Why did you change your mind about this? You seemed pretty adamant yesterday."

"I haven't stopped thinking about you since you showed up late the other night." My heartbeat has quickened, and my hands are literally aching. She smooths the soft pad of her thumb over my jawline. "You walked in, and my brain sort of, like, walked out?" The smile she offers me helps me calm down. "I've never met anyone like you before."

"I'm nothing special."

I can't contain the huff that escapes my lips. "Sure. You've only made me realize I might like women. Definitely not special at all."

My comment seemingly causes her to collapse onto the bed, laughing the entire time. "I'm a gateway drug."

"That is not what I said." I fall backward onto the bed beside her and stare at the ceiling. "You said I make you feel like yourself again?"

"Yeah, it's the truth."

"Well, you make me feel like a person. I've been asleep for most of my life, and then I met you and… I finally woke up." I take a chance and look over at her, at the kindness in her eyes. "I barely know you, and I know I'd rather be near you than anyone else in my life."

"You're insanely sweet, Finnley." She places a kiss on my forehead. My heart sinks. I want so badly to kiss her again. "Let's sleep, okay?"

That same feeling of disappointment floods my veins. I try to remind myself that this is probably just as hard on her as it is on me. Thirty-six hours ago, I thought I was completely straight. I'm still engaged. And she's in the middle of a divorce. It's a perfect storm of wrongs.

God, how can so many wrongs feel so very right?

CHAPTER SIX

Petals for Days has some of the worst books I've ever seen in my entire career, which isn't very long, but still. I've been working there now for one week. In that short amount of time, I've contemplated quitting at least twice daily. This was not what I wanted when I applied for a nice, easy position. I've seen some questionable accounting in my time. And this? This takes the cake. I thought my dad's bookkeeping skills were subpar. I was wrong.

And while dealing with all of that, I'm still trying to keep Steven's texts and phone calls answered in a way that makes him *stay* away. I've been successful so far. I tried the whole *I need to focus on me and my job* conversation with him the other night. He, of course, didn't take it well and declared something about how he was not giving up. Great.

Needless to say, I do need to focus on me and my job, because if this is something I really want to do, I need to make it work.

During a two-hour meeting today with Justine that hasn't been going very smoothly, I tell her she needs to tighten the belt. "I don't think you understand how much money you *don't* have right now."

She has an attitude when she answers with, "Well, I hired you to find the money and manage it."

"Agreed. But when the profits are being spent for your expansion store, it's a little difficult to find *more* money."

"What are you proposing then?"

"You might want to consider running with a skeleton crew at the old store if you want the new store to work and not be in the red for the next two years."

She huffs. "Absolutely not. If we need more money, then I need to have people working on the orders coming in so we can make the money. Who's going to do the work if I have to let people go?"

I raise my eyebrows as I stare at her, hoping she gets what I'm saying without having to actually say it.

"*Me*? I'm already working fifty hours a week."

"Well, you might need to work sixty then."

"And still only make the equivalent to twenty hours a week, I'm sure." She groans. "I thought we had to spend money to make money?"

"Sure, but not when there is no money to spend."

"Can you please explain to me how there's no money? I don't get it."

I flip open the report to the general ledger. "Have you ever learned how to read the ledger? I'm asking a legitimate question, not trying to be rude."

She shakes her head. "It's why you're here."

"Okay, then, look. Here are your sales, which are amazing. You're seriously killing it."

"Thank you," she whispers, as if being proud isn't allowed.

"No, seriously, Justine, these are outstanding numbers. And you're right, you need to keep that up because when you go down the report to your expenditures, things start to fall apart. Rent on your first space is ridiculous. Maybe we can talk to the landlord and work out a better deal."

"No, he hates women. And flowers. The only reason he is still allowing us to be here is because we never miss a payment, and our success has allowed him to fill up the entire complex."

I laugh. "Great. So, not that. Construction on the new place can't be cut because it has to happen. You and the staff can probably do some of the interior work instead of contracting that out. That'll save a little. But ultimately, what's killing you is labor. And, don't take this wrong, but you are cheap labor. Because, as the owner, you don't have to get paid right now."

"Okay, fine. Then who do I fire? Or maybe I'll make you fire the person since you seem to think you know everything."

Whoa. That's a bit much. I take a breath. "Did you hire me to simply do what you've always done, or did you want me to actually help you?"

"I wanted you to do things as I've always done them."

"Well, I wish I had known that."

By the end of the meeting, I am so mad I could spit. I tell Justine I need some time to decompress before we continue. I should have never taken this job. I know not everything is going to be rainbows and unicorns all the time, but goddamn, I didn't realize it'd literally be like working for my dad again. As I'm pacing back and forth on the sidewalk of Wacker Drive, I hear Justine clear her throat from behind me.

"I really need some time, Justine. I wasn't joking about that."

"Listen," she says as she approaches me, her hands held up in mock surrender. "I'm sorry. I really am. I'm not used to someone else being in the books and knowing what's going on. I get away with things because it's what I've always done. But you're right. If I want this to work, for both of these shops to flourish, then I need to change things."

With my arms folded across my chest, I stand and stare out across the Chicago River to the Tribune Building. "I know," I finally answer when she makes her way closer to me. I glance at her, at her curly hair, at the scar on her lip. "I swear I am not going to make you regret making changes. You need to cut costs, though, or nothing will work for you. I'm not being bleak to scare you. I'm being bleak because that's what it is, bleak. I don't even know where you're going to get the sixty-five grand a year you said you could pay me."

She shrugs. "I was going to stop taking a paycheck." The shock on my face must register with her because she points at me and says, "See? I *do* want this. And I do know you're necessary. I'm stubborn. I'm a Capricorn."

"Oh, Jesus. Great." I smirk. "This should be fun."

Justine's face lights up, her cheeks plumping with her wide smile. "So, you'll stay?"

"Yes, I'll stay." I want to add, *But only because I need the money.* I don't, obviously, but only because it's a little too much honesty when I'm getting what I want from her. "No more fighting me when I say you need to make cuts, okay?" She nods her understanding. "And when I make suggestions about marketing and things of that nature, it's because I know what I'm doing. I have an MBA. From Harvard. I'm not stupid."

Her face instantly turns a deep red and she gulps. "You heard that?"

"I did when you were complaining about me to Vivian on the phone."

"I promise you I want this to work and will do whatever it takes, okay?"

"I'll hold you to it." I check my watch, and excitement comes over me. "It's five. Do you need anything else from me?"

"Yes," she says, then gives me a very sheepish smile. "Would you go get a drink with me? I'd love to get to know you better."

I wish I could say no because I'm meeting someone in my very busy life, but it would be a bold-faced lie. "Sure. I'd like that." I silently curse myself as I follow her back upstairs to get our purses. The last thing I want to do is get close to the owner of the business where I do not respect how things have been run. Yet here I am, saying yes without a good excuse in the shoot. I'm such a rookie when it comes to this job stuff.

∼

The closest bar is at the Hyatt Regency. We find a seat at one of the pub-height tables, and before we sit, a platter of chips and dip is placed on the table. Justine thanks the server, and within seconds, a drink is also being delivered by the bartender, who is none other than—

"Blake, hi, how are you?" Justine's voice has a nervous quiver to it I haven't heard before.

"I'm good. I wondered if I'd see you tonight." Blake's hand is on the back of Justine's chair. The way they're standing, shoulders completely facing Justine, blocking me out of the picture entirely, is very telling. If I didn't know any better, I'd be convinced they're *flirting* with her. I'm instantly intrigued. I take a chip and crunch on it, seeing if the noise changes either of their demeanor. Needless to say, I'm not shocked when it doesn't.

"You know me, a Friday night begs for a drink. Especially with the flowers we have to deliver tomorrow for the Kerstin wedding." She hasn't taken her eyes from Blake's. I crunch on another chip. Still no recognition. "Which reminds me, are you still planning to help me?"

"I wouldn't miss it." Blake's other hand is laid flat on the table. Their nails are painted black, the paint chipped, and I'm stunned this bar allows them to get away with it. It seems like a pretty upscale establishment, especially since it's in a nice hotel.

"Are you going to say hi to Finnley?" Justine finally asks Blake.

The way the familiarity in Blake's tone as they toss me a, "Hey, Finn," over their shoulder causes a spark of anger to flare deep, deep inside the pit of my stomach is almost laughable. Almost.

My simple, "Hey," in response was supposed to be biting, but of course my voice sounds way too nice. I really need to work on my tone.

"What would you like to drink, Finnley?" Justine's eyes are still locked on Blake.

"I'll take a tequila and soda with a lime, please."

Blake finally looks at me. "Any particular tequila?"

"Patrón Silver, please."

"Coming right up."

When Blake walks away, Justine's eyes follow them back to the bar. I take another chip and crunch on it. It works this time, and Justine snaps her attention to me. "So, anyway," she demurs.

"Uh, no," I insist. "We'll be discussing *that*."

"No way." Justine lets out a low chuckle. "I barely know you. I'm not dumping the drama of my love life on you." She grabs a chip and brings it to her lips, but before she takes a bite, she asks, "But you'd listen?"

"Absolutely." I hope I don't sound as eager as I feel. Why does the idea of speaking to someone else about a queer relationship excite me so much?

"Good to know." Justine pops the chip into her mouth and chews before launching into the logistics of tomorrow's wedding flower delivery.

∽

It only takes three drinks for Justine to open up.

"I slept with Blake about two years ago," she admits. "It was stupid, and I should have never done it, but I did." She takes a deep breath. "I think they're adorable. I knew them when they weren't identifying as nonbinary. I was attracted to them before, but God, I'm even more so now."

"Well, damn, I knew you two were flirting, but I had no idea you'd already slept together."

"Yeah, so stupid."

"Wait, why's it stupid? Because you're the—"

"The *boss*, for starters, yeah," she says, finishing my sentence. "The owner of the company as well. I didn't want to be that person who would take advantage of an employee. And I sort of… fell into the role, didn't I?" Justine's face twists. "You know what's even worse? When I slept with them, I was married. I'm *still* married actually. Well, separated, I should say." Her eyes fill with tears. "I ruined my marriage for them."

I'm on my third drink as well, so when I bring it to my lips, I briefly wonder if I should try to get out of the rest of this conversation. I can fake a text message from my uncle. I can say I completely forgot I *do* have plans. Or I can sit completely still and let Justine pour her heart out to me.

"Who am I kidding?" She puffs her cheeks. "My marriage was over long before I cheated." Her face twists. "I hate admitting I'm a cheater. Please don't think less of me."

"Oh, God, Justine, I won't. I promise."

I'm not lying. While I've never been a cheater—until my makeout session with Emerson, of course—I have no room to judge anyone who has succumbed to forbidden desire.

"It was stupid, though, because I loved her. I still love her. I always will, I'm sure. She couldn't get over it, though. I don't blame her." Justine is staring at the bottom of her fourth drink. "Isabel was the one who said we shouldn't get married when we did. I'm the one who talked her into it. I should have known, right?" She looks up at me. "Right? Like, when you have to talk someone into something, it pretty much means they don't want to do it." A crazed laugh bubbles from her. "I'm such an idiot."

"Hey," I say as I reach forward and place a hand over hers. "I barely know you, but I do know you are not an idiot. Love makes us do all sorts of things—some of them great, some of them very questionable. At the end of the day, no one gets to judge us for the things we've done because we're in love."

"That's very wise."

I laugh. It's a hearty laugh that makes me bend my head back. "I am so far from wise." What makes her statement even more hilarious is I'm fairly positive I have never been in love with someone else like she was. Like she is... "You shouldn't beat yourself up, though."

"You might feel differently if you knew my soon-to-be ex. She's, well, she's perfect."

"Then, if you don't mind me asking, why? Why did you... y'know... with Blake?"

"Oh, man." She sighs, leans her head back, and stares up at the ceiling of the bar. "I'd love to say Isabel didn't love me enough or like I wanted her to love me. I'd love to say we simply fell out of love. But all of that would be false. She was perfect and continues to be perfect."

"Except for the part where she's not backing down from the divorce."

She nods before taking the final fried mozzarella stick we ordered two drinks ago. She takes a giant bite out of it, then says, around the food in her mouth, "I'm a mess, Finnley. A real fuckin' mess."

I can't help but chuckle at her. She's not lying. She is a mess. But for some reason, especially lately, messy people seem to be my forte. "Luckily for you, I don't mind if you're a mess. I'm here for you. And, hey, maybe this level of honesty will be good for you. You'll be able to heal, to move forward. After all, that's what you need to do in order for your new storefront to be successful."

"You're right. You're absolutely right." She points at me with the half-eaten mozzarella stick. "I have to remember that."

"I'll keep reminding you."

"Thank you, Finnley." Her shoulders fall, her face filling with admiration. "Seriously, I needed this."

"You're very welcome." She invites me to come on tomorrow's wedding flower delivery with her, which sounds like a lot of fun, so I accept without a second thought. She goes on and on about how she wants me to learn the business so I can be an integral part of everything, from the books to the storefront to the events. The last part sounds like a pipe dream, but I keep my head on straight and don't allow my brain to get too far ahead of itself. I have to stay grounded in the fact that this all really could be temporary. I don't want to keep books forever. But maybe, just maybe, it can morph into the position I really want.

The position I really *want*.

Christ. I hope one day that thought doesn't cause my skin to crawl. The past two weeks have been telling. I'm settling into Petals For Days. I'm learning how to navigate Justine's mood swings. I'm using my charm to get Blake to not hate me. I'm letting my guard down and trying to listen to what my heart is telling me.

Is it at all possible that maybe a job isn't what I need to *make me* happy? A good career is what I am supposed to want. But what I want even more than that is to know when it was pounded into my head that a job is what makes a person happy. Because my parents are not a great example of that. And becoming them is not an option. Ever.

I will figure this out. I know I will because I am closer than ever to discovering who I am. And discovering that will hopefully lead to me really understanding what I want.

Is Petals for Days what I want?

Or is this simply a placeholder like Blake originally accused me?

Shit. That is an admission I will not have fun confessing.

Either way, I'm going to continue moving forward. Learning, growing, changing. It's the only thing I can do.

~

Now that I know all about Uncle Mark's line of work, he's rarely home at night. It's obvious that, in the beginning, he wasn't taking calls in an effort to shield me from the truth as long as possible. I'm so glad it's out in the open now, though I do worry about him. I love him so much, and I hope he stays safe out there. Growing closer to him over the last couple of weeks has given me some of the best times of my life. He's kind and fun and incredibly thoughtful. Tonight, he has left me a note in his beautiful, loopy handwriting that says:

Dinner is in the refrigerator. You need to eat. I know you've been skipping meals. I can tell by my lack of needing to grocery-shop. Eat, babycakes.

I smile when I pull out the roast chicken breast, corn on the cob, and salad. He's the best roommate I could ever ask for.

As I'm heating the food, the doorbell rings. My heart starts to beat rapidly. The only person who visits at this time of night is Emerson. I rush to the door, stopping only briefly to check myself in the mirror by the door. Before I do anything else, I pull my lip gloss from my pocket and apply it. Generously.

When I pull open the door, Emerson is standing there, illuminated by the soft glow of the door lamp. Her hair is pulled into the same messy bun it was the night I forgot to put on pants. Sweat is glistening on her bare shoulders, and she's breathing heavily. I'm so turned on simply by looking at her that I forget how to speak.

"Hey," she says, her chest rising and falling with her breathing. My eyes are drawn to her breasts. "You busy?"

Instead of trying to remedy my ability to speak, I reach forward with both hands, grab her, and pull her toward me. When my lips crash into hers, she chuckles at first, but her lips soften and she starts to kiss me back. Her chest continues to rise and fall rapidly against me. How is something as simple as breathing so fucking erotic? I slip my tongue into her mouth, which she accepts. She walks me backward into the house and manages to slam the door behind us. I don't know what's gotten into me, but I take control and push her backward until her back is pressed into the door. Her lips taste like salt from her sweat, and I can smell her deodorant. Lavender and rose petals. I make a mental note to find the exact scent so I can start using it.

She has managed to untuck the maroon blouse from the skinny black slacks I wore to work. Her hands slip under the material, press against my bare sides, and she digs her nails into my skin. "I want to fuck you so badly," she whispers against my lips in between kisses.

Welp. There go that pair of panties. I break from the kiss, rest my head against her forehead. "I know. God, I know. I want that, too."

"We've gotta figure this out." She's still breathless. And it's so hot.

"I know." I whisper the words because saying them out loud seems wrong. I should have already figured this out. Kissing her is incredible. She's soft and sensual and everything I have always wanted but never realized and now... "I missed you."

"Oh, yeah?"

I nod after I pull away from her. "Way more than I thought was possible."

"I missed you, too." Her thumbs are stroking my bare sides. If she keeps that up, I'm going to combust.

"If I knew you were coming over, I would have forgotten pants again," I say as nonchalantly as possible.

She laughs loud, and it warms my heart. "You are hilarious, you know that?"

"I just love making you laugh."

"You're very good at it." She presses her thumbs against my ribs. "You make me *happy*." Her eyes are red-rimmed, and I fear she's going to start crying. "It's been so long since I've felt this way, Finnley. And it feels really good. Like, really fucking good. I didn't realize how much I missed this part of myself until you brought me back. I really like laughing and feeling good again."

"Emerson," I whisper. I place my hands on her cheeks, wipe away the stray tears that have escaped, and place a solitary kiss on her full lips. "You laughing and feeling good is the most beautiful thing I've ever seen."

She leans forward and kisses me again. "Do you think it's possible for us to make out and not have sex?"

"Anything is possible." I grab her hand and pull her toward the stairs. "Of course, you're not going to get your run in. I hope that's okay."

She scoffs. "It's more than okay."

When we get to my room, before I have a chance to turn on a lamp, she pulls me against her. She kisses me deeply, moans into my mouth, and pushes her leg between my thighs. She slides herself against my crotch. I'm ready to combust. How am I supposed to not have sex with her? Is this going to be the biggest test I've ever taken? I went to Harvard, for fuck's sake, and this is going to be the biggest test of my life? What a turn of events.

I need to break it off with Steven before I do this. Don't I?

Or should I just say fuck it? And fuck her? Goddammit.

"Finnley," she whispers. "We can't do this yet."

"I know." I push my hands up under her tank top. Her bare skin is slightly sticky from sweat, and everything about it makes my insides hum. I used to hate touching Steven after a workout. He smelled, and honestly, the slick feeling of his body hair was just not my jam. I now know why. Then I thought it was just a weird tick about myself. Boy, was I wrong.

"Then what are we doing?" She backs me up against the wall next to my bedroom door. When my backside presses against the cool drywall, she leans her forehead against mine. "Because I don't know if I trust us."

"These feelings I have about you are all I trust these days."

She opens her eyes and pulls back from me. "You've got it bad, hmm?"

I let out a laugh. "Um, yeah, you could say that."

She places her hand flat against the wall next to my head. "Don't be mad at me…"

"For what?"

"I'm going to go." She gives me a sorrow-filled expression. "I'm sorry."

"I'm not mad at you." I give her a smile along with my heart and soul. "Patience is a virtue, isn't it?"

"It is." She kisses me before she takes my hand and pulls me with her, back down the stairs to the front door. "Lock this behind me," she says before she gives me one more quick kiss.

And then she's gone, leaving me standing there with every fiber of my being throbbing and begging for release. Guess I know what I'm going to have to do before bed tonight.

I'm not mad at her… but I am severely disappointed. It's hard to be mad when I agree with her. We have to both be in a place where sleeping together isn't happening *only* because we're ravenous. And it gives me fuel to take the steps I need to get rid of Steven. That should be my number one priority.

If I'm mad about anything, it's that I haven't been courageous enough to do it.

CHAPTER SEVEN

Justine tells me I am free to head home at half past five on Saturday. Helping was so much more fun than I imagined it would be. The venue was in Indiana at the Dunes Pavilion with the shore of Lake Michigan as a backdrop. Everything was gorgeous and the floral arrangements Justine, Vivian, and Lydia put together were some of the most beautiful and elaborate I'd ever seen. Bright yellow and orange sunflowers, deep red roses, and purple hydrangeas all pulled together with pops of white lilies of the valley. They looked so beautiful next to the rustic and trendy atmosphere of the venue. I have to admit, learning this side of the business has been way more fun than managing the books.

I also figure out that Blake's change of heart was a temporary thing. They're back to treating me with less than kindness. I'm almost relieved because I won't feel as bad quitting if Petals for Days isn't the last stop of my journey toward career harmony.

Regardless of Blake's attitude, a part of me wants to stay and enjoy the Kerstins' wedding reception, but a larger part of me is dead tired and excited to head home to relax and unwind. My mind is racing with all I was able to witness today. The way

Justine and her team work together is impressive. Their speed, accuracy, and professionalism are top-notch. I can see why she's booked so far into the future. I can also see why she so badly wants to hire more people. It is damn near impossible to do everything that goes into preparing for a wedding and run two storefronts. I need to tell her that, acknowledge that I recognize her desire for more employees. Maybe that will help her see why I'm pinching every penny right now. Because I get it. I understand.

I'm so deep in thought I almost miss my stop on the L. Thankfully, I realize it at the last minute and leap into action, squeezing out the doors just as they're closing.

Once I get home and strip out of the Petals for Days polo shirt and khaki shorts I was mandated to wear, I shower. I've fallen in love with my bathroom, especially the shower. It's over-the-top extravagant, with two heads. One of them is a waterfall, the other a removable one, and let me just say, I may never need a man again. It's given me the best showers of my life, hands down. When I'm done, I pull on a pair of yoga pants and my favorite baggy old sweater, wrap my dark, damp hair into a bun, and head downstairs to wait for the Pasta Bowl delivery I've ordered. I'm starving, too, so they better fucking hurry.

As soon as that thought runs through my head, the doorbell rings. I swing it open, expecting to see a delivery person meeting me, but am completely taken aback when I see Emerson holding the bag.

"Hey," she says, a half smile on her lips. It's been a few days since I last saw her. Every time we see each other, it's becoming harder and harder to not have sex with her. Like right now, all I want to do is kiss her. I want to grab her and make out with her for the next ten hours. I'm an addict. And she is absolutely my drug.

It takes me a few seconds of navigating how to speak around

my heart, which is lodged in my throat, before I can finally acknowledge her. "Hey there."

She holds the bag out to me. "I was going to ask you if you want to go to dinner, but it looks like you already have it covered."

"There's plenty if you'd like to join me." I feel bold, offering for her to come in, though I'm prepared to have my hopes dashed.

"I'd love to," she answers, and my tentative hopes are replaced with elation.

I allow my eyes to follow her into the kitchen, taking in the gentle sway of her hips as she walks, the way her jean shorts are hugging her ass, and the rip in said shorts, right below her right ass cheek. Her body, her curves, her muscles… goddamn. I lean against the kitchen door frame as she pulls containers filled with delicious pesto linguine, spaghettini, and meatballs from the carryout bag.

"I hope I didn't ruin any plans you had." She pauses, her hand on a tin of garlic bread. "I didn't want to be alone tonight."

"Em, you didn't ruin my night."

Her eyes latch onto mine. "Good. I'm glad."

"I wasn't looking forward to an entire night alone either, so you pretty much saved me."

We take our plates to the table and choose seats next to each other. It warms my heart for some dumb reason. I like her way too much for someone who still hasn't broken up with her fiancé, for someone who spent most of her life thinking she was straight as an arrow, for someone who wouldn't know how to have sex with a woman if she were given a million dollars. Speaking of Steven, I keep answering his texts partly to keep him at bay but also because I haven't had the courage to simply call him and break it off with him. I tried a few times, and each time, I chicken out and send a simple response to his *I miss you* texts. Usually it's a smile emoji or a thumbs up. It's not cool and is actually borderline hateful. To him and to Emerson. And hell, to myself. But how do I tell him why when he asks? Because he *will* ask.

I keep sneaking glances at Emerson as she eats. It's weird and probably my dumbest eccentricity, but I find it very hard to watch someone I'm interested in eat food. It makes no sense, but there's an intimacy I feel when I'm eating with someone I care about. Watching Emerson as she twirls linguine onto her fork is way more erotic than it has a right to be. Two years in, and I still can't watch Steven eat anything. Pizza? Fuck no. Pasta? Absolutely not. Salad? Not on my life. When Emerson dabs at her mouth with a napkin, she finally notices my obsessive staring, and the smile on her face is too much for me. The heat filling my cheeks as I look away is telling.

My tongue feels thick with nerves when I take my first bite of linguine. I clear my throat after I swallow. "So, you're not dating anyone?"

What the hell came over to me to ask that question?

She seems to take it in stride, which is comforting.

"Nope, not a soul. I've met a couple of people since everything went down, but I don't know." She chews the forkful of pasta she's placed in her mouth. "Couldn't find someone to take a chance on." Her eyes focus on the dish in front of her.

"That's shocking."

"Really?" She pulls her head back, shoulders straightening. "Why do you say that?"

"Have you seen you? I'm sure women were lining up around the block."

"Like I said," she starts, stabs a cherry tomato in her salad, and then points it at me. "No one I wanted to take a chance on." She pops the tomato off the fork with her lips. "Why? You want to date me?"

I let out a nervous laugh. "Me?"

"Well, I'm a fairly hot commodity, right?"

"This is… I don't even… Come on now." I am tripping all over my words. A nervous, strained laugh fizzles on its way out of my mouth. It's impressive, really, that she has managed to get me flustered without even trying.

"Wow," she says, a giant smile spreading across her face.

"What?"

"That was entirely too easy."

"Please," I protest. "I'm just, y'know, not used to..." When I realize she's going to let me dangle, flailing all the way, I scoff. "Whatever. Don't act like you're special."

"I seem to recall someone telling me I was very special not even two weeks ago." She winks and my heart seizes. "Or were you just trying to get into my pants?"

I swallow around the feeling of being called out. "Um, I have literally no idea how to answer that." My voice sounds far away, as if I wasn't the one speaking. Is this how it feels to be so into someone else? Like the world literally fades away and all that exists is me and her and our heartbeats? I hope so because I never want it to stop. I never want to feel any other way than this. Forever.

Her light laugh is lovely. "You're adorable, Finnley. You know that?"

Suddenly, the weird awkward part of me I thought I had beat into submission years ago takes over and I feel myself clamming up. I open my mouth to respond and no sound comes out. I shrug and hope the heat filling my cheeks isn't obvious.

"So is this normal? You falling all over yourself?"

I want to shout at her that, no, it's not fucking *normal*. Women, very hot, beautiful women, don't usually hit on me. When guys hit on me, it never makes me feel like I have a trampoline inside my body where every organ has a turn, but admitting that would make me sound even more pathetic. I wave a hand through the air, trying to avoid her question. "Let's move on, please."

That damn eyebrow arches. My stomach utilizes the trampoline like a professional. "Hey," she says, her voice soft as she turns her body toward me. "I'm only teasing you."

I try not to look at her. I really do. Because I know the second my eyes lock onto the green loveliness of hers, I'll be a goner. It's impressive, though, how I've tried so hard with *everything* when it comes to her. And somehow, I have managed, in spectacular fashion, to fail.

"You have completely thrown me for a loop." My words and the softness of their tone don't match the conviction I feel. "I feel like a teenager again."

"That's not a bad thing, is it?"

I shake my head. It's all I can do because the compassion, the… *love* in her eyes has taken my breath from me.

"I truly believe, Finnley, that everything in life, every single thing that happens to us, is supposed to happen in the very way it has. Your path, each step you took, unfolded exactly as it was supposed to. You were meant to wind up here, in this chair, next to me. I was meant to go through hell and heartbreak to end up sitting next to you." The air of uncertainty surrounding her as she shrugs a solitary shoulder makes me think she feels small for this admission. "It's the only way I can wrap my head around all of this, around you, around this feeling I have for you." She takes a deep breath and holds it briefly before ending with, "And I barely fucking know you."

"Emerson…" Her name, as it leaves my mouth, comes out breathy. I'm struggling to find the right words because hers have bowled me over.

"All I'm saying is you were supposed to come here to figure out more than your career. Happiness is more than work." She licks her lips, then confesses, "I want to kiss you so badly right now."

"Oh yeah?" It's my turn to raise my eyebrows.

"Whew." She pulls her shoulders back and rubs her face. "I haven't felt like this in a really long time. And you think I threw *you* for a loop," she says with a slight chuckle at the end. "This is going to get messy, isn't it?"

"Probably." I laugh, as does she. "I have one question for you."

"Okay, hit me." She turns, takes a drink of her water, then picks up her fork. It's as if she's readying herself—a carbo-load of sorts—for whatever I'm going to ask.

"Why were you so standoffish when I first met you?"

"Because you are one of the most beautiful women I've ever seen."

My heart is thumping so loudly I'd be shocked if she said she couldn't hear it. "That's... Really?"

She is in the middle of twirling pasta onto her fork, so when she looks up at me with a sheer look of confusion on her face, it's almost comical. "Are you kidding?" she finally asks. "Please tell me you're kidding."

"Um, no, I'm not kidding."

"You don't know how beautiful you are?"

I shrug. Suddenly, I'm the confused one. Sure, guys have told me I'm beautiful, but her? Emerson is one of the most beautiful women alive. How can she think that I'm beautiful, too? It doesn't compute.

"Finnley." She is still frozen in place, fork stabbed into the pasta, eyes locked onto me, disbelief written across her entire face. "I could barely look at you when I first met you because every single time I did, God, I had to remind myself how to breathe, for fuck's sake. Like..." She pauses, shakes her head while putting her fork down. She lays her hands, palms flat, onto the table. "I'm forty-three years old, Finnley. Forty-three. I've seen my share of women, men, trans women and men, drag queens, celebrities, whatever, you name it. But walking in here that night of the dinner party?" She's pointing at the door now, conviction seeping from her pores. Her hand slowly closes into a fist. "Finnley, you shook my entire world. In that blazer, with your hair, and your mind-blowing smile... And your stoned eyes, pupils blown and everything?" She smiles. "You changed everything inside of me by simply existing."

I don't even realize I'm crying until a tear falls onto my hands, which are clasped in my lap. My eyes are drawn to the shape the droplets are creating on my skin, one after another. I should be looking at her. She deserves that much after all the things she's said. There have been some swift men in my life, some smooth talkers with the best pickup lines, but that speech? That passionate speech she gave me? I've never before wanted to drop everything in my entire life and give my whole self to someone as desperately as I do right this instant. As I turn, her hands are on my face. Her lips land on mine, capturing them in a kiss I thought could only ever exist in romance novels. The softness of her lips is a stark contrast to the desire in the kiss. My body, how it's responding, the butterflies, the tingling in my core, the wetness in my panties, I have never experienced this kind of passion before. In the moments after her lips touch mine, I make the decision to give myself completely over to this, to her, to whatever is happening in my heart and mind, body and soul. Because she's right. Everything happens for a reason.

I pull away from her so I can stand. I want better access to her, to her mouth, her tongue, more than my current position allows. She stands with me and pushes her chair away as we lunge at each other. I walk her backward until I hear the gentle thud of her back hitting the wall. She pulls me closer, open-mouthed, soft-lipped, tongue gingerly dipping into my mouth. My lungs are running, sprinting, trying to catch up to my heart, which has a mind of its own and is controlling everything I'm doing. Brain? What brain? Her hands move to my neck, her fingers pressing against the base of my skull, her thumb against the hinge of my jaw. How can a touch so simple be so fucking powerful? I am light as a feather, braced from floating away only by the touch of her. The handful of kisses we've shared up until now have been exquisite, but this? This one has made me believe in true love, in soulmates, in missing pieces fitting together to create the masterpiece of a puzzle I was so sure didn't exist.

My hands also follow my heart's lead and have slipped beneath the Columbia College sweatshirt she's wearing. Her stomach is flat, probably from all the late-night running. The skin along the waistband of her shorts is soft, not rough and hairy like Steven's. Her hips… goddamn, her hips. When I rest my hands on her sides, on the curve of her motherfucking hips, I swear to Christ my knees almost buckle. How can something I've looked at a thousand times before on women have the ability to fan the flames of the hormonal teenager's libido living inside me now?

"I want you to have sex with me," I hear myself say against her lips, around her kisses. "Is that something we can do?"

The low, sexy laugh she does makes my chest ache this time. "Yes." She moves her left hand from my neck to my side, to my hip, along the curve of my ass. "It is absolutely something we can do." She kisses me once more. Twice. *Thrice*… Oh, oh fuck, she is good at this. Her right thumb applies pressure under my jaw, so I lean my head back. She runs her tongue along my jawline to my chin. "But only if you can answer this question with yes." Her lips are on my neck, and she's placing kisses down to the hollow at its base.

"Okay," I manage to rasp.

"Have you broken it off with your fiancé yet?"

Shit. Shit, shit, *shit*. I knew my being a coward was going to bite me in the ass eventually. My simple "no" sounds far away, as if I don't have the courage to admit it, the same way I haven't had the courage to break up with Steven yet. The shame filling my body is palpable.

Her lips are pressed against my ear when she says, "As soon as you do that, I promise you, I will make you come so hard you won't know what happened."

"Fuck." My voice is barely there. I'm pretty sure it has decided to stop working, just like my salivary glands.

"Oh, you better believe it. Because Finnley?" She breathes in against my ear. Chills race over every inch of me. On the out-breath, she adds, "I'm a *very* attentive lover."

"I can't believe we aren't marching upstairs right this instant." Frustration drips from my words.

"That's on you, my dear."

I breathe in deeply, gathering my bearings as her right thumb rubs my cheek affectionately. The sensation pulsating in my core has managed to demolish the clean panties I put on after my shower. "You know that feeling when you're on the brink, and then you stumble and fall and make a complete fool of yourself? Yeah, that's me right now."

"Here, come with me." She threads her fingers into mine. I follow her through the dining room to the stairs, up to my bedroom, where she leads me to the bed. She climbs onto the mattress, to the spot where she slept two weeks earlier. "Lie down." She pats the comforter. "Trust me."

I do trust her. More than I've ever trusted anyone else. I crawl to my spot, feeling like I don't have a pulse.

"Lie on your back."

My eyes lock onto the ceiling after I do as she says.

"Relax." Her whisper is closer than I realized.

"What are you going to do?"

"I'm going to help you out."

I turn my head to look at her. Her face is inches from mine. She's on her side, head propped up with her hand. She is so fucking beautiful it takes my brain a full five seconds before I respond with, "Help me how?"

"By telling you how I would take my hand and slip it between your legs."

Oh. *Ohhh.* "You mean...?"

"I do." She takes my hand from its resting spot on the

comforter and places it on my stomach. "Touch yourself," she whispers.

"With you here?"

"With me right here."

"I've never done it with someone watching."

"You won't be disappointed." She licks her lips. "It'll give me something to think about in preparation for our first time together."

I am a ball of nerves. The same ball of nerves I was when I first met her. But when I look into her green eyes, the nerves dissipate much quicker than they did before. "So, what would you do with your hand between my thighs?"

Her expression morphs to excitement. "I would press against you, feel how wet you are, how you've soaked your panties from the anticipation."

She's certainly not wrong about that.

"I take off your pants, slide them down over your hips, your perfect ass, your thighs."

Well, I guess I should do as she says... I hook my thumbs into the waistband of my yoga pants, lift my hips, and push them down. I lean up and push them the rest of the way off, then toss them onto the end of the bed.

"Damn," she whispers. "I like those," she says, motioning to my black lace panties. "Like, a lot." She is clenching her free hand into a fist, seemingly to keep herself from touching me. It's both a buzzkill *and* a turn-on, and I am completely bewildered as to how that's possible. "I, um, I keep your panties on this time because, well, you're not single yet." The smirk on her lips leaves me even more drenched. "I slip my hand under that hot-as-fuck black lace..." She bites her lip while breathing in. "I feel you, slip my middle finger through your wetness, then my index finger, before I dip inside."

"I'm so wet." My whispered admission sort of shocks me. I didn't mean to say it out loud.

"Show me."

I pull my hand out, and it glimmers in the dim lighting.

"Fuck." She closes her eyes, pulls in another deep breath, and lets it out before opening her eyes. "I slip my middle finger inside you."

When I do as she has said, I moan. The thought that shakes me to my core is this: If my fingers feel this great, how great is it going to feel when it's really her?

"Two fingers," she whispers against my ear.

"Emerson…" I moan softly.

"Pull them out and push them in, slowly."

"I wish this was really you."

"Me too." She kisses me deeply, and I stop gripping the comforter and place my hand on her face. "Rub your clit," she whispers against my lips. "Tell me how it feels."

"So good. So fucking good."

"Are you close at all?"

I nod, and she kisses me again. I keep rubbing as she kisses me harder. Her body presses against me. My nipples are hard, and every time her breasts graze mine, I get closer and closer to an orgasm. She bites down lightly on my bottom lip before she kisses me again. My body tenses and I keep rubbing, harder and faster, until I am coming while she's kissing me. I moan into the kiss, lean my head back, and break from her lips as the orgasm washes over me. I've stilled my hand, pressing it against my clit until the orgasm has passed.

"Holy fucking shit." Little by little, my body starts to relax. "I am calling him right now to break up with him."

Emerson laughs. The sound warms my heart in such a way that I suddenly feel *love* course through my veins.

"You crack me up," she says before she kisses me again.

Once I've pulled my pants back on, I turn and look at her sitting on the edge of my bed. She has removed the ponytail holder from her hair, which has fallen in waves around her face. I'm fully aware I'm staring at her, but at this point, I don't care.

"I can't believe this is happening."

My confession isn't shocking, I'm sure, but the joy on her face is unmistakable.

"I'm really glad it is."

"I am too. But damn, what a turn my life has taken." As soon as those words are out of my mouth, the doorbell is ringing again. "Seriously? Did Mark forget his key?" I groan. "Come on, let's go."

She grabs my hand and pulls me close when we get to the door, pressing me against it before she kisses me. "I don't want him to ruin our night." Her words are said between kisses, between light nips, between her tongue lightly licking my lips.

"We can go back upstairs after this if you'd like," I offer. "I can, y'know, tell you what I'd like to do to you."

"Tempting. Very, very tempting."

The doorbell rings again and startles us both. We both laugh as we pull apart, and I finally open the door. My eyes land on the person standing there. "Steven." I instantly feel like I am going to throw up.

"Finn, hi." He *looks* hopeful, but his tone says he's irritated. I hate to admit that he has every right to feel that way.

"What are you doing here?"

He leans to the side and looks at Emerson. "Who is that?" He's angry now. And accusatory. As if he has any idea...

"What are you doing here, Steven?"

"I came to see my fiancée," he says loudly. "Is that not allowed?"

I can't answer him even though I should. I should say, *No, it's not allowed*. But I don't. Instead, like the groveling people pleaser I am, I open the door for him to walk through.

He stands right in front of Emerson, looks her up and down, and then tosses me a glare over his shoulder. "Can we be alone?"

"No, Emerson isn't leaving."

"Yes," she says softly. She gracefully moves around him. "I'll go. Come see me at the studio tomorrow." She leans forward, presses her lips against my ear, and says, "I'll miss you."

"Don't, please," I beg her in a quiet whisper. "Stay."

"You need to do this." Her eyes lock onto mine when she pulls away. And then she leaves, taking more with her than I even realized I'd given away.

∽

"What the fuck is wrong with you?" Steven's voice is raised as he paces the dining room. "You have called me twice the entire time you've been gone. Twice. That is fucked up, Finn."

He's not wrong. It *is* fucked up.

"I'm sorry?"

"Is that a *question*?"

"Yeah?"

He lets out a huge huff and groans. "You're unbelievable."

"Steven, I told you I wanted to break up when I decided I was moving here. I told you that numerous times, and you kept saying no, no, no. You didn't give a shit that I didn't want to do this anymore. You thought, what? That I'd change my mind when I wasn't around you? That I'd miss you and want you back? Come on."

"Wow." His dark eyes aren't sad; they're furious. I know those eyes. I've seen them before. I've never been frightened by him, but I do know he's going to start saying things to hurt me.

"Well? Do you want me to stop lying to you? I don't want to get married to you. I don't want to be with you. I don't want to be a mom, for fuck's sake."

"Rory loves you."

"I know. I love her, too, but I do not want to be a mom. I've told you that. You don't listen to me. You got angry with me when I told you I wasn't going to come off my birth control. It's like you don't care about what I want. You want me to fit into your little box, and I do not want that."

"I wanted Rory to have a brother or sister since her mother passed away. You knew that." He rubs his hands over his face. "None of this makes sense. Chicago is fucking you up."

"No, Chicago is not fucking me up. It's opening my eyes. Everything here is opening my eyes. I'm sorry it doesn't make sense to you, but all of this makes sense to me. Why would you even want to be with me when I'm finally figuring out that the person I *was* is not the person I am?" He doesn't answer, so I add, "It doesn't make any sense to you because you never fucking listen to me, Steven. Ever. Do you even know how that feels? I listen to everything you say. All of your dreams, desires, hopes… And when I realized my dreams, desires, hopes no longer aligned with yours, I knew it was time."

"Time for what?"

"Jesus. *See?* You don't fucking listen to me. I knew it was time to leave. To go our separate ways."

His shoulders fall as if he has admitted to himself that I am right, that he doesn't listen to me. "I thought you'd come around."

"Come around?" I shout at him. "Steven, do you think that you deserve that? A person who will eventually come around?"

He doesn't answer, just stares blankly at me.

"I'll answer it for you; no, you don't deserve that. The same way I don't deserve to be in a relationship where I'm not happy or comfortable."

"I make you *uncomfortable*?" His defeated tone breaks my heart.

"That's not what I mean! I mean… it's not what I want. I'm really sorry that I didn't realize it until now. I wish I had known sooner. Before the engagement. Before getting to know Rory. I'm sorry. I really am. None of this is what I want."

"What's not what you want? Me? A relationship? What?"

"Exactly. You. A relationship. This," I shout, then head to the kitchen where I pour myself a shot of bourbon and down it. I normally don't drink like this, but he's making me so nervous I need something, anything, to take the edge off. I hear him walk up behind me. "I'm done, Steven. I'm sorry you came all the way up here. I should have had the courage to tell you on the phone, but... I didn't want to hurt you."

He lets out a weird, shaky laugh. "You didn't want to hurt me?" He laughs again. "Why do you want to end this? Don't you love me?"

I pour another drink, but this time, I sip it. "No, Steven, I don't. God, I'm so sorry, but I don't love you."

"That's a lie."

"You need to leave, please. I don't want to do this anymore. I don't want you here. I want to move on and be happy for once. I'm sorry that's not with you. I really am. But I can't keep forcing myself into this when it's not what I want."

"I can't believe you." The anger in his voice is more apparent than it has been this entire argument. "Who was that woman? Huh? Who was that? Some new friend who has talked you into leaving me?"

"What the fuck?" It's my turn to laugh because *fuck* him.

"That's the only reason you'd be doing this. If someone else was talking you into it."

"Wow. You think it's so unheard of for someone to not be in love with you?"

"Considering that I have to turn down students all the time? Yes, it's unheard of."

I literally feel my eyes widen. "Are you fucking kidding me?"

He shakes his head, the pride seeping from him like sweat. "I guess I'll be free of the guilt now."

"So, wait," I say, the nausea roiling in my stomach. "You're saying you were cheating on me with college-age girls?"

"They were all legal," he says, as if that makes this better. Then he folds his arms across his chest. "But yes, numerous times, Finn. You made me do it. You didn't want to have sex; you didn't want me to touch you."

He's not wrong.

"Get out."

"No."

"Get out of here right now." I march to the door and fling it open, point outside, and glare at him. "And to think I didn't want to cheat on *you*."

He scoffs. "Like anyone would ever touch you. You shrew."

"Okay, Steven." I bite my tongue, but the need to put him in his place is overtaking my sanity. "That woman? Her name is Emerson, and you know what? I am going to have sex with her the second you leave this fucking house."

His face falls.

"Yeah. You heard me. I do not want to be with you. And instead of you allowing me to break up with you when I left, you had to make me do it this way. All I want is for this to be over and for you to leave." I pull in a deep breath. "I'm sorry it had to be like this."

He blinks a few times, then steps closer to me. "You're going to have sex with *that* woman?"

"Yeah, I am." I clench my right hand into a fist because the next instinct I have is to punch him. And that won't end well, I'm sure. "You. Need. To. Leave."

His jaw clenches.

"Now, Steven!"

And before I know it, he turns and leaves.

I slam the door behind him.

CHAPTER EIGHT

I'm rushing around the house, fueled by adrenaline, turning off lights so I can somehow track Emerson down, when I stop dead in my tracks. I just broke up with my fiancé. I ended things with him. And he was cheating on *me*? How in the hell did I not know that? Not living with him was part of the reason, obviously, but I was so checked out of our relationship. Is it possible that I didn't even realize the man I was going to marry was sleeping with other people? Wow. How sad is that?

All I want to do is go see Emerson. I want to talk to her, tell her what happened, and then, well, have sex with her.

And I just broke up with my fiancé. What the hell is wrong with me?

It honestly doesn't matter at this point because I have no idea where she lives. I know it's around the corner, but beyond that? No clue. It's Chicago, for Christ's sake, not some Sleepy Hollow town with a population of five. I can't text her; she doesn't have a cell phone. Even if she has a landline, I don't have her number.

Talk about anticlimactic.

I pace back and forth in my bedroom, wall to window, window to wall. What do I do? How do I get in contact with her?

Or do I chalk this up to *everything happens for a reason*? I was willing to believe that earlier; why not now?

I'll tell you why. Because it fucking sucks to be all amped up and need the release only to be faced with the reality that it's not gonna happen. At least not tonight.

It sure says a lot about what I'm feeling for Emerson, though. I've never ever, in the entire history of my sex life, needed release this badly. And, technically, I've already had release.

Holy shit.

What is happening to me?

My phone ringing snaps me out of my spiraling anxiety. I forgot I was gripping it in my hand like a lifeline, and its loud ringer startles me so badly I almost throw it across the room.

"Hello?" I shout into it, not even checking to see who it is.

"Finnley O'Connell?"

I check the number. It's a Chicago area code. "Yeah, who is this?"

"It's Northwestern Memorial's emergency department. We have Steven Hemming here. He's been in an accident. You're listed in his wallet and phone as an emergency contact."

"Steven? What?" It's only been an hour since he left. "I don't understand. How? What happened?"

"Ma'am, it's imperative that you get down here."

My mind is racing. "Northwestern, right?"

"Yes, the emergency department. I'm his nurse, Abby Shepherd. Please ask for me when you get here."

Abby disconnects. I'm frantic as I shove my feet into my Vans, grab my purse, and fly down the stairs. I take off as fast as I can, running toward the Fullerton L station. I can catch the Red Line to Chicago Avenue there.

My lungs are on fire when I burst through the metro station's door and take the steps up two at a time. Shockingly, I don't biff it, which I was fully expecting to do, but the train is there, its doors open, and I don't want to miss it. I squeeze through the doors just as they slide closed, then collapse into a seat, huffing and puffing like I just ran a marathon. A marathon, where the man I just broke up with is waiting at the finish line. What the fuck?

I swipe through my phone as I wait. The need to know what is going on is ridiculous, so I call Steven. No answer. Of course not. Why would he answer if he's in the ER? I check his texts. Fifteen unread. I scroll through them. All apologizing, all telling me how much he loves me, how he never meant to hurt me, how he hates himself for letting it get to this point.

Fuck, fuck, *fuck*.

What have I done?

He loves me. Why was being with him not good enough for me? What is wrong with me? Why am I doing this?

∼

THANKFULLY, I'VE SPENT THE LAST FEW WEEKS STUDYING THE Chicago roads, and I have no problem finding the ER at Northwestern. My legs are like Jell-O, and I haven't been this sweaty since three-a-days volleyball practice in college, but I made it. The front desk attendant, who is the kindest person I've encountered in Chicago, calls the nurse and tells me it'll be just a few minutes. The waiting area is packed. I don't know what I expected, but not all these people. I lean against a wall, breathe in and out to talk myself off the cliff where I am perched so delicately.

The what-ifs in my mind are out of control. I need to stop myself from thinking the worst.

"Finnley O'Connell?"

I cut off the freakout approaching at the pass and rush over to the nurse. "Abby?"

"Yes, come with me."

"How did this happen? What is going on?"

"Listen," she says as she uses her badge to open a set of double doors with the words EMPLOYEES ONLY printed across them in bold, red letters. "He's not doing well at all. He was coming out of a bar, and he walked right out in front of a car. The driver tried to stop, but the way the car hit him, he suffered a lot of injuries. A collapsed lung, broken ribs, a compound fracture to his femur."

"My God."

"He also hit his head very hard. He has a brain bleed they are going to operate on as soon as the doctor gets here." We stop at the door to Steven's room, and she turns to me, concern on her face. "I'm not trying to be bleak, but…." The lines on her forehead, the creases around her eyes, the deep look of compassion displayed on her features all make me think she's been doing this for far too long. "I think you need to prepare yourself for the worst."

I swallow the bile that's rising in my esophagus and nod. She opens the door to reveal him. My heart sinks. Steven has tubes coming out of his chest. He's unconscious, hooked up to monitors, and his leg is wrapped in bandages. I wouldn't wish all this on my worst enemy. I close my eyes and feel Abby's hand on my back. I let her touch comfort me for a second before I enter, holding my breath the entire time.

∼

IT'S HOUR THREE OF STEVEN'S FIRST SURGERY. I HAVEN'T BEEN home. I texted Uncle Mark, Aunt Lisa, and my parents after I returned to the waiting room. I debate calling Rory but I have no idea what to say to her yet. I want to call when I have good news to tell her.

As soon as he can, which apparently is after one of his more needy clients, Uncle Mark arrives with Dunkin' Donuts coffee and my phone charger. "Babycakes," he says as he sits next to me, hand on my back. "How is he doing?"

The coffee is still scalding hot, thank Christ. And black. *Exactly* what I needed. After three consecutive sips, I shrug. "I haven't heard a word."

"That's shocking."

"Tell me about it." I shake my head. "I'm fucking miserable. I can't believe I broke up with him, and then this happens. Like, what are the fucking odds?" I'd love to say I am holding back tears, but I'm not. I haven't cried at all, and I'm not sure if that makes me a monster or not, but I'm struggling more with not knowing than I am with Steven's state.

"Don't do that to yourself, Finnley. This is not your fault." He leans back in the chair, his hand still on my back. "You wanting to be happy has nothing to do with this."

"He was drinking at that bar because I broke up with him. I mean, come on." I look back at him. "Seems like it's my fault."

"You really believe that? You didn't *make* him fly to Chicago. You didn't *make* him walk into traffic."

I drink my coffee, lean forward, and prop my elbows on my knees. "Blaming myself makes it easier."

"Don't do that." His tone is firm with conviction. "You cannot do that to yourself."

"What if he dies?" My question tastes disgusting, but I have to ask it.

"Then he dies, Finnley." Uncle Mark moves from his seat and sits on the floor in front of me. "Does this change the way you feel about him?"

I shake my head.

"Do you want to still be with him?"

"No," I whisper.

"Then? The only thing you can do is hope everything is okay. If it's not, then that's a bridge we cross when we get to it."

"It feels heartless to feel that way, though."

"You're not heartless. You're human."

"Are you sure it's not heartless?" My need to make sure is palpable.

He places his cool hands on my face. "I promise it's not, my love. I'm here for you, okay? Whatever happens."

"Finnley O'Connell?"

I stand instantly. "Yes?"

A man and a woman in matching blue scrubs walk over to me. Their somber expression tells me everything I need to know. The man pulls his scrub hat from his head. "We did everything we could—"

"Is he gone?"

The woman nods. "We're so sorry. We were able to patch up his brain bleed, but he threw a clot and went into cardiac arrest on the table."

"We had him back, but sadly...."

"We are so very sorry, Mrs. Hemming."

"I'm not his wife." *I'm not even his fiancée any longer.* The bile I had been doing such a good job of keeping at bay has reappeared. The doctors give each other a look. "Thank you for everything."

I don't know what comes over me, but I push through them and leave. I leave Uncle Mark standing there, leave the doctors standing there, leave my coffee, my purse, my phone. The elevator isn't working fast enough. I slam my hand on the button as if that will make it come faster. I look around and find the exit for the stairs. My brain is not fully functioning. I know that much for sure. All I can think is that I need to get out of there. I need, need, *need,* but have no idea what.

As soon as the early morning Chicago air hits me, I breathe in deeply, but it only makes me want to throw up more. I rush over to a trash can and toss the top to the ground before I empty the meager contents of my stomach—coffee and a roll of Breath Savers—into the bin.

∽

The first person I want to talk to is Jesse. I am sitting on a bench outside the emergency room door, right next to the garbage can I threw up into. I can't go back inside yet. I can't. I don't know what the fuck to do. All I know is that I need to talk to my best friend. I've tried her two times in a row now, and she still hasn't picked up. I know it's because I never call her this late, so I'm hoping she figures out this is clearly an emergency.

After I hang up the second time, it only takes Jesse five seconds to get the hint. I answer her FaceTime call, but before I can say a solitary word, I break down.

"What the fuck happened, Finn? Are you okay?" She's frantic as she asks these questions.

"Steven is gone."

"Aww, honey, he had to come back to Tampa? I didn't even know he was visiting."

"No, Jess," I say, followed by a sob. "He showed up on my porch, and we fought, and I broke up with him, and then he left. I got a phone call that he was in a horrible accident. They had to do surgery, and he died."

"What?" She scrambles and drops her phone in the process. I hear a few *fucks* and *shits* before she picks it back up and stares at the screen. "Finnley, what the fuck? He's *dead*?"

"Yes," I say through my tears. "I am so fucking horrible. I can't believe I broke up with him and then he fucking died? Like, what the hell?"

"Wait a second, honey. You can't blame yourself for his accident unless you were the one who ran him over or whatever." She pauses. "You weren't the person who ran him over, right?"

Her question makes me laugh. And I blow snot bubbles out of my nose when it happens. "Ugh, you ass," I say while wiping my nose with a Kleenex. "No, I didn't kill him."

"Whew," she says softly. "So, you broke up with him?"

I nod. "I just couldn't do it anymore. And Jesse, God, he told me he had been cheating on me. I screamed at him. I was so angry. And then..." I shake my head and try to find the words.

"Was he drinking? Did he get hit by a car?"

"Yes and yes."

"And he just showed up on your doorstep? You had no idea he was coming?"

"No," I groan. "I had no fucking idea. He literally just showed up. And fuck, Emerson was there and..." I can't continue.

"And what?"

"Nothing."

"Finnley... did you have sex with her?"

"No." I close my eyes. "But she watched me."

"Watched you what... Oh!" She lets out a loud laugh. "You mean she watched you masturbate? Fuck, that's hot."

I am so ashamed. I can't even open my eyes to look at my best friend. "Yeah, well, karma arrived and killed my ex only minutes after I broke up with him. So there you go."

"Oh, my fucking God." Jesse groans this time, and I open my eyes finally. "Stop right now. This is not karma. Did you want to marry Steven?"

I shake my head.

"Did you love him?"

"I mean, I loved him, but—"

"Were you in love with him?"

I shake my head again.

"So you broke up with him. You needed to. You're not being punished for breaking up with him. Stop thinking that. It's not okay, and it's not fair to your heart. You and Steven were not meant to be. You know this. Hell, I knew it but was afraid to tell you." She laughs gently. "I mean, I'm sad he's dead, but what the fuck? He cheated on you? Fuck that asshole."

"Jess, it's a little soon to be cursing his name."

"Fine." She shrugs. "I'm just saying... don't let go of the fact that he purposely hurt you. You tried to break up with him a few times before this. Take some deep breaths, okay? Try to remind yourself that this isn't your fault. You're a casualty of his stupidity unfortunately. It sucks. It's not okay. But it's the truth."

I try to respond but my, "Okay," gets lost in my throat.

"Finn, babe, please don't let this ruin you." Her whispered plea makes me cry again. "He doesn't deserve it."

"I won't." After a couple beats of silence in which Jesse stares straight ahead at the camera and not at herself, I finally say, "I'm sure I'll need to come back to Florida for the arrangements."

"Well, when you do, we will get together and we will have some fun to take your mind off things, okay?"

I nod. "I love you." The admission crumples my face again, like used Kleenex.

"Oh, honey. I love you, too."

I hang up and lean back on the bench. If I had anything left to throw up, the thought of going back upstairs would have me retching again in the trash can.

∼

SOMEHOW, AND I'M NOT EVEN SURE HOW, UNCLE MARK IS ABLE TO get me back to his house. I manage to shower and put on fresh clothes. The bag of Steven's belongings and his suitcase, which we had to retrieve from the Holiday Inn where he was staying, are sitting in my room. Staring at me.

I open my phone to call my parents, but the last thing I want to do is talk to them. My mom will be kind, but my dad? He *loved* Steven. He thought he was God's gift to humanity.

My procrastination of calling Rory slams into me. Fuck. I waited to call so I had good news and now this… She's probably with Carla, Steven's sister. Christ, I need to tell Carla too.

I collapse onto the bed, slide to the floor, and take a deep breath while I stare down at Carla's contact information. Telling Rory trumps my parents. "Now or never."

The phone rings once, twice, three times. My heart is beating so hard I can feel it in my throat as I wait for Carla to pick up.

"Finnley," she says by way of greeting. "I'm surprised to hear from you."

"Carla," I manage to say. "I have to tell you something."

She shouts at her kids and Rory to settle down. "What's up?"

"Steven came to visit me."

"Yeah, I know. I have Rory."

"I know."

"Okay… so, what's going on?"

"Steven, um… he got into a horrible accident and… he… um, he didn't make it."

I hear her drop the phone, say "fuck" a few times, and then pick it up again. "Finnley, what are you saying?"

"He's gone. He died."

"No, that's not… that's not possible. What the hell happened, Finnley?"

"We argued. And he left and I guess went to a bar near the hotel he was staying at. And…when he left the bar, he stepped into traffic."

"What the *fuck*?" Her voice is covered with the tears she's crying. I can hear them; I can almost feel them myself. I want to cry with her. I want to offer her that much, but all I can do is listen as she sobs on the other end of the phone. "I have to call our stepdad. I have to—oh God. Rory. I have to tell Rory. Oh, God."

"Do you—" I say, then stop because I don't know what I want to say, what I want to offer. I have no idea what to do. "Do you want me to tell her? I know she loves me."

"No. Absolutely not. He…" She sniffles, chokes, and starts to cough. "What the hell, Finnley? What did you argue about? And why did you let him leave? Why weren't you with him?" The anger in her voice is apparent.

"Carla, I… I… wasn't. I just *wasn't*." I can't tell her. I can't bring myself to say that I had broken up with him. "I am going to come home with him, with his body."

"Don't, Finnley. He's not your problem. He's mine." She sounds so angry. It's almost like she…

"He told you, didn't he?" I'm filled with dread. I knew there was a reason she was being so short with me.

"Of course he fucking told me. He called me the second he left you, Finnley." The force with which she spits my name is intense. I actually move the phone away from my ear in an effort to protect my heart. It's futile, though, because she also says, "You are the reason this fucking happened."

"Carla, stop, please."

"You used him for his money."

"His money?" I let out a laugh. "Are you kidding me? He was broke!"

"He had our dad's money."

"No, he didn't, Carla. He blew that. He blew everything. You don't even know."

"I'm hanging up. Good luck, Finnley."

And the line disconnects.

CHAPTER NINE

My parents immediately hung up the phone with me and hopped on a flight. I told them at least eight times I was fine. I didn't need them to swoop in and save the day. Them saving the day ultimately means I'm going to be more stressed out. I love them, but Jesus, they really know how to occupy space. When I told Uncle Mark we were going to have visitors, he brushed it off and told me it was fine. He had fully expected it. I think he was still nervous, though, which worried me. He and I have never spoken about his relationship with my parents. The only thing I know is they're not super supportive. And I also know never to tell them he's a high-end escort.

"The main issue is my third bedroom only has a pullout," he says. We're standing in the kitchen the day they're meant to arrive.

I shrug as he hands me an old-fashioned. "They're the ones who didn't listen when I told them I was fine."

"Are you, though? Fine?"

I take a sip of my drink. The bourbon doesn't burn like it normally does. What does that mean? Am I not okay? Am I numb? "I have no fucking idea," I finally answer. His face morphs from supportive to sympathetic as he pulls me into a hug. "I'm sure I'm fine." My voice is muffled against his shoulder.

He pulls away. "Have you cried yet?"

I shake my head.

"Oh, great." He sighs. "When you finally do, it'll be like opening the floodgates. I should probably stock up on Kleenex."

I let out a laugh when he winks at me. "I'm sad, don't get me wrong. I just… he was so careless. He didn't love me. I don't know why he said he did because, in the next breath, he was telling me he was sleeping with his female students. I loved him. I wasn't in love with him any longer, but goddammit, I never wanted to hurt him like that."

"So, now what?"

"Carla said she would handle it." I sigh. "I am not going to push my involvement when she clearly said she doesn't want me there."

"You're allowed to be involved if you want to be."

"I know," I whisper. I look down at my drink, at the ball of ice, at the dark liquor. "I haven't spoken to Rory at all."

"Can I ask you…" He considers his words, then states simply, "Why did you start dating someone with a kid if you never wanted kids?"

"Remember when I told you I had found a part-time job as a math tutor?"

"I remember that well. You had said it was the one thing that was keeping you sane while working with your parents." He laughs. "Hindsight, eh?"

"God." I shake my head. "Yeah, well, I tutored her for algebra. Meeting her dad seemed like a safe thing to do. She was so excited to introduce me to him, I didn't know how to say no." I take a drink of my old-fashioned. I still cannot feel the alcohol, and it is starting to worry me. "We started seeing each other more and more until, one day, we were a couple. And then he asked me to marry him and I didn't know what to say. So I said yes. Honestly, I love Rory. She's a fantastic kid. But it never changed my feelings about—"

"Becoming a mom."

I raise my glass. "Exactly."

The doorbell rings, and Uncle Mark's face falls. "That'll be your parents."

"I'm so sorry."

He laughs, waves a hand through the air, and grabs his own beverage before leaving the kitchen. "Don't worry about it. I have plenty of alcohol."

"Thank God," I say under my breath as we head to the door together. "Thank you for doing this, by the way."

"Don't thank me. You live here with me. This is your house too. We will get through this together. Okay?" He holds my hand and squeezes it. "Now, brace yourself for the next two days. We're going to be so ready for them to leave."

I laugh as he swings the door open. My mom and dad are standing there, one suitcase between them. My dad is wearing a Make America Great Again baseball hat, and my mom is wearing a very worried facial expression.

"Dad, what the fuck is that?"

"What?" he asks as he tries to hide his smile. "What's wrong?"

"You're an asshole. Take that off immediately." I reach for the hat, and he dodges me.

"No way. I love this hat."

"Dad, you cannot come in here if you have that on."

"Okay, okay, it was only a joke, Finn. Don't be so serious." He takes it off and hands it over to my mom, who rolls her eyes at him. I still have no idea, after all the issues they have had, why they decided to stay together. Especially when he pulls things like that. Always trying to rile me up. "Come here, kiddo. Let me hug ya."

"You jerk," I whisper as I hug him.

"I'm so sorry you have to go through this." He pats me on the back lightly. That's not like him. Normally he's very gruff. My mom must have lectured him from the second they left Florida.

"Baby," my mom says softly when I pull away from Dad. She pulls me into her. She's shorter than me, rounder than me, and definitely a stronger woman than me. "I know you weren't happy with him, but this isn't what you wanted. I know that."

"Floodgates open yet?" Uncle Mark asks with a low chuckle. There's a box of Kleenex being held in front of me while I'm still hugging my mom.

I start laughing when I wave him off. "When I finally do cry, a national weather service announcement will happen."

"Come in and stop moping around on the doorstep, please." He pulls us gently inside and shuts the door. "I'll put your suitcase in the spare room."

It hasn't escaped me that neither my dad nor my mom has hugged Uncle Mark or even said hello to him. They're being disrespectful to him in his own house, which irritates the hell out of me.

"What is wrong with you two?" I say as we sit on the couches in the living area.

"Nothing, dear," Mom says. "We're just happy to see you."

"Whatever. Neither of you are being kind to Uncle Mark. You realize he's been the most incredible person ever to me, right?"

"They're still not super comfortable with me being a big, gay man, Finnley." Uncle Mark has returned to the room and sits on the opposite couch. He crosses his left leg over his right, and rests his highball glass on his knee. "Isn't that right, Sarah?"

"Mark, stop. That's not it." My mom sighs. The glare she shoots at him is unmistakable. I've seen that glare a thousand times. It means *don't push your luck*. "So, Carla is coming to get him?"

I nod.

"And then what?"

"What do you mean, Dad?"

"Are you coming home?"

"For what?" I let out a puff of air. "Carla told me I'm not welcome at the funeral."

"Oh, geez," my mom says dismissively. "She'll cool off."

I shake my head. "She won't. And she doesn't need to. I don't want to deal with any of this." My dad's face shifts after I say those words. "What's wrong?"

"Nothing," he states.

I narrow my eyes as I look at him, then at her. "What the hell is going on?"

"Well, we spoke to Carla on our way here. Apparently, in Steven's will—" My dad stops when my mom places her hand on his knee. He clears his throat and looks at her.

My mom takes a deep breath before she says, "Rory is supposed to go to you."

"I'm sorry, *what?*"

And what was that choice of words? I think to myself. *"Go to me"? Rory's a human being, not an antique vase!*

"According to Steven's will, you are Rory's legal guardian. So you are going to need to come home to handle that."

"Handle what exactly? Are you fucking kidding me?"

My dad groans. "You have got to stop being like this, Finnley. You are not the only person who exists in this world."

I feel my mouth fall open as I glare at him. "What is *that* supposed to mean?"

"Well, you picked up and moved here—"

"Because *you* fired me! And *Mom* told me I should come to Chicago!"

Uncle Mark stands up quickly and grabs my hand. "Come with me, please." He pulls me from the couch and leads me into the kitchen. "You have got to calm down." His eyes are locked onto mine. "You are going to need to take care of this. This will not simply go away. If you want me to go with you, I will. Okay?"

"Uncle Mark, I don't want to be a mom," I whine. "I don't want this."

He pulls me into another big, comforting hug. "I'll help you through this, okay?"

I can't respond because I am beyond words. I am past the point of understanding what is happening. If everything happens for a reason, what am I supposed to think now? What reason is behind *this*?

∼

After twenty-four hours with my parents, I am ready to kill them both. How did I put up with them on a regular basis before all of this?

We are having dinner in tonight because neither of them wanted to leave the townhome.

"Chicago is so dangerous," my mom said when we asked them where they'd like to go. I had to hold back my eye roll.

Uncle Mark, on the other hand, did not hold back. "Okay, Sarah, what would you like to do then? I can order in and have some sinister man *deliver* the food or we can go out? It's up to you." His attempt at being passive-aggressive missed the mark because both of those ideas were nixed.

He's in the kitchen now, plating the filets he made with parmesan polenta. "And salad, of course, which your father won't eat, but whatever."

"I'll eat his portion. I haven't had anything in a day and a half."

"Finnley," he says, followed by a low growl. "You cannot starve yourself."

"I know. I didn't feel like eating, okay?" Things have calmed a little since I found out about Rory. I actually spoke with Carla and had a decent conversation with her. I also spoke to Rory, who wasn't nearly as freaked out as I was. Sure, she's sad. *Obviously*. She lost her mom years ago, and now her dad. What else can this poor kid go through? She's way more resilient than I would be, that's for damn sure. I'm leaving tomorrow to go to Florida for a few days with my parents and Uncle Mark. I will go see her then, and we will figure it out together. I'm nervous about it, but I feel better. I've slept. I've thought. I've planned. We'll see what happens next.

I had to call off from work for the past two days too. Justine was very understanding and actually asked me if I needed her to help in any way. I thought it was very kind of her, considering she barely knows me.

The only person I have not spoken to is Emerson.

My entire life has changed since I last saw her. She left thinking I was going to break up with Steven, and now? How do I even begin to tell her not only that Steven got into a horrific accident, but that he also died? Oh, and by the way, I now have custody of his daughter. *Still wanna date me?*

Ugh.

My stomach twists at the thought of her running straight for the hills when I unload all of this on her. "Mark, before we go out there for yet another uncomfortable dinner with *your* sister and her husband—"

"Who are also *your* parents..."

I chuckle. "You had them first." And so does he. "Have you spoken to Emerson?"

He stops tossing the salad. "I haven't. Have you?"

"No. I keep meaning to, but then it slips my mind. I feel like I'm a horrible person for not talking to her yet."

"Well, we need to let her know."

"I know she lives around here, but I don't know where. And I felt weird just stopping by."

"Lisa can get a hold of her. She'll be here shortly. We'll get her on the case. Sound good?"

A weight lifts. "Yes, that sounds perfect."

"Okay then. Let's go eat with these weird people neither of us wants to claim." He winks as he carries out the giant salad bowl. I grab the smaller bowls and follow him, worried that my life is going to take yet another turn after I talk to Emerson. Dealing with the roller coaster that my life has become is not fun. I wasn't loving the twists and turns to begin with, but now? Now I'd very much like to get off this ride, please.

~

"SARAH AND HANK, HOW THE HELL ARE YOU BOTH?" AUNT LISA HAS arrived and joined us in The Oasis. She is either high as a kite or drunk as a skunk. I can't tell which, but it's one of them. I don't blame her for whichever route she chose. Honestly, I am a little jealous.

"We're good. Living the dream, y'know, since we are running the business all by ourselves again." He's being sarcastic, but it comes off like *I* abandoned *them*.

"Because you wanted to run it all by yourselves, of course. Don't forget that." Aunt Lisa tosses me a smile after she drops that line. My heart grows three sizes, all for her.

"Well, yeah, right." My dad clears his throat. "It's good to see Finn *trying* to succeed on her own."

My mom, who has never really stood up for me before, nudges him. "She's doing great, Hank. Don't take that from her."

I'm grateful but also unsure how to take her kindness. "The new gig is fun. I am learning a lot and think I might actually like to take the flower shop route." My dad scoffs. My mom elbows him. *Hard*. I give her a grateful look. "You know horticulture was always my real love. Not that I don't appreciate the Harvard MBA."

"And the thousands of dollars you put us in debt." My dad's condescension makes me want to scream. I try to contain my eye roll, I really do, but it's useless. And, unfortunately, my dad sees it. "Don't you roll your eyes, young lady."

"You fired me. You remember that, right?"

"Because you were so unhappy. Not because I wanted to."

"Wait a second. You told me to leave because you thought it was what I wanted?"

I feel my mom's hand land on my knee. She squeezes gently. "Finnley, honey, I told him to let you go. If you're going to be angry with someone, be angry with me."

"Mom, what? Why?"

"Because I know what it's like to be unhappy and stuck and have absolutely no way out." She pauses, glances at my dad. "No offense."

Holy shit. Did she really just say that? Out loud? I am flabbergasted as I wait for my dad's response.

He scoffs yet again. "Thanks, I think."

"I wanted to see you smile. See you enjoying yourself. See you find real happiness and chase your dreams."

"Well, look how that has worked out for me." My shoulders slump. "As soon as I felt like my life was going in a great direction, all of this happened."

"Everything happens for a reason, right?"

I perk up at the familiar voice. My throat tightens at the sight of Emerson standing there, hair pulled up in a messy ponytail, different colors of paint all over her clothing and Birkenstocks.

I'm across the space between us and throwing my arms around her in no time.

She chuckles, low and deep, before whispering, "Shh, it's okay," in my ear. I realize then that I am finally crying.

～

EXPLAINING EMERSON TO MY PARENTS IS... INTERESTING. MY MOM is unfazed but also distant. Her reaction makes sense, especially after recalling Uncle Mark's declaration that my mom always thought I was a queer kid. My dad, on the other hand... I want to punch him more than once. I'd like to believe his erratic behavior is because Emerson is one of the most beautiful people to ever exist, and maybe that *was* the reason, but ultimately, he acts like he doesn't know what to do with himself. He keeps speaking at a super loud volume. He laughs at the most inappropriate times. And at one point, I have to ask him if he realizes he is gesturing wildly for no apparent reason.

It is comical, sure.

But it is also really annoying, considering I am hoping to impress Emerson, not scare her away. At least not before I've unloaded my ten tons of baggage on her.

She clearly isn't going anywhere, though, which is a load off my mind. I should be surprised that she is handling my parents with such poise and grace, though of course she is. I have never met anyone like her before. She's sure of herself, but she never comes across as cocky. Is it the artist in her, or is it her age that allows her to have the wisdom and courage not to shrink in situations where shrinking would be a go-to for me?

After she arrived and I disappeared into the house with her, she hugged me and informed me that Lisa had told her everything.

"Are you okay?"

"I don't know," I respond honestly. I really have no idea.

"Talk to me. What's going on in your head?"

I groan. "I wish I could put it all into words. I feel like an asshole. I went and fell for someone else while I was supposed to be with him, and I stupidly didn't just end it with him when I should have, and now…" I can feel myself starting to cry. "It just makes no sense. I feel like this is all my fault. I killed him."

"Finnley," she says, a soft smile on her face. "Honey. You didn't kill him. You did what you needed to do. You cannot control how he reacted to it."

"But if I would have just done it sooner, he would have never come here, and I wouldn't have flipped out and—"

"Stop." She calms me by holding my hands. "You had no way of knowing this would be the outcome. And what do I always say?"

I breathe in her question. "Everything happens for a reason."

"Yes." She gives me a gracious smile. "It sucks that this happened. It's not fair. You're right. But you did not cause this. You have to try and stop thinking that way. It does no good for you or anyone else."

I listen to her, process her words, and do as she says. I *try* to stop thinking this way. "I'm just so... torn. A huge part of me, fuck, feels relieved. And the weight of the guilt I feel because of that is crushing me."

"Completely understandable." She places her hand on my back and starts rubbing small circles there. "This is going to take time, Finn."

"The last thing I wanted was for something to derail us, though."

She chuckles. "Are you serious?"

"What?"

"Honey," she says, her voice low. "Nothing is going to derail us. Especially not this."

I nod as I look at her. "Will you come with me?"

"To Tampa?"

"I know, it's a lot. And you can say no. I mean, you should probably say no. But everything about your presence calms me. I don't want to do this without you. Is that weird?" I cringe. "I'm a mess. I'm sorry."

"Don't apologize. I can absolutely come with you." She leans forward and places a kiss on my forehead. "I'm honored, actually."

And if it's possible, I fall even more for her.

Later, when I tell Uncle Mark, he is completely on board with the idea. "She will be a good buffer," he says. "I trust Emerson's ability to remain calm. And calm is what you're going to need."

"You don't think it's too soon?" I ask as I pass him the tequila. He's making margaritas again. My mom asked for one. We're not having Mexican food—she just wants one. "What if it becomes way more than she wants to handle?"

"Then you won't spend the next few months wandering around in a relationship, wondering if this is the person for you. You'll know. Like, right away." He pauses to vigorously shake the drink shaker. Moments like this, when he's so authentically himself, make me love him so much more than I ever thought possible. He is so real, so flawed yet perfect, that he inspires me to leap into action, to make that jump, to fall and then hopefully soar. When my life feels so tragically fucked, it helps to know that I have him in my corner.

"If she is saying she will go, I wouldn't question it. I don't want to get your hopes up because I realize this is very new for you, but she likes you a lot. She would never have said yes if she thought this wasn't what she wanted. I know Emerson like the back of my hand. She is not into beating around the bush, so to speak." He laughs. "And she's gonna be honest with you. Hey, tell you what?" He hands me a margarita for my mom and another old-fashioned for me. "I'll come with too. It'll be just the three of us, traveling and taking your mind off the stress. Well, the three of us and your parents."

"You mean *your* sister and her husband."

"Oh yeah," he says, sparing no sarcasm. "This is gonna be a fun trip, for sure."

CHAPTER TEN

Tampa International Airport's call sign is TIA. More like UGH. I am so not in the mood to be back in the sweltering heat and oppressive humidity. I know I'll miss warm Florida winters, but I am enjoying not dying from heat during the summer. I have fallen completely in love with Chicago, too, which is another reason the idea of going back to Florida makes me sad.

Uncle Mark, Aunt Lisa, Emerson, and even my parents have all been super supportive. Even so, my anxiety is off the charts. I don't know what I'm going to walk into when we arrive at Carla's, but I have a pretty good feeling it's not going to be a welcome party.

My relationship with Rory... I tried to explain this to Emerson last night. It's not that I don't like Rory. She's a great person. And even though I have never wanted to be a parent, I found myself enjoying the time I spent with her. She's sixteen. She's not a child. And Steven did a remarkable job raising her. She loves *Saturday Night Live,* playing Monopoly, and listening to Taylor Swift. What's not to like about her, right?

When I start to think about why I don't want to be a parent, my first thoughts always head right to my own parents. To the way they raised me. To the way I never felt like I was good enough. To the way I was always dying to get away from them. I don't want to be that person for someone. I don't want to be the reason they are eager to leave, excited to be gone, ecstatic to be *free*. I love my parents, I do. But I don't like them very much. And that's hard.

Maybe knowing what I don't want to do means I would make a terrific parent, the same way I know how to run a business because I know what *not* to do. Ultimately, it doesn't matter what I tell myself; the desire, the instinct, has never been there.

So, I love Rory, but I never wanted to be a parental figure to her. I wanted her to like me because it was easier on her father if she did. I wanted her to like me because it made my life easier.

Isn't that fucked up?

I'm a disgusting human being.

"Hey," Emerson says as we climb into the back seat of my parents' Land Rover. "You're going to combust if you don't settle down."

Her hand on my back, then the back of my neck, is helping, but it's not stopping my runaway train of destructive thoughts. "Just nervous," I whisper when I glance over at her. Her supportive eyes make my heart ache. This person barely knows me, and she's here. With me. Now. During the most fucked-up moments of my life, she has shown up.

Uncle Mark sits next to me and rests his arm along the top of the seat behind me, so I lean my head against the crook of his arm. "We are all here for you, Finnley. Don't forget that. We're all in your corner."

"This is not going to go well. Carla was so angry with me."

"Can you blame her?" My dad's gruff response comes from the driver's seat.

My mom backhands his arm. "Hank," she says harshly. "Let it go, you asshole." She looks at my uncle over her shoulder, and he rolls his eyes. "Don't listen to him, Finn. Everything is going to be fine."

I don't know when my mom decided to be one of my supporters, but I've decided that I'm not going to push her away like I normally would. It's not worth it anymore. I'm going to need all the help I can get if Rory decides she wants to come stay with me.

That's another thing. What if she decides she'd rather not come with me? That's a real possibility. She loves her aunt and her cousins. If that's the case, if she decides that she'd like to stay with them, then what? The thought sort of scares me. But why? That would mean I'm off the hook, right?

Off the hook?

I have *got* to stop thinking like that.

I look down at Emerson's hand, at the veins beneath her pale skin, at her bare nails. She is no longer wearing her wedding ring, but a faint tan line remains. How can something so tiny, the absence of something that at one time held such significance, bring me so much peace? How did this woman come into my life and change everything?

"Carla said to come on in," my mom says as we pull up to their Seminole Heights bungalow. We all climb out of the Land Rover.

"Is it always this humid?" Emerson asks, and we all answer with the same groan. "Why would you ever want to live here?"

"Why do you think I love Chicago so much?" I whisper my question, but Uncle Mark must have heard me.

He looks back at us and nods enthusiastically while tapping his nose. I chuckle. "See?"

"It's an acquired taste," my dad says before we get to the front door of the house.

"Agree to disagree," Uncle Mark says, then looks at me. "You doin' okay?"

"Sure."

His gracious smile is exactly what I need. "One minute at a time, okay?"

I nod my response. I have to conserve my words because I only have a few more left in me before I either combust or freak out. Emerson's fingers intertwine with mine. She squeezes; then, as quickly as it happened, it's over. I'm grateful that she realizes holding my hand right now is probably not the best decision, but I also miss her instantly.

Walking into Carla's is like a slap to the face. The front entryway has an easel displaying a giant portrait of Steven. She did that on purpose, I'm sure of it. He was so handsome with his red hair and brown eyes. The sight knocks the wind out of me, and anger floods my body. Anger because I wasn't happy with him. Anger because of the situation. Anger because he didn't clear any of this with me regarding Rory. Anger, anger, *anger*. A lot of fucking anger.

"Carla, we're here," my mom calls from the foyer.

"In the kitchen," Carla shouts back.

"Finnley?"

I look up the stairs at the sound of my name. Rory is standing halfway down the steps, her hair pulled back from her face, just like Steven liked it, and her club volleyball uniform on.

"Rory," I say softly, and she rushes down the stairs and leaps into my arms.

"I'm so glad you're here," she says into my shoulder. "I didn't know if you were coming or not."

"Of course I'm here. I would never not show up for you." It sounds like a lie, but as soon as I say it, I realize it's one of the most honest things I've ever said.

"I know," she whispers. "But Aunt Carla said—"

"Don't listen to anything she's said, okay? I'm here now, and that's all that matters." I pull away from her and look into her dark eyes, the same color as Steven's. "Let's go get this over with."

THE KITCHEN IS A COMPLETE DISASTER. THE COUNTERTOPS ARE covered with casserole dishes, presumably from people who are sending cheesy potatoes along with their condolences. Carla's red hair is a mess when she looks up from the stack of papers that is holding her attention. The curls are out of control from the humidity, but it's also clear she hasn't had a moment to catch her breath or tame the frizz. Her face softens when she sees me. I'm not going to lie, it shocks me, the kindness in her eyes as she rushes over to me.

"I'm so sorry," she whispers as she throws her arms around my neck. "I'm so, so sorry."

"Carla, stop." I smooth my hand over her back as she sobs in my arms. I've always tried to find peace with her. She was the voice of reason in Steven's brain for as long as he could remember, and now, she's the voice of reason in Rory's ear. It's astonishing how older sisters naturally pick up the pieces when parents pass. Carla has done so effortlessly and without complaint. "I'm sorry that you have to go through this. That we all do."

She pulls away from me. "No, Finn, I tried to make you feel bad, but..." She covers her hand with her mouth. "He was a mess." She does a sweeping motion toward more stacks of paper. "He was in debt up to his eyeballs. He blew every cent our parents left him. I'm disgusted by it all."

"Rory, honey, why don't you show me around?" Emerson's voice brings me back to reality. It also makes Carla tilt her head and stare at her, then me.

"My friend Emerson."

"Oh," Carla says softly. "Yes, Rory, please show her around. And take Uncle Mark with you."

Rory nods, and when I find Emerson's eyes, she gives me a look that says, *Take your time. I've got this.* My mom busies herself by focusing on the dishes in the sink. My dad is looking through the papers on the table.

"Let's take a look here," he says, and I want to smack him. Like he has any idea what he's even looking at.

"Dad, stop," I say as I push him away from the papers. "None of this is your business. Not your lawn business or your actual business, so please step back."

"It's okay, Finn," Carla says while sitting at the table. "I need help with it all."

"Yeah, well, he is not the right person to decipher anything to do with money. Isn't that right, Dad?"

He groans. "I bounced a few checks. So sue me."

"A few? Jesus. He had over thirty thousand dollars in bounced check fees while I was in Boston." I look at him. "Go help Mom."

"I don't need help," I hear her say as he walks over to her. "Go sit outside with Barry."

"Yeah, my husband needs the company," Carla offers. "He's been a fucking lunatic since this all went down. Like I needed another fucking person to look after, y'know?"

I place my hand on hers and squeeze. "Carla, we have to talk about Rory."

"I know, I know." She sounds defeated, as if this is the last thing she wants to talk about but she knows we have to.

"What does she want to do?"

"I have no idea." Carla pulls out a cigarette from a ratty old pack that looks like she found it under the couch. When she lights it and inhales, she shakes her head. "I quit these fifteen years ago. Fifteen. And now look at me. I had to barter my fucking life away to get this pack from Barry."

I let out a low laugh when she does. It seems appropriate. I can only imagine the stress she's under. "I can talk to her, to Rory."

"I know you can. She loves you so much, Finn."

"I know. I don't want to move back here, though." Carla's eyes land on mine. "I will want to take her back to Chicago."

"Okay," she says so very softly. "I understand that. Florida's education system is a fucking mess."

"No shit." I borrow her cigarette and take a drag from it, then hand it back. The smoke billows from my mouth, and I hear my mom groan. "What do you want to do?"

Carla sighs. "I love Rory so much. I just want her to make her own decision. If she wants to stay? Great. If she wants to go with you, I'm okay with that too. I know you'll take care of her, even though..." Her voice, the way it trails off, makes my stomach churn. "I know you didn't want kids. I don't think that has to change because he left guardianship of her to you."

It means the world to me that she gets it without me having to voice it.

"Did he even tell you that he did that?" Her question isn't accusatory, but her tone is. She's pissed at him. I get it because, yeah, *same*. I shake my head, and she sighs. "He should have told you, Finn."

"Yeah, that would have been nice."

"What do you want to do?"

I sigh. "I have no fucking idea."

"I get that."

I feel a hand on my shoulder before my mom sits next to me at the table. "Can I offer you some advice?"

I stare at Carla. Her gracious smile calms me. "Sure, Mom, offer away."

"I think you should have Rory come stay with you for a week and see how it works out. She may decide Chicago is not for her." My mom is rubbing small circles into my back. It feels strange because she has never been touchy-feely with me. But at the same time, it feels nice... It's something I think I've craved and have never realized until now.

Carla shrugs. "It's not a bad idea."

"That's a fantastic idea." Uncle Mark shrugs at our surprised faces after he sits next to Carla. "I decided to eavesdrop if that's okay."

"You sure?" I say. His words are a load off my mind, but I'm still hesitant. I am literally living *with* him, and now I'm going to move a teenager into his home? Talk about changing someone's everything.

"I'm positive," he says. He smiles at me. "It might be fun."

"She's a hormonal teenager." Carla laughs. "I can assure you, it will not be fun."

And we all descend into laughter. For the first time since everything happened, I feel like maybe, just maybe, I can see light at the end of the tunnel.

∼

"Ybor City, hmm? You think that'll help get your mind off of things?" Uncle Mark straightens his tie after he pulls into a parking spot behind Seventh Avenue in downtown Tampa. "It does look like a good time down here." Ybor City is the oldest part of Tampa. The old cigar-rolling district, it's now home to hip restaurants, trendy bars, and tattoo shops. And it also has a few of the city's best gay bars. He glances over at me. "Finnley? Are you okay?"

"Yeah, I'm good." I take a deep breath. "I couldn't talk Jesse out of it either. She was like a dog with a bone."

"She just wants to meet me," Emerson says from the back seat. "Because I'm sure you've told her about me, right?"

I can feel the heat rushing into my cheeks. "What gave you that idea?"

"That deep red blush in your cheeks." She is leaning forward now, a smile on her face. "You're adorable, you know that?"

"Get a room," Uncle Mark says with a groan. He climbs out of the Land Rover and claps his hands together. "We need a game plan, okay? An exit strategy, if you will."

"He's not wrong." I stand next to him. "Jesse is wild. She'll want to stay out the entire night."

"Well, lucky for the both of you, I'm sober, so I'll be the DD."

"That's not the point." I shake my head. "If we don't have a plan, we'll never leave. It'll be awful."

"And this chick is your best friend?" Emerson laughs. "She sounds like a hot mess."

Uncle Mark points at Emerson. "Exactly! But we all know that Finnley here loves herself a little hot mess."

"Whoa, whoa," Emerson protests. "Does that mean that you think *I'm* a hot mess?"

"Hm, almost divorced? Maybe a smidge." Uncle Mark laughs good-naturedly as he puts his arm around Emerson's shoulders. "But you're, like, an angel on earth, so we all forgive you."

"You really think I'm a hot mess?" She's looking at me now, a breathtaking smile on her beautiful face.

"Absolutely not," I answer. She ditches Uncle Mark's arm and throws hers around me.

"Thank you." She kisses my cheek, then quickly kisses my lips. The touch lights a fire in my abdomen almost instantly. "Seriously, thank you." Her warm whispers tickle. "You have no idea how you've changed everything in my life."

"You think I've changed your life?" I let out a small puff of air. "What are you even talking about?"

"This." She takes my hand and places it on her heart. I can feel the gentle thumping of the muscle, and a chill erupts all over my body. "You made it beat again, Finnley."

Uncle Mark groans yet again. "Come on, you two."

Before I met Emerson, it was rare for me to be rendered speechless. I have so much I want to say, after all, but every word seems so insignificant when I'm standing in front of her. Like, how do I tell her that I feel the same way about her without it seeming like a cop-out? How do I tell her I've never been more excited about a future that is more unknown than I ever thought possible? How do I tell her that I've fallen in love with her in two weeks when I spent most of my life struggling to know what love even is?

"Let's go meet Jesse," she says after she kisses my cheek again. "I wanna know the people who are important to you."

"Aside from me, of course." Uncle Mark's shout from about ten paces in front of us is well timed. He tosses us a look over his shoulder. "Hurry up before we miss out on all the action."

The action he is referring to, of course, is the drag show "Diva Royale" at Southern Nights Tampa. Jesse suggested it, and Uncle Mark leapt at the opportunity. "Drag in Florida? Sign me up," he shouted when I told him earlier.

Walking in takes me back instantly to turning twenty-one and celebrating at Club Czar. The rainbow of flashing lights, the smell of stale cigarettes, my shoes sticking to the floor, all of it. The music is exactly what I remember too. Britney Spears and Beyonce at full volume. I get exactly why Uncle Mark was a tad skeptical that a night in Ybor was the right course of action. I am sure I'll regret the decisions that future Finnley makes in the next four hours.

Jesse is standing near the bar, of course, with her arm around a guy, also of course, and a drink in her hand, again, of course. She looks like she stumbled off the pages of a nineties magazine, though, and I briefly wonder if I missed a memo about the dress code. Mid-drink, she finally sees me and squeals, causing her drink to fly everywhere. She drops the rest of it, plastic cup and all, on the guy she is with and zigzags through the crowd over to me.

"I am so happy to see you," she says after she throws her arms around me. She won't let go of the hug. She has always been way more touchy-feely than me. Right now is a perfect example of that.

"Jess, babe, you're gonna smear your makeup." I feel her laugh vibrate through her small frame. "I'm okay. I promise."

"Are you sure?"

She's *still* hugging me. I pull away from her a bit. "I swear. Look at me. Don't I look okay?"

"Yeah, but bitch, he died. Like, poof. He's gone."

Welp, she's drunk already. Great. "How many have you had?"

"What? Vodkas? Oh, y'know," she says. I've seen the face she's making before. She's tallying them in her head. "Like, five?"

"Wonderful." I make sure the sarcasm is thick because, completely sober, she wouldn't pick it up. I lock my gaze onto her blue eyes. Her makeup really does look flawless, so I'm glad she managed to stop the fury of tears that were threatening to ruin it. "Are *you* okay? Maybe that's the question we should be asking."

Her hands on my shoulders clench into fists, taking my shirt with them. "I don't think so."

"Jess," I say with a small laugh. "Come on." I make apologetic eye contact with Emerson and Uncle Mark. They understand immediately. I lead her through the remaining crowd and exit the bar into the humid night air. "What is going on?"

She slumps against the brick wall and groans. "Dude, *death*. Am I right?"

"Jesus."

"I just—he was young."

"Jess, he didn't die of a heart attack. He got wasted; he walked in front of a car. He did it to himself." *Whoa*. I hear the irritation in my voice, feel the heat of anger flare in my chest, and realize for the first time that maybe I'm not okay either. I lean against the wall next to her and take a deep breath. "It all sucks, doesn't it?"

"Yeah, it really does." She slips her hand through the crook of my arm and pulls herself as close to me as possible. In any other circumstance, I'd push her off because it's too fucking hot for close contact. But now? Now all I want to do is melt into my best friend and cry for days. "How long are you staying?" Her voice is so small, soft, unlike her. I don't know if it's the boom of the bass or the hustle and bustle of Seventh Avenue in Ybor. She's always sure of herself. Her upbringing, her parents' money, her beauty, all of it adds up to Jesse Cale.

"We leave tomorrow." I'm already not looking forward to potentially being hungover on a plane.

"Is she going with you?" She picks her head up from its leaned-back position on the bricks and looks at me. "Rory, I mean."

I sigh. It's much deeper than I intended. I can't decide if I don't want to talk about this or if I really, really do. "I have no idea."

A laugh bubbles from deep within me, but before I know it, I feel warm tears sliding down my cheeks. "Jess, I don't want to be a mom. I don't want this. I don't want any of it. And I feel like the most selfish asshole in the world. He just died, for fuck's sake, and all I can think of is how fucking angry I am at him. For not letting me break up with him. For just showing up in Chicago. For leaving me as Rory's guardian without telling me. Like, who the fuck does something like that?" I pull away from her and dab at my eyes with the sides of my index fingers. I don't want to ruin my makeup either, dammit, but it's happening, and I can't fucking stop it apparently. I groan as I pat my face dry. The last thing I want to do is go inside and watch a drag show. What the hell was I thinking? I should have listened to Uncle Mark. He'll be thrilled to learn that, I'm sure.

"Can I say something?" Jesse turns so her shoulder is now leaning against the bricks. I turn to look at her, at her crop top, mom jeans, and white Air Force Ones. She's thirty-two, but she looks twenty-five. Shows what a life without stress will do for you.

"Of course, Jess. Please. Say something. Because I can't keep wallowing."

"Well, yeah, that's what I was going to say."

My mouth falls open.

She starts laughing. "I'm kidding, you asshole. I was going to say that I think you need to have this conversation with Rory. Not me. She's sixteen. She'll understand."

"You honestly think a sixteen-year-old who has lost her mom and now her dad will understand that the only other person in her life that is supposed to want her doesn't?"

Jesse opens her mouth to protest, then closes it promptly. "Well, shit. You make a good point."

"Yeah, see? I'm a selfish dick."

"First of all," she says as she pushes away from the wall, "stop fucking saying that you're selfish. I'm selfish. You are not. So stop. And second?" She smooths her hands down my biceps, forearms, until she's holding both of my hands. "You do not need to feel bad for not wanting to be a mom. Society has really fucked us, hasn't it? Just because you're a woman doesn't mean you should want to, y'know, birth a baby from your loins and raise it. That's fucking patriarchal bullshit, and you know it. Personally? And this is just me, selfish me, if I were Rory, I'd much rather you talk to me now than years from now when you resent me for being burdened with me."

"Burdened?" I smile at her. "You're not a burden."

"You know what I mean."

"You sobered up pretty quick," I say in admiration. "You're a great friend too. Not nearly as selfish as you think you are."

"Yeah, well, ditto."

"We should probably go back in there."

Jesse pulls me away from the wall and wraps her arms around me again. "Are you sure you're okay?"

"No," I say softly. "But I'm really hoping that I will be."

"I like the honesty, but I really was hoping you'd lie to me some more. It's easier." She grabs my hand and yanks me toward the entrance of the club. "Let's go. You need to introduce me to this woman you're gonna bang. Which, by the way"—she stops and looks at me—"is so on brand for you. Do you even realize that?"

"Um… no?"

"Jesus, Finn, you were *so* unhappy, weren't you?"

I know she's saying that from a place of love and caring, but it *rips* my heart out.

"I'm really sorry, babe. Really, really sorry that I didn't see it. I'm your best friend."

"Yeah, well, we already determined that you're selfish, so are we surprised?"

A beat passes before she laughs. "Yeah, yeah, you're right. Well, let's go in and embrace this new happy person you are." She leans in closer to me, incapable of letting this go. "You're so into women. How has it taken you until now to finally get that about yourself?"

"It's called denial, Jess." And a whole lot of repression. Ugh.

"It ain't just a lake."

"A river. It ain't just a river, for fuck's sake."

Jesse laughs again as she heads back into the club, pulling me behind her.

CHAPTER ELEVEN

At five in the morning, I roll over and bump into a body. After I peel my eyes open and see that it's Emerson, I feel better…

…until I remember that I'm at my parents' house. And Emerson isn't just my friend. And they know that.

Oh God, oh God, oh God. I roll onto my back and stare up at the ceiling. I should have never sublet my apartment. Wait, that's dumb. Calm down, Finnley. Stop being irrational.

Who cares if she's in your bed? If your parents do, then oh fucking well. You're thirty-two years old. You're an adult.

I look over at her again. She's sound asleep. Her mouth is open slightly, her hair is a mess, and her white tank top has moved just enough to expose almost all of her left breast. The heat that erupts in my center is so powerful that I have to *literally* tell myself to look away from her.

The drama that has unfolded since our one encounter has been *intense*. If I were to tell a random person the story, they'd probably tell me that I'm lying. Or that I've embellished parts to make it more interesting. And I'd have to tell them to get bent.

Why the hell would I make this shit up? Why would I choose to go through all of this?

The only reason, of course, would be if it means I end up happy at the end of the drama, right? Otherwise, why go through it? If everything happens for a reason, as Emerson says, then all of this has to be so I can figure myself out. If it's not, if it's for some other reason, I'm going to be so upset.

My dad firing me started a chain reaction of events that I never thought I'd experience, that's for damn sure. I was so mad at him at first. God, I wanted to kill him. But now I'm actually thankful. I heard him telling Barry how stressful the business has been lately, and for the first time in my adult life, I felt the joy of knowing I didn't have to worry about it.

Moving in with Uncle Mark, what an impeccable decision that has been. I feel so at peace in his home. I feel at home, and before this, I hadn't felt at home in a space in years. Maybe not ever. Holy cow, how is that possible? How can I have lived my entire life and never have felt completely at peace somewhere?

Meeting Emerson… I still haven't been able to wrap my brain around that one. She breezed into my life wearing a suit and a hot-as-fuck attitude and completely rearranged my world. I don't often think about forever because, truthfully, the idea of it freaks me out. But forever with Emerson sounds absolutely tremendous.

I allow myself to look at her again. I am in love with her. There isn't a doubt in my mind. I'd love to say I have no idea how it happened, but I know exactly how it happened.

I figured myself out. Finally. And goddamn, it feels unbelievably good. I think back to my conversation with Lisa, to whether or not I'm a lesbian or straight. "Why do you need to label it?" She's right, yes. Labels aren't necessary. But in this particular moment of my life, I want to label myself. I want to slap a giant LESBIAN label on my forehead for the entire world to see. I want to come out of the closet wearing a genuine smile on my face instead of the smile that, up until now, I've been faking.

And I want to start *this* life, where, sure, I'm nervous and scared, but I'm also excited and... *happy.*

I'm happy.

I'm really fucking happy.

Guilt seeps in the second I remember why I'm here.

Steven.

Rory.

How fucked up is it that I'm able to admit I'm finally happy in spite of dealing with the shit show that has unfolded?

"Your thoughts are so loud," Emerson whispers. She licks her lips, opens her eyes, and gives me a sleepy smile.

"I'm sorry." Working on not apologizing all the time has been at the top of my priority list, but right this second, I really am sorry. I know I can be a hot mess when I'm obsessing.

She scoots closer to me. Her tank top has shifted and is exposing even more of her. "Don't be." She runs her fingers down my cheek, along my jawline, then lightly across my lips. "You're really going through it, aren't ya?"

"That's putting it lightly."

"Do you want to talk about it?"

"I don't know what to tell Rory." My voice sounds far away as I see the words wash over her.

"That's understandable. Having her live with you will change your entire life." She pauses. "Again."

"Is it wrong that I don't want to do this?"

"No, it's not wrong." She tucks her hair behind her ear before folding her hands together and resting them near her face. I notice again that she isn't wearing her wedding ring. I want to ask if her divorce is final. Has she moved out? Or has her ex-wife moved out? My drama has had a monopoly on our attention for the past week or so. "When are you talking to her?"

"Noon. We're going to go back over to Carla's before the flight."

"What is the main reason you *want* to do this?"

"The main reason?" I shake my head. "Guilt."

"That's not a good reason to do it."

Her bare shoulder is all I can focus on. "I know. It's the worst reason imaginable."

"I still think having her come stay for a week would be good for you and for her." She shrugs her bare shoulder, the one I can't stop focusing on. "You can still be a part of her life. That doesn't have to change."

"True."

"Finnley, can I tell you something?"

"Of course," I say softly. "You can tell me anything."

"Justine is my wife… my ex-wife."

Everything in the room skids to a halt as if the earth simply stopped spinning. I blink the confusion away, but it's useless. "What?"

"I'm Isabel. Emerson is my last name. My maiden name."

"What?"

"I knew you were the one she hired after it happened. She told me about this woman from Florida with a Harvard MBA and how she was going to save the business. It didn't take me long to figure out who she was talking about. I know Chicago is big, but that's pretty specifically *you*." She takes a deep breath and lets it out. I want to focus on her morning breath, so maybe it will help me be as angry as possible with her, but all I can do is be thankful that she's telling me the truth. "I'm sorry I'm just now telling you. I should have told you immediately. But I liked you way too much to risk you hating me."

"And what about now? Do you not care if I hate you now?"

She inhales deeply, and her eyes fill with tears. "Now I like you way too much to keep lying to you."

"Does she know? Does she know that you… me…" I can't say

the words. I don't know why. Maybe because I don't even know what to call whatever is happening between us. I've fallen in love with this woman, and I can't even describe our relationship.

"Yes."

"Oh."

She holds up a hand, all business. "Your job is safe."

I let out a soft chuckle. "Do you think I give a fuck about that job? Accounting is not my passion. You know this."

Her smile makes my heart hurt. "I know, Finnley."

"So, now what? You just come into my life and change everything about it, drop this bomb, then leave? Is that what's going to happen?"

Her face shifts. She's no longer concerned. She's confused. "What are you talking about? Do you think I would have come to Tampa with you if I planned on telling you the truth and leaving you? Are you out of your mind?"

"I don't even know what is happening between us, Emerson. Or do I call you Isabel?"

"Stop." She sits up in an instant, then huffs because of her tank top. She looks back at me, exasperated. "You couldn't have told me my breasts were popping out of this? What the hell?"

"I liked looking at them." It's all I can say because, well, it's the truth. Why start lying now?

A smile slowly appears on her lips before she looks away, hiding her face from me. "You can call me whatever you want to call me. I told you all of that because the last thing I want is to lose you. Besides, you would have found out eventually."

The tank she is wearing has ridden up at the back, and the hem of her black panties is showing. It's a real mindfuck that I should probably be asking her a hundred questions, but all I can think is that I want to fuck her. I want to undress her and kiss every inch of her body and taste all of her, catalog every single flavor, the dried sweat on her hairline from our night out dancing to her hot, wet center and everything in between.

I reach out and run my index finger along the hem of her panties. She stiffens under the contact before relaxing into it. I place my hand flat against her back, then move so my fingers are wrapped around her side above her hip. I pull myself toward her, lift the back of her tank top, and place a kiss on her lower back. The skin there is so soft, untouched by the conditions of the world, and I breathe in the sweet smell of her skin. I sit up behind her and slowly pull her tank the rest of the way up until she's no longer wearing it. She looks at me over her shoulder. Her wavy hair is hanging against the bare skin of her back. I move it gently to the side and kiss her shoulder blade.

"You sure you want to do this now?"

"I've never been more sure of something before."

I scoot as close to her as possible and slide my hands around her body to her bare breasts. When she leans her head back onto my shoulder, I kiss her cheek, her jaw, her neck. I cup each breast, use my forefinger and thumb to tweak her nipples, which harden as soon as I start playing with them. She pulls in a sharp breath when I pinch maybe a little too hard. She's leaning back fully into me, though, and I love how new this feels, yet also as if we've done this a thousand times before. I'm not nervous. I'm not hesitant. I know what I want, and I want to feel her. I move my right hand down her sternum, over her abdominal muscles, to the hem of her panties.

She stills my hand for half a second with her own. "I haven't done this in a while…"

I smile into her cheek as I whisper, "I haven't done this ever." Her hand moves with mine as we slip beneath the black cotton. She's unshaven, and her soft pubic hair feels phenomenal. When she removes her hand from mine, I take that as my cue to take charge. I'd love to say that since I just recently figured out I like women, I have no idea what to do, but I know exactly what to do. I've masturbated a million times. I know what I want. I just hope it's also what she wants. Slipping my fingers through her wetness is one of the most erotic things I've ever done in my life. For obvious reasons, but also because I never thought I'd be here with her. It causes my throat to ache. I curl a finger and slip it inside her, then another after she spreads her legs to give me better access.

"I can take my panties off," she says between heavy breaths. "If you want—oh, holy shit." She stops talking the second my fingers find her clit. "Never mind."

I let out a low laugh as I keep my attention focused on the small circles I'm doing. She has her hands on my thighs, her fingertips digging into my muscles. "Does this feel okay?" I whisper the question next to her ear, and she nods enthusiastically.

"But harder, please." Her instruction is said in a voice that practically makes my own orgasm rear its head. I do as she says and rub harder until suddenly she is shaking, clasping her thighs together, clenching her jaw. I finally still my hand when the force of her thighs makes it so I can't move. When she relaxes, she lets out a breathy laugh. "Okay then." She leans forward and turns, so she's now facing me. "What the hell was that?"

My eyes are drawn to her bare breasts. Her areolas and nipples are a stark contrast to the rest of her pale skin. The size of her breasts, though, is absolutely everything I never knew I wanted. "I wanted to touch you." I shrug, my gaze never wavering. "Is that a crime?"

"My eyes are up here," she says as she places her hand under my chin and tilts my face upward. "Take that shirt off, please."

"Yes, ma'am," I whisper. I pull my sleep shirt up and over my head, then toss it on the floor next to the bed.

"Panties too."

"Same to you, Miss Thing."

"Don't you worry about me." She pushes me gently backward until I am flat on the bed. She takes the hem of my panties and pulls them down my legs when I lift my hips. I'm so wet, it's almost laughable. I've never been this wet when it comes to sex with men. I can't take my eyes off hers, which in the early morning light are so emerald in color that I can barely handle it. She gently pushes my legs apart before she kneels between them. There have been many times in my life when I haven't remembered to tidy things up downstairs, but thankfully this is not one of those times.

"What is this from?" she murmurs as she runs a finger over a deep scar on my thigh.

"The one and only time I played soccer. I had a run-in with the goal."

"The goalie?" she clarifies.

"No, the actual goal. The net. I don't know. I told you, I'm a klutz."

She chuckles and leans down to kiss it. "You're adorable." She places another kiss on my other thigh. "Can I tell you something else?"

"Not if you're going to tell me you're also in a relationship with Blake or something."

She freezes. "Blake still works there?" She looks up at me. "Seriously?"

"Um…" Oh shit. "Yeah…"

"God," she says as she sits back on her feet. "Wow."

"Emerson…" I sit up and place my hand on hers. "Don't. Okay? It's not worth it."

She looks at me, right into my eyes, and I feel it deep inside my stomach. "I think I am falling in love with you." Her voice is smooth, full of devotion, and it causes my breath to catch. "I hope that's not too much truth for this early in the morning."

"I feel the same way about you." My own truth comes out in a whisper, doused in emotion. "I hope that's not too much truth considering we're both naked."

The soft laugh she gives as she lunges toward me and kisses me has me feeling like I could fly.

We lie back on the bed together, and she straddles my hips. I snap the elastic of her panties and she yelps. "I thought I told you to take these off." I raise up to my elbows and watch her as she stands, slips them off, then tosses them haphazardly over her shoulder. "Goddamn." I'm admiring her body, the curve of her hips, the dark color of her pubic hair, the way her quads are defined in the early sunlight. "You're perfect." She straddles me again, pressing her center into me, and I reach for her. I want to finger her again, make her come again. "I want to put my mouth on you."

"You're going to have to wait." She takes my hands, holds them together, then pins them above my head. Her breasts are right by my face now, so I lift my head to get my mouth on her. She moans when I suck her left nipple into my mouth and bite down lightly. "Do the other one." She hovers right above me, so I have access again. When I do it, she grinds into me. "If you keep doing that, I'm going to come again."

"And that's a problem, why?"

"It's not," she husks right by my ear. "But I want to make you come."

"What are you waiting for?"

Her eyes widen before she moves one of her hands down my body, to my breasts, where she starts to play with my nipples, one at a time. "I'm going to move my other hand. Don't touch me, okay?"

"Why?"

"Because I want to focus on you."

"Okay…" I smile when she releases my hands above my head. I leave them there and watch her move down my body, watch her hands as they caress my breasts, watch her place kisses along my body. I move so I can see her better when she settles between my thighs. She locks her eyes onto mine, then leans in and places her mouth over my center. I feel her tongue dip inside, then feel it on my clit. She is moving against it, fast, light, and I'm so close already that if she continues like this, I'll be coming in no time. Her fingers slip inside me, and she starts to thrust, slowly, angling them in just the right position so that she's hitting my G-spot. I am a goner. Holy fucking shit. The thrusting is harder now —her tongue is flicking my clit harder too. I am so very close. She thrusts again and again until it suddenly slams into me. I buck my hips off the bed and hear her chuckle into my wetness. I'm shaking so hard I can barely see straight. My calf muscles are shaking so badly that I fear I'm going to get a cramp. She hasn't stopped either. She's still thrusting, still flicking, and another one crashes into me.

After what feels like a lifetime, I fall onto the bed, panting, completely spent.

"Holy fucking shit," I say between breaths. "Holy fucking shit."

"You okay?"

"I don't know."

"Anything I can do?"

"Yeah, you can do it again and again."

She moves her fingers inside me. "I'm in a great place to start if you're ready." She slowly slides them out, then pushes back in. I'm already ready to go again. How the hell is she doing this to me?

"I can use my fingers this time," she says as she positions herself next to me. "Like this." She slides her fingers out and places them on my clit. "And you can come while I'm watching you this time." Slowly at first, then slightly faster, she rubs me. It's not going to take much.

"Emerson..." Her name sounds like a prayer. I've never been religious, yet I'm ready to sacrifice myself to her. "I'm so close."

"What will this be?" She kisses me. "Number three?" And it hits again. This time, though, I completely come apart and actually come... all over her hand.

"Oh my God." I felt it happen. Add this to my list of embarrassing moments, for sure. I cover my face by folding my arms over it. "I am so sorry."

"Finnley," she whispers. "Stop, please." She pulls my arms away from my face. "Don't apologize. Do you have any idea how happy this makes me?"

"But that's... a lot." The shame is coming on fast. "I have never... I am sorry."

"Okay, stop." Her tone is one I feel she reserves for when she's very serious. "This has been amazing. Absolutely amazing. And you completely letting go like that is part of the reason. Don't ever apologize for letting go and being with me like this. Please."

I lick my lips and nod.

"I mean, I *did* tell you I was going to make you come so hard that you wouldn't know what happened."

I start to laugh then because she did tell me that. I pull her down to me and kiss her as deeply as possible. She has become everything important and wonderful in my life. And to top it off, she wasn't lying when she said she's an attentive lover.

∽

CARLA'S HOUSE LOOKS LIKE A COMPLETELY DIFFERENT PLACE WHEN we arrive at noon. The kitchen no longer looks like a tornado went through it. All the papers are in neat stacks, and the overabundance of casserole dishes have been dealt with. She places cups of coffee in front of me, Emerson, and Uncle Mark at the table, then does a sweeping motion with her hand. "A clean house brought to you by cigarettes and caffeine."

"And Adderall?" Uncle Mark's question is asked with nothing but love.

"I may have stolen one from my eldest's stash. Don't tell him."

Maybe I shouldn't leave Rory with her. Damn. "Whatever works, right?" I say.

"Exactly." Her nervous behavior makes more sense now than it did when we arrived. "So, how was your night?"

I tense. "Um, good."

"Yeah, it was good. The drag show was very fun. And it was great to meet Jesse," Emerson says. Her addition is perfectly timed, thank God. It's not like it looks like I've been freshly fucked, so I don't know why I'm acting weird.

"Jesse is a handful, isn't she?" Carla chuckles. "I love that girl."

"Yeah, she's fun," I say. Emerson has her hand on my bobbing knee now, and she squeezes it, clearly urging me to calm the fuck down. Carla isn't stupid, though. She can see right through me. I can feel it. "So." I clear my throat. "Rory."

"Yes. You need to speak with her."

"I do." I pull a breath into my lungs and hold it for a few seconds before I say, "I think it'd be best for me to talk to her alone, though."

Carla's facial expression shifts as she lets out a breath of her own. I can tell the need for privacy deflated her, but she agrees. "I think that's probably best."

"Is she—"

"Upstairs, yes. Go on up." Carla's demeanor is like a light switch. What was she expecting, though?

I leave the table, carrying my coffee with me, and head upstairs to the room where Rory stays whenever she's here. When I get up there, the door is closed. I knock gently and wait for her response. Her soft "Yes?" makes my heart ache.

"Hey, beautiful," I say after I poke my head in. "Can I come in?"

She nods, but the same light that was in her yesterday when she saw me is not nearly as bright.

I sit on the desk chair facing the bed, where she's sitting cross-legged. Her dark hair is hanging loosely around her face. She's struggling. Obviously. "How are you?"

"I want people to stop asking me how I am, that's how I am."

I nod. "Understandable. What would you like to be asked instead?"

"How about no questions at all? How about just say what I know you want to say?"

Okay. Wow. "Right. Let's discuss you and me."

"Let's."

"What do you want to do, Rory?"

"I don't know, Finnley. What the *fuck*?"

"Whoa there."

Her face softens. "I'm sorry. I just... I don't want to come live with you."

The elephant-size weight camping out in the middle of my chest lifts. It's like I can breathe again. "Rory, honey, that's okay. You don't have to."

Tears start to pour from her eyes. "It's not that I don't love you. I do. I love you so much. But we both know you weren't in love with my dad."

Her words smack me like a two-by-four across the face. "Oh." It's not very eloquent, but it's all I can say.

"I don't think it was fair of him to just dump me onto you either." She is still wiping at her tears when she says that last part. "The last thing I want is for you to hate me because you *had* to take me."

"Oh, God, Rory." My stomach has officially abandoned me and is in full protest of the conversation. One false move and I'll be using her trash can like I used the one outside of Northwestern. "Can I come sit by you?" She nods.

"I need you to listen to me," I say as I sit and make sure to get her full attention. "My feelings for your father have nothing to do with my feelings for you. Sure, I wasn't in a good spot with him when I left. And yeah, a lot happened between us that I wish wouldn't have. But all of that aside, I could never *hate* you. Never. If you were coming with me, I would love you the same way I love you now. Hell, I would love you *more*. I would be whatever you needed me to be. There is nothing in this world that can replace the love that your parents had for you. I know that. But I am ready and willing to be that person for you if you want me to be. But if you don't want to move, if you want to stay here with your aunt, if you want to visit, whatever it is that *you want,* I am also cool with that. This is not an obligation on your part or mine. Okay?"

"Thank you for saying all of that." She sniffles. "I am going to stay. Aunt Carla is my family. She sort of became my mom when I lost mine. You're so lovely, and we have so much fun together, but… it's Aunt Carla." She shrugs. "But I think I would like to visit. Eventually."

"Come here," I say as I pull her into a hug.

She softens to my touch, and we allow ourselves to cry. Cry for the situation. Cry for her father. Cry for the weight that has been lifted off both of our chests.

CHAPTER TWELVE

One week has passed since the trip to Tampa, and the conversations I like to refer to as "gut-wrenching" have unfolded. I've spoken to Rory every day, which is odd, to say the least. I know a lot has changed, and not just for me. I have never spoken to her this often before, but I'm actually... *enjoying* it.

My first week back at Petals for Days has been interesting. Justine's demeanor is exactly as I thought it'd be: cold, bordering on mean. In the five days I've been back, I've almost resigned as many times. Especially when she asked me to do a bouquet for a customer that needed black dahlias, burgundy and yellow roses, and ten sprigs of lavender. I know what all those flowers mean: betrayal, hatred, jealousy, and distrust. She is bitter, and I do not blame her.

Blake also pissed me off this morning when they thought it'd be so cool to be a dick to me when I asked about a customer order. When it turned out I was right, the customer wanted something for congratulations, not a funeral, Blake refused to apologize. Their disdain didn't surprise me so much as confuse me. Why would they hate me? Wouldn't my presence make it easier for them to get Justine all to themselves? And speaking of being confused, why would Justine be mad at *me*? She's the one who cheated. She said so herself to me over drinks that night. Did she want to keep Emerson on a leash, just in case? The more I have heard about their relationship from Emerson, the more I have questioned my loyalty to Justine and Petals for Days. As much as it pains me to say this, the best part has been Emerson never saying a cruel word about Justine or their years together. She urges me not to be biased. "We both have our own versions of the story, Finnley. Don't ever forget that."

It's hard for me to believe that she could ever be the villain in her own story, but if a stranger were to peel back the layers of my story, I'd probably be labeled the same way. It would make sense too. I can only imagine the headlines: *Thirty-Two-Year-Old Woman Leaves Perfectly Fine Fiancé Behind to Sow Her Wild, Lesbian Oats in Chicago*. The article would be chock full of misconceptions and lies, I'm sure, but threads of truth would remain. I may not have sown many oats, but I did figure out that I like women.

I wish I could go back and handle everything with Steven differently. I wish I could tell him how much he meant to me even though I couldn't get to the same place as him emotionally. I wish I could tell him that love has many layers, and while I may not have been in love with him, I loved him so much. I wish I could tell him that I miss him. And I wish I could tell him that I have no right to miss him.

Life would be so much easier if every person came with instructions and a background history provided. Making genuine connections regardless would be the ultimate test, wouldn't it?

Now it's Friday afternoon and I am finally leaving work, leaving Justine's shitty behavior and Blake's mean-spirited attitude at the door. The only thing to keep me company is my obsessive thoughts, per usual. Leaving on a Friday has always been my favorite moment of the week, so I decided to walk home after work. I've mastered a route that takes about an hour. After the day I've had, I need the decompression such a walk will give me.

There's a large part of me that wonders if I am having a hard time with Justine and Blake not only because of the weird circumstances, but also because I've literally only ever worked for my family. I don't know how to handle other people. Handling people like Justine and Blake is proving to be a lot for me. I'm going to need to have a conversation with both of them. After the past few weeks, it's the last thing I want to do.

The next few days will be a welcome reprieve. Uncle Mark is having people over tonight to kick off the Fourth of July weekend . After the last dinner party, I am going to make it a point not to get trashed. Or too trashed. With the current state of my mind, though, who knows? Anyway, I am looking forward to forgetting about my problems for the evening.

When I finally make it to Uncle Mark's, the front door is propped open, and his music is blaring. For six o'clock on a Friday that isn't out of the realm of normal, but the song of choice is "Someone Like You" by Adele. *That* is not normal for him. I fly inside to find him sitting at the dining table, a half-empty bottle of an expensive scotch in front of him. He finally looks up at me, his eyes red-rimmed, a bag of peas held to his face. When he moves it, his left eye is horribly bruised.

"Finnley, babycakes, how are you?"

"What is going on?" I pull the bottle of scotch away from him before I sit down. He has a death grip on the glass, so I don't attempt to move it, but I do turn his face gently toward me. "Are you okay?"

He gives me a half-hearted nod as pulls away from my touch. I cannot explain it, but his pulling away breaks my heart in two. "I will be."

"Uncle Mark?"

"Mark," he corrects, never making eye contact. Giant tears slide down his cheeks, and he hisses when he accidentally wipes his bruised eye. "A client's husband found out. She was my favorite."

I open my mouth to speak, but I have no fucking idea what to say. *How* did this happen, *what* exactly happened, *why* did this happen, *who the fuck did this to you*... But none of those answers are my business.

"I'll be okay, Finnley. I promise." He breathes in a thick snort through snot and tears. "Life is full of twists and turns, isn't it?" When he lifts his drink, I notice his knuckles are bloody. "It's okay." He offers me a smile I wish I could decline. My heart feels like it's in a goddamn vise. Seeing him bruised and bloody is one of the toughest things I've ever witnessed. "He didn't win if that's what you're wondering."

I let out a small laugh. "I'd hate to see what he looks like then."

"Let's be thankful this guy didn't have a gun."

"Jesus *Christ*." I try to hold back my gasp, but fail. "Please tell me he doesn't know where you live."

His expression softens. "I promise. They never know where I live. Except for Emerson." He knows the second the words left his mouth that he fucked up. "Wait, it's not what you think."

I lean back in my chair. "Hand me your drink, please."

"Finnley—"

"Now, Mark. Right now." He reluctantly slides it across the wooden tabletop. I down the rest of it as soon as it's in my hands. It tastes vile. I detest scotch. "Thank you," I say as I wipe my mouth with the back of my hand. "That was awful."

"Please let me explain."

"I don't know if I want to know that my... whatever she is... slept with my *uncle*. It's like a Shakespeare play."

"Hold up there," he says, slicing his hand through the air. "We did not sleep together."

I instantly feel better, though I have a whole new line of questions. "Oh."

"We knew each other at the high school, y'know, before all

this." His small smile as he pulls up his memories is totally not helping me jump to conclusions. "When I left, we sort of lost touch. She was married to Justine—"

"Who is my boss, by the way. Thank you for telling me."

"She swore me to secrecy."

I sigh as I wave my hand at him. "Of course she did. Carry on with your story, please."

"Well, I was doing very well with the escort gig. No one knew about it at the time either. Not even Lisa. I got a call one night, so I got ready and met the person at the Renaissance downtown." He pours another drink, but he keeps the glass right in the middle of us. "I didn't know who it was until Emerson opened that door." He shakes his head. "We were both shocked shitless. She was so embarrassed, and I was, well, I guess you could say I was confused."

"I can only imagine," I say quietly.

"Needless to say, all we did was talk. And laugh. And she told me everything that was going on with her and Justine, which I am not going to repeat. Client-escort confidentiality, you know."

I feel my face twist. "Is that a real thing?"

"Yes. I mean, it is for me." He places his hand over mine. "She was scared and lost, and Justine was the only person she had ever loved. If you ask her, she'll tell you."

"What else am I going to find out? I was so cool when she told me about Justine. I didn't get mad or upset because I like her so much. For the first time in forever, I have hope for my future with another person. And now this?"

"Finnley," he says with a laugh. "Come on. We were like each other's therapists that night. For what it's worth, that has continued. She's one of my favorite people in this entire world. Aside from finding out that her name is Isabel, and she almost slept with an escort, you know everything else."

I can't handle looking at how swollen his eye is becoming, so I reach for the peas and gently hold them up to his cheek. "I think

I'm in love with her." My tone holds far less confidence than I intended. "Actually, I don't think. I know. I'm in love with her."

The happiness in his uncovered eye and the sly smirk on his lips is enough of a response for me.

"I don't want to lose her."

"You won't."

It's my turn to get emotional. "I'm so scared."

"Don't be. It's not like you'll have a piece-of-shit husband trying to beat you up."

I slowly shake my head. "Too soon, Mark."

He sighs deeply. "I really loved that client. All she ever wanted was for me to hold her. No kissing, no sex, just me wrapping my arms around her while she slept." A tear rolls down his cheek. "Straight men are the worst."

"Two months ago, I would have fought you on that."

"Would you help me up the stairs? I have to get ready for the party."

"I think you should cancel."

He gasps. "Never! The show must go on, my dear. And you'll be helping me with the coverup process, so ready the artillery."

I wish I could say that his enthusiasm was contagious. Unfortunately, I would be lying.

∾

Aunt Lisa is furious when she sees Uncle Mark's face. "I'm going to kill the son of a bitch. Give me his name, number, and location. Right now."

"Do you truly think I have all that information?" He's staring at her in the mirror as I help apply the concealer. I'm doing a decent job, so if she'd been twenty minutes later, I doubt she would have even noticed. "Calm down, okay, Lisa? It's not worth it. Hazards of the job, y'know?"

"Hazards of the job?" She huffs. "Hazards of the *job*?" She spins around in the bathroom and shouts toward the ceiling, "Did you hear him? Hazards of the job, he said."

His eyes land on mine in our reflections. "My hero," he says when he rolls his eyes. "Settle the fuck down, Lisa. Right now."

"Mark, baby, you cannot just let this go."

He turns toward her, ripping his face away from my makeup sponge. "I will, Lisa. I will let it go. And so will you. I am not stopping, and you will have to find a way to deal with it."

After ten seconds of the most intense eye contact I have ever witnessed, she nods and says, "I'm sorry." His stoic expression doesn't budge, though. I'm so uncomfortable standing there that I take a step back and swallow the lump in my throat.

Uncle Mark returns to the mirror. "Finish my makeup, please," he says softly.

∼

THAT OLD SAYING ABOUT WAITING FOR THE OTHER SHOE TO DROP? I've never met someone who hasn't experienced that feeling of impending doom. Things are going great, everything's coming up roses, and then *bam!* Something happens that reminds you that reality is inescapable and happiness is fleeting. I often wait for the other shoe to drop. Things don't often go swimmingly in my life for too long before something happens. I got a great MBA and a couple years later got fired from my job. I had an okay fiancé, but I broke it off with him. And then...

My mouth feels like the Sahara as the thought of Steven's passing fills my mind.

Needless to say, I have been waiting and waiting for the other shoe to drop when it comes to Emerson. Things are too great. She's too exquisite. Too beautiful. Too everything. And my life doesn't know how to handle exquisite without adding a dash of catastrophic.

I'm trying to keep my head on straight. I don't want to

constantly worry that something bad will unfold with Emerson. I'm not dumb. I realize every person's first isn't always their last. This might not work. She might not want me in the end. I may not want her.

Who am I kidding, though? I do want her. I've never wanted anyone else like I want her. It baffles me, really, the desire I feel coursing through my body whenever I think about her. Her hands. Her body. Her lips. Her mouth. Her eyes. Goddamn, *her eyes*. They're gorgeous. I could get lost in them. Hell, I have. Multiple times. But of all the times I've stared into them, tonight is the first time I figure out why I love them so much. It's not just the color—which, don't get me wrong, the green is otherworldly and completely worthy of the compliment. It's the kindness that makes them the most beautiful eyes I've ever gazed into.

In the span of six weeks, Emerson has become the most important person in my life. Next to Uncle Mark, of course. She's everything I never knew I wanted and needed. She's funny and smart and talented. She's sexy and a phenomenal kisser.

She is perfect.

Except for the fact that she is, indeed, still married.

And as I stare at Justine, who has barged into Uncle Mark's, caused a scene in The Oasis, and has now burst into my bedroom wildly waving the divorce papers she *still* hasn't signed, that fact is driven home. Hard.

Thank Christ, we are both fully clothed. The whole scene could have been significantly worse.

"Justine, you can't just come in here and act like this." Uncle Mark is standing in my doorway, glaring at the back of Justine's head. His face is red, and he is breathing heavily. "I'm sorry, but you're going to have to leave."

Justine's eyes are filled with rage. She narrows them and throws a look over her shoulder. "Mark, this won't take long."

"Justine—"

"Mark," Emerson says, her hand raised. "I'll take care of this."

"You'd better." He turns and leaves my bedroom.

"What are you doing here, Justine? You can't just break into parties you aren't invited to." Emerson's tone is so much calmer than I think it should be. But she's obviously used to dealing with Justine. I only hope she knows what she's doing.

"You realize," Justine shouts, her eyes boring holes into Emerson, her face beet red, "that I am still your *wife*, Isabel. And you think it's appropriate to be doing whatever you're doing with her? With Finnley? A *straight* woman?"

"Whoa, whoa, whoa, I am *hardly* straight," I say, and if the look I get from Justine doesn't do some sort of long-lasting internal damage, I'll be surprised.

Emerson is standing in front of Justine now, her hands up, her stance ready for anything. "You *said* you signed them and turned them in, Justine. What was I supposed to think?"

"Yeah, well, I didn't. And you." Justine is pointing at me over Emerson's shoulder. "You can find a new job. You're fucking fired."

"What the hell?" My question is quiet, but Emerson hears it. She shakes her head as she looks over her shoulder at me.

"Do not take this out on her," she says. "That isn't fair or right, and you know it."

"I don't know what I'm supposed to do here, Izzy. Am I supposed to walk away? After everything? After in vitro, after every miscarriage, after renewed vows? You want me to just throw in the towel?"

Emerson's deep breath is unmistakable. "Yeah, you are. You already did once. You can do it again."

"But I still love you."

"Do you?" Emerson lets out a puff of air. "Sure you don't still want to have sex with Blake?"

Justine's face falls. Her eyes rake over Emerson's features before she glares at me over her shoulder. "Did you *tell* her?" She spits her accusation at me. I don't answer. She knows I did. "Did you? Huh? How else would she know if you didn't open your little whore mouth?"

Emerson steps to her left so she's directly in Justine's line of sight. "Do you have any idea how fucked up that question is? You told me you let Blake go. You promised me. And then I find out that Blake is still there and that you lied, and it's Finnley's fault?" She clenches her hands into fists, presumably to stop their trembling. "You are *ridiculous*."

"I don't want us to be over." Justine's pleading is making my stomach churn. I saw how she was with Blake. I heard her talk about them and her relationship with them. To hear her now causes anger to flare inside me, an anger I have never felt before. "I love you," she whispers.

I can't take it anymore. "No, you don't," I say as I approach them. "If you loved her, you wouldn't have lied."

"Not now, Finn." Emerson's gentle touch almost pisses me off, except I know she's doing it for my own good. "Thank you, but I got this." Her eyes, her kind eyes… I take a deep breath and shut myself up. "We've both done things we shouldn't have, Justine. It's time. You know it, and so do I."

"We're just going to give up? After ten years?" Justine is crying now. Seeing her tears makes me want to scream, *You did this!*, but I hold back. This isn't my fight. I hope it never is. "Will you please just come back to the house with me so we can talk?"

Emerson's shoulders slump the tiniest of amounts. I can feel her giving in.

Don't. Don't do it… please don't do it.

She turns, places her hands on my arms, and looks into my eyes. "I'm going to go back with her."

"Em—"

"I have to do this."

I can't protest. She does need to do this. But what if it doesn't go the way I'm wanting? What happens if tomorrow I get some sort of excuse about how this was fun but not what Emerson was looking for? The truth is, all of that is possible, and I have to find the patience and trust to allow things to unfold as they should. Everything happens for a reason, right? The only reason I can find right now, as Justine reaches for Emerson's hand, is that karma is a bitch because Emerson doesn't flinch, doesn't yank her hand away. That's when my heart nearly flatlines. I stand there, mouth hanging open, wondering what the fuck just happened.

"But what about us?" My question falls upon the deafening silence of my empty bedroom.

The only answer is that the other shoe finally fucking dropped.

CHAPTER THIRTEEN

Time heals all wounds. Except it doesn't. I don't think it ever has. I think that saying was invented because people continued to hurt, and some jackass figured it would be great to give people hope that as each day passes, things would get easier.

Things. Do not. Get. Easier.

Period.

It's been three weeks since Emerson left with Justine. Three weeks. I figured I wouldn't hear from her at all, honestly. But I've heard from her a few times. The first time she called to explain. She needed time. Some space. To figure this all out. I was as kind as possible, which, as it turns out, is not kind at all. The second time, I apologized for my behavior. She told me not to apologize. She told me how sorry she was and how she promised to keep me updated. The third time, she told me to be patient. Patience, as you know, is not my best quality. I was at the end of my rope, so telling me to be patient only meant that it was time to start moving on. After all, in my mind, of course she didn't want to be with me. Of course I was just a rebound. Of course I didn't mean a thing to her.

So, yeah. I was a mess. Not being able to at least text her had been probably the hardest part. Because heaven forbid Emerson live in the goddamn twenty-first century and have a motherfucking cell phone. And I refused to send her an email. Who even emails anymore? I'll tell you who. People who don't own cell phones. That's who.

The only benefit to all of this is that it pushed me to go out and find something to do with my free time. I applied to a place that specializes in tutoring and quickly had an entire roster of math students. It's so funny because, for the longest time, I thought I hated math and numbers. But really, I just hate accounting. I actually love math and teaching it to students has been really rewarding.

The worst part about Justine firing me, aside from the horrible feeling someone hating me has caused deep down in my gut, is that I was actually enjoying learning about her business. The flowers, the customers, the events. All of it. Even the staff. Well, minus Blake. But I would have done whatever it took to turn that job into a passion.

Now here I am. Tutoring students in math. *Again.* Hoping I don't meet a dad whose kid needs a mom. *Again.*

I stare at my reflection in the mirror in the bathroom at Uncle Mark's. Life is going to toss me a shoe. I can feel it. Why? Because we're going to Emerson's art studio tonight for the show she's been curating. She postponed it once. Uncle Mark says he had no idea why. Even he hasn't spoken to her in great detail for the past three weeks. He's not happy about how things unfolded with Emerson and me—*Listen, buddy, neither am I*—but I'm allowing him to be upset. Apparently, he needs it, and I can't always be the only one carrying around every emotion, locked and loaded.

For the first time since the night of the party, the one where Justine fired me—the one that changed everything—I have put on makeup. I couldn't go out without it; I was starting to look like a ghost. Even Uncle Mark said I was not allowed to leave without putting on at least a little rouge. I'm going to see Emerson tonight, but I'm sure I'm going to see Justine too. I don't want to look like death warmed over.

After I grab the sparkly gold jacket I bought the other day when I was trying to get myself out of my funk, I head downstairs. Aunt Lisa has arrived. The sight of her stops me in my tracks. Her long, dark hair isn't pulled back for the first time in forever. She's wearing a beautiful maroon A-line dress, and she looks stunning.

"Wow, look at you," I say as I head over to get a hug. "Your hair looks gorgeous."

"Just had it done." She poses, then pulls her hair over her shoulder and runs her fingers through it. "I had four inches cut off. It feels lighter. I love it."

"You look stunning."

"Babycakes, so do you." She places her hands on my face and gives me a quick peck. "You getting excited about Rory and Jesse's visit?"

Jesse called a week ago and asked if she could come with Rory. I said yes because I figured I needed the company. But now, as I force myself to smile, I am regretting my decision. I am not excited one bit. "Yeah, absolutely. It'll be great to hang out for the couple of days they're here. I only hope Jesse's influence on a young sixteen-year-old won't be detrimental. She's a live wire, that's for sure, but she also has great self-esteem and loads extra to share with the people around her. She used to make me feel like I was unstoppable."

"Hmm, judging by your very unconvincing level of excitement, maybe you could use some Jesse in your life too? I take it you're not feeling that much better?"

I shrug. "I'm trying to be patient but I'm losing hope."

"You're too lovely to stay down forever. Like I said before, you can be sad, you can mope, you can wallow in self-pity for as long as you need to, but eventually, your heart is going to want to smile again. I know you, and that frowny face is not your go-to."

Frowning *is* the worst. "Thanks, Lisa. You're very right."

"Mark, did you hear that? I'm right," she shouts. "Actually, I'm *very* right."

Uncle Mark laughs from the kitchen. "Finnley, don't give her an even bigger head." He breezes through the entry with three old-fashioneds. When he hands me mine, he winks. "For the nerves."

The drink feels heavy in my hand. I haven't had a drink since that night either. "You think I'm nervous?"

"Does a bear shit in the woods?"

"No, isn't it, 'Is the pope Catholic?'"

"Whatever," Uncle Mark says. "Anyway, yes, my dear, I think you're nervous, and like Lisa here, I am very right." He raises his eyebrows slightly. "Aren't I?'

"Does the pope shit in the woods?" I ask, then groan. "I do not want to go to this. Can't I bail?"

Aunt Lisa leans forward and hugs me. "Oh, Finnley, we'll be there with you the whole time. Unfortunately, though"—she pulls away and turns my face so I am looking directly at her—"this is an important night for Emerson. It's her biggest show yet. I know it'll be hard, but I think you need to be there. Not just for her but for you. So you can show yourself that you can do this; you can stand up tall and be okay."

"Why do I need to be there for her when she hasn't been there for me for the past three weeks?" I hear my question, my tone, how spoiled I sound, and I grimace. "That was the worst thing I have ever said."

Aunt Lisa's scrunched face is all the response I need.

"Listen," Uncle Mark says after sitting at the head of the table. He pats his palms on the surface as if beckoning for my full attention. "I'm sure if someone asked you if I was a role model, you'd say yes—"

Aunt Lisa huffs.

He glares at her. "You would. Not because I have been present for every single second of your life but because I'm amazing." He giggles. "I mean, right? Wait, don't answer that. Let me finish.

"The point I am trying to make is that I'm not a role model. I'm stuffy and weird, *and* I'm an escort, for Christ's sake. I'm not the picture of wealth because I'm a lawyer. Or a CEO. Gross." He shudders. "I'd die, honestly. But I digress. I may not be the world's best role model, but I will try to teach you this: We show up for the people we love. Period. It doesn't matter what kind of love it is. You show up. This is not going to be fun. You have every right to be nervous, to be worried, to be filled with wonder. But to not go, to not show up for the woman you are still very much in love with, would be a total dick move."

I chuckle. "A dick move, hmm?"

"Absolutely." His smile warms my heart. "We'll be with you the whole time, just like Lisa said."

I take a deep breath and nod. A silence falls among us as we focus on our drinks, the large, solitary ice cubes clinking in unison. Uncle Mark's *ahhh* after he finishes is perfectly timed. He does it after every drink he finishes, I've realized. Aunt Lisa always runs her index finger around the rim and comments on the superb mixologist she let get away. I usually laugh because her statement makes me feel awkward, and laughing when I'm awkward is my favorite defense. But today, I reach over and grab Uncle Mark's hand before he stands.

"Wait," I say softly. "You are one hundred percent my role model. And I'd tell anyone that." His eyes soften and fill with tears. "I just thought you should know."

He stands, pulls me from my chair, and hugs me tight. I can tell by the shaking of his shoulders that he's crying. It's not until I hear Aunt Lisa's sniffles that I realize she's crying too.

∽

Parking at The Living Room is a madhouse. We barely find a space, and even then, we have to shell out fifty dollars instead of twenty-five because someone price-gouges us. Uncle Mark mumbles something about telling Emerson, but Aunt Lisa calmly tells him that it's not worth it.

"Let her enjoy the evening, Mark," she says as she pats him on the back. Everything about them is still so very much the aunt and uncle I remember from my childhood, so them not being together is hard to wrap my brain around. Especially given how they are around each other. I'm thrilled they coexist so effortlessly, though. They don't have to be together romantically to realize how perfect they are together platonically. It gives me hope for my future.

Even if I'm assuming Emerson and I are done. Not seeing her has been a blow to my heart I didn't ever want to experience. It's easier for me to protect myself and just assume the worst. To love hard is to lose hard. My life has been such a whirlwind for the past few months. I didn't need or want her to essentially disappear from my life, yet here we are.

And here I am, showing up for her, for someone I love. My internal groan is deafening.

In keeping with the parking situation, the inside of The Living Room is packed. After waiting in line for fifteen minutes and paying our entry fee of five dollars, we finally make it inside. We maneuver through the people congregating around Beth Weber's paintings. She is standing front and center, speaking about her time painting abroad. Her auburn hair is pulled away from her face, and I feel connected to her. Is it her artwork that strikes a chord within me, or am I just a raving lunatic these days, searching for any thread of queerness so I can prove that Emerson is not a one-off? And to whom would I be proving it? Myself? That's just pathetic.

Me spinning out of control is really the issue at hand. I'm sad and mad and disappointed and depressed that Emerson chose

Justine. After everything—me being so worried that she would think all I wanted was to experiment, me essentially coming out to my parents, me taking her with me to meet my dead ex-fiancé's daughter.

Maybe that's why she chose Justine. My life is a veritable minefield of drama and issues. Why the fuck would she have chosen me?

"Keep walking," Uncle Mark whispers as he tugs on the sleeve of my jacket.

I follow him, keeping my eyes peeled the entire time. There is so much to see. Almost too much. I want to go to every artist's booth and tell them how much I admire them, their courage, their talent. Respect builds in me with each new exhibit we pass. The ceramic work, the drawings, the illustrations, the paintings, the sculptures, the photography. Emerson has made sure to cover all her bases with multiple artists. They are all equally mesmerizing. How did she manage to find so many phenomenal artists and put them into the same show? She's impressive.

I'm settling into my surroundings. Finally. The sights and sounds have a strange, calming effect on me. Or maybe it was the low-dose edible my uncle passed me as we walked out the townhouse door. Whatever the case may be (let's be real, it's the edible), the thought enters my mind that maybe I am having a good time. It's been a few days since I haven't had the weight of my emotions dragging me down into the pits of despair. Being more depressed over losing Emerson than I was over losing Steven has been quite the journey. I want so much to be distraught that my ex is gone. I want to cry into my pillow, yell and scream at the heavens, curse God for taking him too early. And while I am very upset about it all, I find every ounce of sadness within me is because I finally stood back and admired the tapestry of my heart, and in the next instant, it was shredded to bits.

Jesus. That was deep. I chuckle to myself as I take in the

artist's work before me. A young photographer who captures the wildlife of the national parks is explaining his process to the couple standing next to me. The DJ at the side of the room is spinning a remixed version of ODESZA's "Higher Ground."

I am enjoying myself.

Finally.

I'm smiling. I can feel it in my cheeks. God, it feels good. I glance around as the song changes to "Get Lost" by Bearson. The words of this song... It should be the anthem of my life. I did have to lose everything to figure out what I wanted.

Dammit. This edible is making me far too introspective right now.

Just as those words pass through my mind, my heart leaps into my throat. I see the paintings that Emerson showed me hanging close to where I am standing. The skeleton, the one she named *deComposition Paper,* has a tag next to it that says SOLD. I smile. Of course it sold. It's fucking incredible. *Breath of Life* has a tag on it as well. I take a few steps to see if she ever finished the heart, and I gasp. She did.

I swallow around the lump in my throat. It has a similar vibe as the other two, but there is something about this one that has literally taken my breath from me. The flowers surrounding the heart, the grass, the moss, the ray of sunlight shining through it, all of it has made this painting one of the most beautiful pieces of art I have ever seen. I'm close enough now that I can see that there are words pasted onto it. Large typewriter font says "patch-work tapestry." I can't speak. How is it possible that moments earlier, I was all in my feels about my own heart being a tapestry and here she is, reading my fucking mind? Is this another moment when I have to put all my questions aside and chalk it up to everything happening for a reason? I will if I need to, but, goddamn, this is the most intense thing that has ever happened to me.

I look around, trying to find Aunt Lisa and Uncle Mark so I

can talk to them about this, and that's when it happens. I see Emerson through the sea of people. And she looks *breathtaking*. Tears sting my eyes. I want to look away, if only to compose myself, but I can't. Her hair is falling in waves around her face. She has black-framed glasses on, which is new but so fucking hot. She is wearing a black blazer over a tight, black shirt with jeans. The sight is, *wow*, spectacular.

Someone runs into my shoulder and shakes me out of my reverie. I steady my footing and quickly look around to see if anyone saw me almost run into an exhibit. And that's when I see the other person I knew I was going to see. Justine. She's standing near a row of sculptures. I guess I should be grateful. Seeing her has dislodged my heart, which has now successfully sunk like an anvil right into my ass.

Great. She looks good too. Of *course* she does. She wouldn't show up to an event looking awful. She's actually too pretty to look horrible. And the curator's significant other needs to look presentable, doesn't she?

"Focus," Aunt Lisa says softly as she comes up to me with a beverage. "Vodka, soda, lime. Take it. Drink it. Don't argue."

"Jeez," I say under my breath. But I take a sip. And another. And one more for good measure. It's strong. Not Aunt Lisa's best idea, but at this point, with Emerson looking like a fucking model and Justine looking like she belongs on her arm, what else am I going to do?

"Did you see that painting she did?" I point at it. "Aunt Lisa, I literally thought those same words moments before, that my heart is like a fucking tapestry, and then she painted it. She painted my heart."

She looks at the painting, then back at me. "That's intense."
"That's exactly what I thought."
"Wow."
"I *know!*"
She shakes her head. "I mean... wow. I guess this will seem

like small potatoes then, but also, I just confirmed that they aren't together."

My head snaps toward her. I choke on the piece of ice I am sucking on. "What?" I cough for air. "Are you sure?"

"I'm positive." She winks. "Trust me. I'm good with reconnaissance."

"She really is." Uncle Mark has flanked my left side, holding his drink. They must have smelled my fear. Either way, I'm so very grateful for them in that moment.

"What do I do?" I steady myself, using them as both physical and emotional crutches. The fact that I've replaced my parents with an updated, and far cooler, set hasn't escaped me. Should I feel bad about it? Probably. But my parents are the ones who pushed me out of the proverbial nest. Is it wrong that I found a new set of birds to fly with?

"You wait."

"Patience is a virtue, my dear," Aunt Lisa says. "It's hard as fuck, but it's a virtue."

"She'll see you. Don't you worry—" Uncle Mark gasps. "Ah, there it is. She saw you."

I try to be nonchalant. I really do. But my eagerness takes over, and my resolve breaks. When my eyes find hers across the crowd, the room comes screeching to a halt. The people seem to fade away until it's only her and me and the lights strung above us. The smile that spreads across her perfect lips stops my heart. Is this the moment? The one where I forget everything that happened and forgive her, without her having to say a word to me? Am I that much of a pushover?

She nods. Her eyebrow arches. She bounces the tiniest amounts on her toes.

"See? You show up for people you love," Uncle Mark whispers. "Look at her. She's happy you're here."

I can't feel my knees. "She is?"

He scoffs. "Jesus, Finnley, it was a five-milligram gummy.

How high are you? Yes, she's happy. *Look* at her. Her smile just lit up the goddamn room." He motions to her with his empty hand.

I gasp and grab his arm. "Oh my God, don't embarrass me."

He straightens his sand-colored linen jacket. "Excuse me; I am not an embarrassment. I'm simply a great wingman."

"Yeah, you really are." I snake my arm around his waist and pull myself close to him. "Thank you for always being so lovely. You have no idea how much it means to me."

He returns the side hug before looking down at me.

"Thank *you*, Finnley, my dear. Having you here has made my life significantly better." He pushes me away. "Now, go talk to her. I can't deal with you moping around the house one second longer."

As soon as I take a step away, I feel the calmness I had secured slip through my fingers. I'm not ready for this. I'm not prepared to see her face to face, up close and personal, in front of people. What if I cry? What if I fall and rip my tapestry even more?

～

I DON'T MAKE IT ALL THE WAY UP TO EMERSON. SHE'S BUSY, AND I'm too shy to interrupt. I also don't want to annoy her. What if I'm reading the signals wrong?

And what about Justine? Why is she here if they're not together? I have a million fucking questions and no goddamn answers. So I have to talk to her. I have to do this. If for no other reason than to get closure.

And that's okay. It has to be.

I find a semi-quiet spot near the side of the exhibition, so I lean against the wall and put on my patience cap.

My phone vibrates in my purse, so I maneuver my drink and pull it out. I need to occupy my impatient mind, so I might as well check the text that arrived. It's from an unknown number. That's weird.

I like your outfit. The Fleetwood Mac shirt is a nice touch.

What the heck? Who sent this? While I'm searching my memory bank, another text appears on my screen.

Give me two minutes. Please don't leave.

And then it dawns on me. I look up at Emerson across the room. She smiles at me, holds up an iPhone, and shrugs. I can't help but smile back.

"What are you smiling about?"

I jerk my attention to the person standing next to me. "Blake, hi." Seeing them standing there wholly shocks me. "What are you doing here?"

They smile as they lean against the wall next to me. "I'm here with Justine."

"Oh?"

They nod. "Well, like that, but also to deliver some arrangements. Anyway, I feel like I need to apologize to you."

"No, not at all."

They tilt their head and furrow their brow. "Come on."

"Okay, fine. You probably do."

"Thank you." Blake smiles. "I'm sorry. Sincerely. I was angry and awful to you."

I nod. "For what it's worth, I'm not mad at you. I get it. You were going through some shit, I'm sure."

Their eyes move from mine to where Justine is standing. "Yeah, apparently, patience is a virtue."

"Odd. I just heard that saying today. Must be new and catching on."

Blake laughs. "Right? It's a new one for me, for sure."

"So," I say, wondering how much I can ask before I overstep. "You and Justine are together?"

"Yes, we are. I know she's quite a bit older than me, but I've always felt like an old soul. And I might actually be happy now, which is so not like me." They shrug and raise their glass to me. "To being happy?"

"To being happy. Or eventually being happy, for me, at least."

"Can I tell you something?" Blake pushes away from the wall to stand directly in front of me. "Justine doesn't hate you. In fact, she wants you to come back but doesn't know how to talk to you about it. And regarding your happiness?" They smile, and it makes me sad that we've spent so much time disliking each other instead of getting to know each other. "Emerson loves you. Probably more than either of you realizes. Don't give up on her."

"Thank you, Blake," I say softly. "That means a lot to me."

"Good." Blake extends their fist, and I bump it playfully. "I'm gonna go get Justine out of here. These flowers can take care of themselves now. Take it easy, my friend."

And they're gone, just like that.

CHAPTER FOURTEEN

It's the longest two minutes in the history of time, but when Emerson excuses herself from the group of people she was speaking with, it really has been only two minutes. She squeezes through the crowd of people, head held high, smiling and saying thank you to whatever compliments they're giving her.

Her smile... I can't get over how much I love seeing it again.

Finally, she is standing in front of me. The air surrounding me fills with her signature scent. I'm a fucking goner. I can't believe I'm so easy.

"Hi." Her voice cracks. She reaches for her throat. "I'm sorry. Too much talking." I hand her the water bottle I've acquired. She takes it and drinks. All I can do is watch the way her lips press against the opening, the tiny droplet of water at the corner of her mouth, the movement her throat makes as she swallows. I want to rip her clothes off. "How are you?"

"Okay," I lie.

"Okay?"

I sigh. "I've had better months, Emerson. I've definitely had better months."

She takes a step closer. She's standing only inches from me now. My eyes are drawn to her sharp jawline. "I know."

"Em, is that painting..." My voice has abandoned me.

"*Patchwork Tapestry?*"

"Yeah," I start, then stop and breathe. My eyes have filled with tears. "Emerson, that is gorgeous."

"It's all for you." Her voice is velvet smooth, soft, but so genuine. "You need to know how sorry I am."

"Emerson—"

"No, wait. I need to say this."

My entire body is aching to kiss her. To tell *her* to shut the fuck up and kiss *me*. To tell her to take me into her studio, lock the door behind us, and fuck me up against a painting. Holy shit, what is *wrong* with me?

"You need to say it *here?*" I finally say. And after I pull myself from the gutter that is my dirty mind, *she bites her fucking lip*. I cannot handle this.

She intertwines her hand with mine and pulls me with her as she weaves in and out of the crowd. Did she hear my thoughts? Did I say all of that out loud? Where is she taking me?

She pushes through the back door of the exhibition hall and through the warehouse that was bustling with people the last time I saw it. Now it's dead quiet, and the only sounds are our footfalls as she pulls me after her.

We get to her studio.

She has to have heard me. *Oh my God.*

The door slams behind us, and she turns, her chest rising and falling rapidly.

"Emerson, what is going on—"

"I know I already told you I think I'm falling in love with you. But, Finnley, I am *in* love with you." She pulls a deep breath into her lungs and lets it out slowly. "I have loved you since the second I laid eyes on you. I know it doesn't make sense. Love at first sight sounds so cliché and stupid, but fuck, it's *real*. I've given up fighting it." She shrugs. "Listen, I *know* I disappeared. It was wrong to leave like that. But I wanted, and needed, to ensure that my life was fixed before I went any further with you. I wanted you to know, without a shadow of a doubt, that I am not going anywhere *ever* again. I want this… with you." She has her hand on my face now, her thumb is lightly stroking my cheek, and her emerald-green eyes are filled with tears. "You are everything I have ever wanted."

That is all the talking I need to do. I lunge at her, probably too aggressively, but I have lost the ability to care. My teeth and lips crash into hers. She has her hands on my hips, carefully walking me backward until my back gently slams against the door. I put my hands on her face, pulling her all the more deeply into one of the best kisses of my entire life. I both want to savor her, little by little, and to have her all at once because it's been far too fucking long. I press my fingers into the back of her neck, near the base of her skull, and she moans softly into my mouth. Like I needed another reason to ruin this pair of panties I'm wearing.

Her tongue slides into my mouth. Everything about her is my version of heaven. The slickness of her tongue, the slippery surface of her teeth, the sweetness of her saliva from the breath mint she had been sucking on. I lean my head back, and she captures my neck with her lips, pressing kisses down it before she flattens her tongue against it and licks her way back to my chin.

"Emerson?" I whisper before she kisses me again.

"Yeah?" She looks into my eyes, and I feel it in my vagina. The sensation almost makes me laugh; I have never been this whipped before.

"I'm in love with you too."

A smile spreads across her lips as she leans forward and kisses me. I feel her unbutton my pants. The zipper pulls apart, and then her hand slips beneath the waistband of my black jeans, under my panties.

"You're so wet." Her sultry voice is so sexy against my lips. "Can I fuck you?"

I let out a small giggle. "If you don't, I'm going to pass out. So, yes, please do."

She pushes two fingers inside of me with ease, the entire time keeping her gaze locked onto mine. The moan I release doesn't even sound like it came from me. She pulls out and pushes back in, eyes never leaving mine. I can't look away from her. She has me in a trance, and it is the most stunning feeling I've experienced.

"What if I told you I want to fuck you with a strap-on?"

Her question, the way she asked it, the hesitation in her voice, makes my entire body scream, *Yes! Yes, yes, please do.* But I compose myself and say, "I would tell you that I would love every single second."

"What if I told you I have one here?"

I swallow the trepidation that has suddenly manifested inside me. "Why do you have one here?"

She laughs. It's way too light and airy for the topic, but for some reason, it fits. "I've never used it on anyone else. But I wore it for a photo shoot for an artist."

"Oh? So you *are* a model?"

The confusion on her face is adorable.

"I thought you were a model the first time I saw you." I shrug, and she thrusts her fingers inside me, which causes me to moan again. "Goddamn, Emerson… I don't know if I need anything but your fingers." It's the truth, but I don't know if I would have typically been so forthcoming.

"I am very good with them," she whispers before she thrusts again.

"Does this door lock?"

"It does."

"Get the strap-on."

EMERSON NAKED, WEARING NOTHING BUT A STRAP-ON, IS unequivocally the sexiest thing I have ever seen. She smiles when she looks at me. I'm also completely naked, sitting on one of the countertops in her studio. I am not usually this comfortable in my own skin, but being around her has changed me in the best ways. The imperfections I have aren't annoying to me any longer. Now I find myself sexy because she does. Sadly, I needed someone else's approval to see my attractive qualities. I'm glad that someone else is her, though, because she makes me feel like the most beautiful person in the world.

"It feels weird. Can you fix it?" She turns and shows me her ass, where one strap is all twisted. I slide off the counter and kneel to untwist the soft leather. Her skin is flawless. The contrast of the black leather against her pale ass cheeks makes me so hot.

"There. Fixed." I lean forward and kiss her left cheek. She lets out a low chuckle. I don't know what comes over me, but I push my hand between her legs. She gasps but doesn't protest when I slide my fingers through her wetness, then gently slip two inside her. She spreads her stance the slightest amount, which gives me more access, so I stand behind her, pressing my body against hers. She looks over her shoulder, a smile on her face.

"I thought I was going to fuck you?"

"You are." I pull my fingers out of her, reach around, and grab the dildo by the base. I move my wet hand over the length of it. Her chest starts to move up and down more rapidly. "Gotta get it wet now, don't we?" She gulps so loudly that I hear it. I let out a laugh as I turn her around. Her eyes are on mine; then they move down to look at the dildo. I pull on it, and a smile spreads across her lips. "I like to be fucked from behind."

Her eyes jerk up to mine. "Holy *fuck*." She reaches forward and pulls me into her so quickly that I start to laugh. She kisses me with enough force to make me stop laughing but not enough to be anything other than sensual. She places her hands on my breasts, massages them, tweaks each nipple, then breaks the kiss to get them in her mouth. She runs her tongue around each nipple, nibbles them, makes me even wetter since she knows I like them to be played with. Foreplay with her quickly moves up the list of the top ten things I don't want to live without.

Emerson understands what I want and need, and she doesn't hesitate to provide. Her fingernails dig lightly into my hips before she flips me around. When she presses her body against me, her bare breasts press into my back, and the dildo rubs against my ass. I'd love to say the sensation was confusing, but in reality it was erotic as fuck. She moves my hair over my shoulder, kisses the back of my neck, all the while massaging my breasts from behind. I'm so eager to feel her inside me that it's becoming an obsession. She slides her hand over my stomach, my crotch, to my wetness. She dips her fingers in, rubs my clit with my own slickness, and then bends me forward with her other hand. "Are you ready?"

"God, yes," I hear myself pant. I am ravenous. I want her so fucking badly. When I feel the tip of the dildo dip inside, I gasp. She jerks away as if she's hurt me.

"Are you okay?"

"I swear you won't break me, so please don't stop."

The only response I get is her pushing into me very slowly. She takes her time, making sure my wetness completely covers the shaft. I brace myself, gripping the edge of the countertop for leverage. The compressed wood doesn't seem strong enough for what's about to happen. Or maybe *I'm* not strong enough... I don't care, one way or another, because I am so ready for her to break me. Emerson pulls my hips against her as the dildo slides inside me. "Are you okay?"

"Yes," I gasp out. "I'm so okay."

She starts to move her hips, pushing the dildo deeper, and I moan. *Loudly.* She lets out a low chuckle. "Don't forget we aren't the only ones here." She knows damn well what she's doing to me because her thrusts are picking up speed and intensity. I can't contain my moans. It's not possible. It feels so fucking good. She is completing every thrust with precision and accuracy, and the angle of the dildo is hitting my G-spot perfectly. I don't usually come from penetration alone. I just *don't*... but this? Emerson fucking me with a strap-on? This is most definitely getting me there. And fast. I start to move with her when she slows a bit. I've dealt with enough penis in my life that I know how to help myself out, which I'm sure will help her out too.

"Jesus Christ. That's fucking hot." She thrusts again, faster now. I'm so close, but something makes me stop. I slide off the dildo. "What's wrong?" she asks. "Are you okay?"

"I'm perfect. Lay down, please."

"On the floor?"

I laugh. "Yes, on the floor. Now." Once she does as I've commanded, I straddle her and slowly lower myself onto the dildo. Her eyes go wide when it completely disappears. I start to bounce on it. I will come in seconds like this. I want her to see me. I want to see her. She has her hands on my thighs. I bend forward and place my hands on either side of her to brace myself. She thrusts her hips in time with me.

"You're so fucking gorgeous," she whispers, and my orgasm crashes into me like a tsunami. She keeps thrusting, though, and I keep coming. It's amazing. It's incredible. She's amazing. She's incredible. I come again, but I feel tears falling from my eyes this time. Another fucking first... My orgasm hasn't finished, but I collapse on top of her when it does. The dildo pops out of me, which causes a shockwave to rip through my body. I laugh through my tears as she rubs my back.

"Shh," she says softly against my ear. "I got you."

And she does. She has me. And I have never been happier.

∽

We've been back at the townhouse now for a few hours, and I've spent most of those one hundred eighty minutes memorizing every single inch of Emerson's body. She's sleeping now on her stomach, her bare backside uncovered. I've mapped out her curves with my eyes because even though she said she isn't leaving again, there's a voice inside me that keeps saying this isn't going to last, that the damned other shoe is going to drop.

A conversation still hasn't happened. It needs to, and I think we both know that, but ultimately we wanted to fuck each other's brains out, as displayed by the romp at the studio and then the three hours straight of sex back here at the house. Needless to say, I've never been more excited that Uncle Mark left after the event to go on a call than I was last night.

I want to wake her up right now. I want to touch her. I want to feel her wetness and bury my fingers inside of her.

A wave of heat rushes over me as memories of doing just that flood my mind. Watching her arch her back while she came, begging me not to stop… Jesus. I have to keep pinching myself to make sure this is really happening. It wasn't a dream. She's lying *naked* in my bed right now. And I'm naked next to her.

Next to a woman.

A woman I have fallen madly in love with.

I've stopped asking why this is happening. Adopting Emerson's view that everything happens for a reason is the only way to view this. I came here to figure myself out, to find happiness, to learn how to love myself and hopefully someone else. And I have done all of that.

Emerson stirs next to me, changing positions, so she's on her back now. Her breast closest to me falls the tiniest of bits to the side. Gravity is such a tease.

"Are you watching me sleep?"

Her question startles me in the quiet of my bedroom. "Am I gawking too loudly?"

She smiles, eyes still closed. "Not at all." She reaches over, and when she finds me, she pulls me until I move closer to her. "Are you ready to go again?"

"I have a feeling I'm going to always be ready when it comes to you." I run my fingers down her sternum to her stomach, her navel, her pubic bone. I cup her warm center and find that she's deliciously wet. "Well, look at that." She breathes out a small laugh. "The question should actually be, are *you* ready to go again?"

"Why? You wanna fuck me again?" Her sexy tone of voice makes my insides combust. Her eyes slide open. "Because you can if you want to."

"Oh, yeah?" I slip a finger inside of her. She bites her lip and nods before she spreads her legs, giving me easier access. "You feel so good."

"God, Finnley... baby, so do you." She is gripping me now, so I push another finger inside her. She leans her head back and moans my name. I don't care what else happens, her moaning my name is the sexiest sound I have ever heard in my entire life, and I guarantee it will be until I die. It doesn't take long to get her to orgasm. I am learning my way around her body with as much ease and speed as I learned the city streets of Chicago. Learning *her* has been exponentially more fun, though. Hands down.

She lets out a laugh as she's coming down from her orgasm. "You're good. Like, really, really good."

I am beaming with pride. I can feel it radiating from me. "Well, thank you. You've been a remarkable teacher."

She rolls onto her side and faces me as she pulls the covers up around us. "Do you think we should talk about everything?"

"I have heard that a healthy relationship starts with communication."

"That is very true."

I take a deep breath. "I'll go first."

"You didn't do anything wrong, though." She lays her hand on my face. "I can go first."

"No, I do want to say something before you go. I think it's important for you to know this about me." I take her hand and kiss her knuckles. "I know we are going to both go through a lot in the next however many days, weeks, years, whatever. I can't believe I'm saying this because when I landed here in Chicago, I was spinning out of control, hating the path I was on, fearing the path in front of me, and simultaneously running from a commitment that should have been my forever. But, Em, you have to make me one promise. If we are really going to do this, I need you to tell me when you're ready to leave me. I don't want you to ghost me again. I can't handle that. My heart can't. When you're ready to leave me, which I'm sure will happen, tell me. I won't stand in your way. I won't beg you to stay. I will let you do what you need to do. But I need that one thing in return. Okay?"

Tears start to fall from her eyes. Big, sloppy tears. She wipes at her face with her free hand, then looks up at the ceiling. "Finnley, what the fuck?"

"What? What did I say?"

"Why would you think that? Why would you assume that I am just going to leave you?" She is still looking up at the ceiling, using both hands now to wipe her face. She presses the heels of her hands into her eyes. "I've never—" The words must get stuck in her throat because she coughs and sits up. The covers fall from her as she leans forward. "I would never just leave. Ever."

"But you left Justine."

"No," she says through tears, followed by an incredulous huff. "She left me." She looks over her shoulder at me. "She gave up first. I'm just the one who had to give up completely. Do you understand the difference?"

I nod after I sit up so I can see her better in the pre-dawn light. "I'm sorry."

"Don't. You don't have to apologize, Finnley. Don't ever apologize for being honest with me, for telling me what you're thinking. I need to know those things because, unfortunately, I can't read minds." She gives me a small smile. "It'd make it a lot easier if I could."

"Yeah, you would have known right away that I was hot for you."

"Oh, I *did* know that right away." She chuckles. "Completely straight women don't look at me the way you did."

I gasp. "Seriously? What? How did I look at you?"

"Like you wanted to rip my clothes off."

"No way."

"Are you telling me you *didn't* want to rip my clothes off?" She moves so she's facing me, and she motions to her body. "You didn't want to see all this?"

I can tell instantly that I'm blushing. "Well, it's impossible to argue with my stupid red cheeks giving me away."

"Yeah, that's what I thought." She's sitting with her legs folded, and if my comforter wasn't covering her, I'd have perfect access.

"So Justine's an idiot is the moral of the story."

The soft laughter she gives me is adorable. "I'd like to think she made the decisions she made because she, too, was searching for her happily ever after. No one is perfect. I did things that weren't honorable in the search for happiness. I was twenty-five when we met. We didn't start dating until I was thirty-three. After the third date, she didn't leave. And that was it. Typical lesbian shit, y'know?" She smiles. "Well, you *will* know. Not that you *have* to be lesbian. You could be bi or pan."

I grab her hand. "It's okay. You didn't offend me."

"Whew." She squeezes my hand. "When I left you after the Fourth of July party?" The mention of that night has me staring into a downward spiral I don't want to jump into, so I breathe in and wait for her to continue. "I'm not going to lie to you. I thought we were going to maybe make it, her and me. It was stupid. But you spend so many years of your life with someone, and it's *comfortable*, familiar. Staying in hell is easier when you recognize all the landmarks."

"Oddly enough, I know exactly what you mean."

"There was one thing I kept thinking about. It didn't matter what we were talking about, our future, our past, our house, our jobs, our money. This thing kept popping into my mind and wouldn't leave me alone."

"What was it? This thing?"

"I guess it was more of a person than a thing. It was *you*, Finnley."

My chest tightens.

"I could not shake you. You made me feel things again. You made me laugh, made my heart beat again, made me want to be happy again. You did that. And after a couple days of Justine and me talking and talking and *talking* about our future, ugh, I couldn't do it anymore. She knew it. She was done, too, so it wasn't a difficult conversation. Or at least not as difficult as I thought it was going to be. I think we were both scared to do life without each other when we've been in each other's lives for so long." She is still holding my hand, her thumb rubbing soft circles on the top. "She signed the divorce papers the next day and started moving out. And then I needed to get my own shit in order. My money, my business, my artists, everything. Basically, I want you to know that I didn't stop talking to you with the sole purpose of never talking to you again. I needed to get myself to a place where nothing was holding me back. Because"—her eyes lock onto mine—"I want you, Finnley. All of you. I want to date you, sleep next to you, laugh with you, watch movies with you… *fuck* you…" Her eyebrow arches, and I feel it in my stomach. "And I did not want you ever to doubt me again."

"Emerson…" My voice cracks. I lick my lips and hold back the tears I can feel riding this emotional roller coaster with me. "I don't—"

"Wait," she says. "I have one more thing to tell you." She pulls a very deep breath into her lungs. Her eyes instantly fill with tears. "When Justine mentioned in vitro that night? It was me who was trying to get pregnant. Not her."

I swallow. "Okay."

"It was a last-ditch effort to try and save our marriage. She wanted kids. She can't have them. I tried. And it never..." She stops, purses her lips. Her eyes, her kind eyes, are filled with so much sadness that it makes my throat ache. "I needed you to know that."

I lean forward onto my knees and wrap my arms around her. She hugs me back, pulling me until I'm sitting on her lap, straddling her waist. "I got you," I say before I kiss her. She parts her lips and slides her tongue into my mouth. She drags her fingertips down my back, over my ass.

"I want to put my mouth on you again," she says between kisses. "Can I?"

"Oh, Emerson." I kiss her deeply before I add, "You seeking consent is so hot. Yes, for fuck's sake, yes, you can put your mouth on me."

Within seconds she has me on my back, legs spread, feet flat on the mattress, while she presses her tongue into my very wet center. The way she licks me, flicks me, pushes into me, is incredible. I prop myself up so I can watch her. I want to remember every single moment of this night into the morning. And I want to spend the rest of my days creating new memories with her. With Emerson. The love of my life.

CHAPTER FIFTEEN

Around noon, after we showered together and had, oh, I don't know, maybe *the* most phenomenal shower sex, we headed downstairs to get something to eat. As someone who has enjoyed sex for most of my adult years, I find it very odd that sex with Emerson has awakened something insatiable inside me. I cannot get enough of her. When she pushed me against the wall of the shower and fingered me until I almost collapsed, I still wanted more. And when I did the same to her, made her come with her foot propped on the built-in seat, the water rushing over her magnificent curves, I, again, still wanted *more*.

However, I was also ready to gnaw my own arm off. It'd been a hot minute since I'd had anything to eat. Truthfully, I didn't eat dinner or have a single hors d'oeuvres at the art show. I was ready for sustenance. And, unfortunately, Emerson's body wasn't enough at that point.

In the kitchen, Emerson takes stock of the cabinets. It's almost like she lives with Uncle Mark and me. As with everything else concerning her, it makes me so happy to imagine one day living together. Waking up next to her, showering with her, making breakfast—or in this case, lunch—with her. It only freaks me out a tiny bit that I can see myself living a life with her, and the only reason that tiny bit exists is because I feel like it's entirely too soon. Maybe also because I was engaged to a man before, but who's counting?

"Do you like to cook?" I ask as she chops a red pepper into pieces. I'm sitting on the counter, legs hanging over the edge, watching her every move like a hawk. Her profile, her concentration, her fingers, her grip on the handle of the knife. How is holding a knife sexy? I have no idea, but the way she's doing it is only amplifying my horniness. I'll never understand this attraction I have to her. I really won't. "Like, is this something I won't have to worry about if we ever live together?"

The lighthearted chuckle she gives me makes me want to kiss her. "I do enjoy cooking. It's sort of like art, y'know? I can do what I feel and hope for the best. Nine times out of ten, it turns out beautiful."

"And the tenth time?"

"Meh. I've thrown out my share of masterpieces." She winks. "But yes, I'll take care of the meals if you'd like."

"That is totally fine with me. Especially if I get to watch you while you cook."

She picks up the purple onion she managed to find and slices the top off. I can't get over how beautiful she looks with her hair pulled back in a messy bun and no makeup. No lip gloss, no mascara, no blush, no eyeliner. Just *her*. The tiny lines at the corners of her eyes make me love her even more.

I hear the front door close. "Uh-oh," I say with a chuckle and wait for Uncle Mark to walk in and see us in his kitchen, cooking, clearly having spent the night together.

"Well, well, well," he says before he even gets to the doorway. "Look what we have here." He appears, a giant smile on his face. "Did we finally kiss and make up, ladies?"

Emerson tosses me a glance, a smile on her face, before she answers with, "Oh, we did more than that. Multiple times."

He giggles, smacks his hands, and rubs them together. "That is exactly what I was hoping to hear." He strides across the kitchen to me, places his hands on my cheeks, and kisses my forehead. "I'm so happy for you."

"Thank you so much, Uncle Mark." I'm holding back tears. Why? Who knows? I can't control anything these days, which is maybe exactly how it should have always been.

"I'll allow 'Uncle' this time, babycakes." He moves to Emerson next, his hand on the small of her back as she turns to hug him. "It's about time," he stage-whispers into her ear when she wraps her arms around his neck. "You deserve this, y'know? Emerson, you deserve this."

"I love you, Mark." Her whisper sounds strained, as if she's holding back tears. Their love for each other is what some people go their whole lives hoping to find in a friendship. It's beautiful.

He pulls back from her and grins. "Want me to take over cooking?"

"He hates people being in his kitchen. Has he told you this yet?" Emerson rolls her eyes and steps aside.

"I don't hate it; I just know I can do it better. So, what are we making? Omelets? Toast? Did you find the Canadian bacon in the fridge? Oh, and I have these phenomenal goat cheese crumbles." He swings open the Sub-Zero refrigerator and peers into it. "Yes, yes, let's do that. Okay, you two." He waves at us. "I've got this."

Emerson shakes her head before she washes her hands and dries them. She backs herself in front of me, the perfect position for me to wrap my arms and legs around her. When she leans her head against me, I kiss her temple. "You were doing so well at chopping."

She sighs. "I know. And he had to come in and ruin it."

"Hey now, you know this omelet will rock your world. Don't

hate the player." He holds the knife up while he's speaking. "Hate the game, y'know?"

"Yeah, yeah. Tell us how your night was, Mark. Enquiring minds want to know." While Emerson's speaking, she's rubbing my knees, and while it feels really great, it's also making me way too horny for a conversation with my uncle.

"Had a lovely client last night. First time together. Escaping an abusive marriage." He's so methodical as he tosses the veggies into the pan to sauté them. I've watched him cook numerous times, but this morning, he seems lighter than the last few times he's come home from a client. It's great to see him like this. "You both know I don't talk about details, but suffice it to say, when a client hires me just so she can feel safe in the arms of a man, it emphasizes why I continue to do this. Y'know, after getting the shit kicked out of me that night—"

"Whoa, whoa, what? What did he say?" Emerson's head pops up, her hands still on my knees. "Mark? What happened?"

"You didn't tell her?" He's looking at me when he asks.

"Um, no," I say, trying to convey the reason why on my face so I don't have to bring it up, but he's not getting it. "That was the night. Y'know, *the* night?"

His face softens. "Oh, yeah." He shrugs. "Em, it's okay. I'm fine. You know how some of these women's significant others get. Normally everything is fine. But my favorite client's husband followed her, and well, he got physical with me."

Emerson's body stiffens. "Mark—"

"I'm fine, Em," he says, his hand slicing through the air to stop the onslaught he must know is coming from her. "I promise."

She takes a breath, then relaxes, but only slightly. "I worry about you."

"I do, too," I add softly. "I know you're not going to stop. Maybe you need a bodyguard."

Emerson laughs. "I'll be your bodyguard. I know tae kwon do."

"Do you really? That's so hot."

Uncle Mark groans while popping a piece of red pepper in his mouth. "Get a room."

"Seriously, Mark, I just want you to be safe. Okay?"

"I know. And I am very safe. Believe me, I protected myself. I only had a black eye. The other guy looked way worse." He pulls his shoulders back, making himself look broader across the chest. "I take boxing classes for this very reason. I promise you don't need to worry." He scoffs. "Now I'm actually glad you didn't tell her, Finn. Let's stop talking about it. Tell me about your night."

I feel my eyes widen, and Emerson lets out a small chuckle. "Um," she starts. "We talked. And made up."

"Exactly." I clear my throat. "Talked and made out." She squeezes my leg. "I mean, made *up*. Up. Not out."

His eyes are filled with so much happiness when he looks at us while cracking eggs into a bowl. "I love you both so much."

"It was a really great *conversation*," she says as she leans back and looks at me. "Right?"

"The best conversation I have ever had in my entire life."

"I have a feeling *conversation* is code for fucking, but I'm not going to push the issue." He shakes his head. "And everything is done with Justine?"

Emerson lifts her head. "Completely done. She moved out. Divorce papers have been signed by both of us and turned in. It's over." There is a hint of sadness in her voice that would have bothered me before all of this, but now, I get it. The end of a relationship is hard. Feeling like a failure is inevitable, especially after they were in each other's lives for as long as they were. She squeezes my knee again. "Toward the end, all I wanted was for both of us to be happy."

Uncle Mark points his spatula at Emerson. "That's a real grown-up way to think about it."

"Well, I am forty-three. Figured it was time."

"She looked happy last night. That's all that matters."

She breathes in deeply and slowly lets it out. "The end of an era," she says quietly.

"The start of a new one," I whisper next to her ear. I can see her cheeks lift when she smiles. This right here is all I have ever wanted. This feeling of being content, knowing that I'm making someone else happy, but also actually feeling that happiness within me. I wouldn't trade it for anything in the world.

~

I ask Emerson to go with me to meet Jesse and Rory at the airport, but she says she has to get back to the studio to help with the cleanup. "Y'know, since I sort of bailed last night," she says as she pulls her jeans on, then hands over the pair of shorts I had loaned her. "Not that I am upset with how everything turned out."

"I completely understand. I promise." I pull her toward me and kiss her. What starts out innocent quickly escalates. She manages to pull my shirt up and expose my breasts before pushing me backward onto the bed and yanking me toward the edge. Within seconds, she has my shorts and panties off, is kneeling before me, and has her face buried in between my legs. Her tongue dips into me, and then her fingers replace her tongue, and she starts flicking my clit. I moan her name and push my fingers into her hair as I press myself into her. I'm already on the edge of my release. She is so fucking good at this.

"Come for me," she whispers when she breaks away from me. I look down at her, at her smile, the love in her eyes, and the wetness on her face. That's all it takes for me to jump off the edge. I come so hard that I get a cramp in my calf. I yelp as I stretch it, but I'm still coming, and I can barely handle the pain combined with the pleasure of release. When it subsides, she pulls her fingers from me. "Are you okay?"

"My calf," I say with a laugh. "I have a cramp. Oh my God."

She rubs it while chuckling. "I've never given someone a cramp before."

"Well, lucky me." I am still laughing even though my calf is killing me. "You're ridiculous, you know that?" I prop myself up on my elbows. She's fixing her hair, pulling it back into the messy bun again, and it takes literally everything in me to not lunge at her and devour her. "Fucking *gorgeous*, but ridiculous."

She looks at her watch. "When do you need to leave?"

"By two."

"Say less." She pulls her shirt off while standing, then undoes her jeans and pulls them off again. "We've got plenty of time."

She's on top of me in seconds, her fingers are inside of me, her mouth on mine, and the entire time, all I can think is that I love her more and more with every passing second.

∽

SEEING RORY WAS CATHARTIC. SHE LOOKED TERRIFIC WHEN I grabbed them from the airport. Her hair, her skin, her adorable outfit. It was almost as if she was completely healed. I am positive that isn't the case, but witnessing the transformation a few weeks can garner was great.

She and Jesse were both starving, so we went straight to lunch. They both wanted pizza. And who am I to argue?

The server at Pequod's laughs at their expressions when the pizza is set in front of us. Jesse's mouth is hanging open, and Rory says, "Holy shit."

I love them both.

"Enjoy, ladies. And by the looks on their faces, I'm sure you all will." The server laughs again as she leaves.

"Dig in," I say. They both do, but only after both posting pictures to their Instagram accounts. I roll my eyes. They're sixteen years apart, but you could never tell. No wonder they get along so well. "So…"

"How's Emerson?" I know Emerson was with me when I saw her in Florida, but Rory's question still takes my breath away. "She was so cool. Like, weirdly so. I kept getting lost in her eyes, like, what the heck? How do people have such spectacularly colored eyes?"

Jesse shrugs. "Bro, right? Like, they're so green."

"Bro?" I start to laugh. They are the same person. "She's really great. She was going to come with me to pick you up, but she had an art show last night and needed to go help with the cleanup."

"How was the show?" Jesse wags her brows. "Art show, I mean."

I roll my eyes. "It was awesome. It's happening again tonight if you two want to go."

"Without you?" Rory doesn't sound pleased that I implied they should go alone.

"No, I'll go with, silly."

"Okay, good. I want to hang out with you." She shrugs. "I miss you. A lot more than I thought I would."

"Same." Jesse sighs. "I wish you were moving back to Tampa."

I take a deep breath. Being missed feels good. I hate admitting that. But... "Girls, I'm never moving back to Florida."

"Like Taylor Swift's song, 'We Are Never Ever Getting Back Together'?" Rory grins. "I've been listening to her nonstop since *Midnights* came out."

I place my hand over my heart. "Oh, Rory, you have no idea how much that means to me. I told you you'd love her if you gave her a chance."

"Yeah, Finn, she's so freaking incredible. Like, she writes all her own lyrics. Did you know that?"

I chuckle. "Yes, I did. Pretty fantastic, isn't it?"

"And she composes the music. How does she do it all? I am so sad I've been sleeping on her this whole time."

"But lucky you, you essentially got to listen to all her albums as if they were brand new. Pretty awesome if you ask me."

Jesse groans. "Y'all need to listen to Beyonce too."

"I do," Rory shouts. "I love Queen Bey. *Lemonade* is one of the most groundbreaking albums of all time."

Jesse's eyes fill with tears. "Rory, I do think we were separated at birth."

"Yeah, but I think you're sixteen years too old," I add.

"Right? Like, seriously." She high-fives Rory.

The conversation continues about music and songs and how much they all mean to us. Rory, bless her heart, has started her own therapeutic process of finding the saddest song she can and listening to it once a day so she can cry. Then she turns it off and moves on with her day. I wonder if I should do the same thing; it sounds smart. Get it all out so I can focus on more important things. Because, yeah, I was over Steven when I broke up with him, but his death broke something inside of me. Trauma is an untamed beast if not handled correctly.

I tell them about Petals for Days and getting fired from that job too. They both laugh because it is a little comical when I sit back and think about it. I went from not needing to worry about a job ever to not being able to find something. And when I did find something that I was starting to enjoy, I got fired because I was sleeping with the owner's soon-to-be ex-wife. My life really could be a movie.

Rory is super pumped when I ask her about the volleyball club where she'll be playing this fall and winter, though. Her eyes light up, and she asks a thousand questions. She's been training hard at the club in Florida, so she's ready for the season to start at the end of August. I have always been impressed with her talent. She's tall, all arms and legs, and one of the best left-handed setters I've seen. She'll get a scholarship if she plays her cards right. My only hope is that Carla allows her to leave the state of Florida.

"Finn, I have a question." Rory slides a third piece of pizza onto her plate. "Are you and Emerson, like, dating or whatever? It's totally cool if you are. I can sort of, like, tell that she's into you. I know I've only been around her a couple times, but it's pretty obvious."

How do I handle this? The daughter of my ex-fiancé. My ex-fiancé who is dead. My ex-fiancé who was her dad. "Um…"

"Yes, they're together," Jesse answers for me, and my eyes snap to hers. Irritation bubbles under my skin, but the love, the understanding, the commitment to our friendship in her eyes has it dissipating within seconds.

"Okay, cool. That's cool." Rory shrugs.

"I'm sorry." I hear the words come out of me. It's been a while since I've apologized for something that isn't my fault, so it makes me cringe. But the apology feels necessary.

Rory's eyes soften. "Don't be. You deserve to be loved." She leans forward. "My dad loved himself more than he loved anyone else. We both know that."

My throat tightens after hearing her statement. "Rory, honey, I don't think that's true." I'm lying. I do think it's true. But he was her dad. And I loved him, and so did she, so I must try to protect that, right? "He loved you so much."

"He did, I know. It's okay for me to come to terms with the fact that he wasn't a great dad, but still love him and miss him." She smiles. Probably at the expression on my face, one of shock and admiration at the handle she has on her mental health. "Therapy, baby. Dr. Eggan has taught me so much about grief."

"Wow." It comes out as a whisper. She has bowled me over with her honesty.

"Also"—she leans forward over the table—"I mean, we both know he wasn't completely faithful."

Jesse's eyes almost pop out of her head. "I'm sorry, what?"

I tried to catch her before she spoke, but I wasn't fast enough. "Yeah, um, I didn't tell you any of that. I'm sorry."

"What the hell?" Jesse glares at me, then looks at Rory, then fixes her glare on me again. "When did you find this out?"

I shake my head. "Jess, not now."

"No, I want to know. What the fuck? I'm your best friend." She motions to Rory. "Fuck, I'm practically *her* best friend."

Rory chuckles around a mouthful of pizza. "Truth."

"I leave you two alone for three months, and this is what happens?" I sigh. "I found out when he came here to, I don't know, surprise me? Except he was angry with me because I was ignoring him." I look at Rory. "I'm sorry."

"Don't. It's okay."

"Yeah, well, I told him I think we should be done, and he went on a rant about all the college girls he slept with. Ugh, Rory, I'm sorry again."

"Finnley," she says with a small laugh. "I have ears. I would hear them."

I gasp. "And you never told me?"

She tilts her head. "You're joking, right?" Sarcasm is dripping from her statement. "What would I have said to you? 'Hey, Finnley, by the way, my dad is hooking up with college chicks when you aren't here, so you might want to practice safe sex with him'?"

I widen my eyes as my mouth drops open. Jesse lets out a loud laugh. "And this is why we're best friends," she says, putting her arm around Rory's shoulders.

"Well, shit." I shrug and raise my beer. "Touché, pussycat."

"Like I said, it's okay for me to think he was kind of a bad dad. Doesn't mean I don't miss him."

"Both things can be true, hmm?"

Rory smiles, and it lights up her eyes. "Exactly."

"Probably should go to therapy, shouldn't I?"

She scrunches her nose. "I mean, it couldn't hurt."

"Think they have a two-for-one deal?" Jesse asks before drinking from her freshly delivered 312.

And we all descend into laughter. It feels so good to be with them both. To not have to censor ourselves or our feelings. What a concept.

∼

Rory falls instantly in love with The Oasis. She asks if she can sleep outside under the stars. I don't see a problem with it. Uncle Mark confirms that he's fallen asleep out there more times than he'd like to admit, so we pull out the air mattress for her.

Jesse, on the other hand, says there is no way in hell she is giving up the space next to me in my bed, so "Emerson better watch out."

Emerson laughs as she holds her hands up in defeat. "You win, my friend. You win." I'm a little bummed, though. I was so looking forward to sleeping next to her again. "We have the rest of our lives," she whispers to me, presumably sensing my disappointment. Her soft voice and words help, but the idea of not having sex with her tonight fills me with a longing I didn't realize existed. "She's your best friend. She misses you. It's okay. I promise."

She's sitting next to me on the outdoor couch, her hair still a mess, her skin still free of makeup. Her feeling so comfortable with me brings me a lot of joy. I feel honored I'm one of the few people she allows herself to relax around. "Tomorrow then, okay?"

"And every night after that?"

Her smile causes my heart rate to bottom out.

"Yes, please."

"Can we watch a movie out here?" Rory's question snaps us both back to reality. "A scary one?"

"That's a great idea. What about... *Hereditary*? With Toni Collette. That movie fucked me up." Jesse plops down on the air mattress next to Rory. "Whoa, this is super comfy. Maybe I will just sleep out here."

Emerson nudges me. I hold back my grin. "How about a rom-com? *It's Complicated* or *Sleepless in Seattle* or something?"

"Meryl Streep," Uncle Mark says under his breath while clutching his heart. "I'd take a bullet for her. I'm one hundred percent in for *It's Complicated*."

"*Bridges of Madison County*." Emerson points at Mark. "Best Meryl movie."

"Rip my *heart* out, Clint Eastwood." He gasps. "Who would have ever thought he would be charming? Certainly not me."

"I love her in *Adaptation*. But I'm also a huge Nic Cage fan." I shrug when they all look at me. "What? I like Tom Cruise too. So sue me."

"We may need to reevaluate this," Emerson says with a low voice. "I don't know if I can watch Tom Cruise."

"Oh, come on. *Mission Impossible*? Those are some of the best movies ever. Please tell me you've at least seen those?"

Her face is completely void of emotion.

"*Top Gun*?"

She smiles. "Okay, okay, I'll give you *Top Gun*."

"I've never seen *Top Gun*," Rory says. It's now her turn to get the death stare. "What? I'm sixteen. Y'all are a lot older than me."

"You're gonna sleep on the cold, hard ground in a second, kiddo," Uncle Mark says, followed by a smile and a wink. "Let's introduce her to Maverick and Goose. Shall we?"

"I'm in," we all say in unison.

"I'm in too." Aunt Lisa is standing in the doorway, holding two giant tins of Garrett's Popcorn. "And I brought snacks."

"My hero." Emerson stands and rushes over to her. They hug each other for what feels like days. Aunt Lisa kisses her on the cheek.

"Oh, Em, we have a lot to talk about, my dear." Aunt Lisa breaks from the hug, looks Emerson in the face, and smiles. "You do look really good, though. A whole new woman."

"I *feel* really good."

"I'm so glad." Aunt Lisa's eyes meet mine. She points at me and says, "I told you I was right."

I chuckle as she walks over to me, passing the popcorn tin to Jesse and Rory on her way. She pulls me into her and hugs me like she's never hugged me before. "Don't break her heart. I know you're my niece, and I love you, but I'll fucking murder you if you hurt her."

I let out a laugh. "I promise I will not hurt her."

"Good."

CHAPTER SIXTEEN

After forty-four hours of hanging out with Rory and Jesse, who indeed ended up sleeping next to me not one but two nights, we are on our way back to O'Hare. The last two days have been a godsend. I needed it way more than I realized. The laughter with Jesse was so healing, and being around Rory was exactly what the doctor ordered. She is a great person, and the more I'm around her, the more I love her.

When the Blue Line stops at O'Hare, we climb off the L and head toward security. "Okay, you're both checked in," I say. "Neither of you is checking a bag, correct?"

As if on cue, they say in unison, "Yes, Mom."

I roll my eyes. "Y'know what—"

Rory cuts me off, though, as she leaps into my arms, hugging me as tight as she's ever hugged me. "I need a mom, so I'm cool with it." Her voice cracks at the end of her sentence. If she cries, I'm going to bawl like a baby.

I breathe out and continue hugging her until Jesse wraps her arms around us in a giant group hug. "I'm going to miss you so much," she says. She is definitely crying. I can hear it in her voice.

"I'll miss the two of you too. Please come back." I pull away and look at them both. "Both of you. Rory, if you ever change your mind..." My voice snags in my throat. I'm overcome with so much emotion that I can barely feel my legs. I cover my mouth and shake my head. "I'm sorry. I don't know why I'm so emotional."

"*Stop* apologizing," she says as she hugs me again. "You're amazing, and I love you."

Jesse grabs my hand and squeezes. She knows me. She knows I never cared about something like this or needed this. I still don't need it, but I also never realized how much I cared *for* this girl until right this second, as I'm preparing to let her go back to her aunt, uncle, and cousins. The road of life is so very strange, isn't it? Nothing is mapped out. There is no GPS. We simply have to pay attention in order to not wreck as we drive like hell to get where we are going.

"All right," Jesse says softly. "We gotta go, Rory."

Rory pulls away from the hug. "Text you when we land."

"And when you get through security. And get on the plane too."

"Man, you really are like a mom." Jesse laughs as she gives me a final hug. "Go get Emerson. Don't let her go," she whispers. "I love seeing you like this. Happy and safe." She pulls out of the hug and takes off toward the entrance of the airport, waving at Rory to keep up.

While I know this isn't the *end* of anything, it still feels like the start of something. All I have to do is grip the steering wheel and hope like hell that I don't wreck.

∽

ON A COMPLETELY STUPID WHIM, I DECIDE ON MY WAY BACK TO THE house to stop at Petals for Days. Blake's comment about Justine wanting me back hasn't left my head. My obsessive need to fix everything that happened is running rampant, but I was also really starting to love working for Justine. We were getting to know each other. She was on the same page as me, finally, and good things were starting to happen, things that were going to lead to big returns on investment.

When I walk into the downtown location, I hear Vivian gasp, then let out a loud, giddy giggle. "Oh, please tell me you're back for good." She rushes up to me and throws her arms around me with such force that she nearly knocks the wind from my lungs. "We have missed you so much."

"Wow. That's quite the reception," I say as I hug her back.

"Finnley, my dear, you're back!" Lydia must have seen me too. "Please tell me you're back."

I pull away from Vivian's grasp and hug Lydia next. "I hate to disappoint, but no, I'm not. I want to talk to Justine. Is she around because—" My words are cut short, though, when I see Justine appear at the back of the store. I pull in a deep breath.

Lydia pats my back. "You got this."

"Yeah, you can do this." Vivian does the same, and I start walking back toward Justine.

"What are you doing here?" Her question could be construed as accusatory, though her tone is anything but. She seems genuinely shocked. It gives me an ounce of hope.

"I wanted to talk to you. Do you think I could have a minute or two of your time?"

Her facial expression morphs from confused to composed. "Sure, come on back." She turns and maneuvers through the small hallway. There are buckets of flowers everywhere. She's clearly getting ready for an event. "Sorry for the mess. It's been a whirlwind since those TikToks we posted of the Kerstin wedding went viral." She adjusts her tortoiseshell-framed glasses with the back of her gloved hand as she leans against the planting table in the back room. Her dark, curly hair is pulled back, and she's wearing a Boho Bandeau headband. She looks dead tired. I may have caught her at the perfect time. Or the worst. The jury is still out.

"So, what's up?"

Ugh. It's the wrong time. "Well, I wanted to come by to talk to you. Blake mentioned something about me coming back and… I don't want that, but I want you to know how thankful I am for having been given the opportunity to begin with."

My statement stuns her, but not in the way I was preparing myself for. Her wide-eyed stare is accentuated by a soft puff of breath. "Well, that's not exactly how I thought this conversation was going to go."

"Really?"

"Yeah, I figured you'd leap at the chance to come back."

There's no point in beating around the bush. "Y'know, I'm *really* good at accounting and numbers. But… it's not my passion. At all. And you need someone who's going to stay for the long run."

A silence falls between us and goes on for a good thirty seconds. Her gaze hasn't left mine the entire time. I feel like a science project under the lens of a microscope. I don't move for fear that movement will disrupt whatever is happening. "That's really professional of you to admit," she finally says.

I shrug. "I'm not super happy that you fired me, but in the long run, you sort of did me a favor."

She laughs. "Man, I didn't see this on my yearly bingo card: my ex's new lover thanking me for firing her."

I can't help but join in on her laughter. "Yeah, this year has been a real mindfuck, hasn't it?"

"That's putting it mildly."

"Well, thank you, Justine, for taking the time to speak with me." I start to leave—I don't want to chance anything else—but her soft "Finnley?" stops me in my tracks.

"Yeah?"

"There are no hard feelings. Okay?"

I nod.

"She loves you." Her voice cracks. "A lot. And I can see why." She gives me a smile, one I feel she only gives people when she's vulnerable.

I turn and leave as fast as I can.

∽

"Wait a second."

Emerson rolls onto her side. She's naked. So am I. Because I cannot handle myself around her. It's the first time I've ever been to her house, too, which meant only one thing: christening every single room. We're in the living room now. The kitchen was fun. Her sprawled out on the center island was a scene directly out of my fantasies. The powder room wasn't bad either, but the living room has been the best. Probably because it's the first time we've actually come at the same time. At least, that's why I think it has been the best.

Emerson props herself on an elbow and levels me with a stare. "You're telling me that she was cool to you? And didn't act like a jerk?"

"Yep, you heard me right." I'm staring up at the ceiling. The hardwood floor was cold at first, but now it's helping to cool down my very hot body.

"Wow." She runs her fingers down my sternum, then under and around my left breast. "What a turn of events."

"I mean, I already have what I want. But I wanted to make sure that I didn't leave that relationship in shambles. Y'know what I mean?"

"And what is that you want?"

I look at her, at her green eyes, and smile. "This—you and me like this forever—is what I want. Everything else? It's just icing."

"I agree," she whispers before she leans over and kisses me. "I've never had this much sex in my entire life."

"And it's only like day five. Imagine how much more we are going to have." I feel like a teenager. "Should we do another room?"

She laughs her beautiful laugh I've come to love so much. "How about I take you up to my bedroom, and we can get off the floor?"

"Em?"

"Hmm?" Her eyes lock onto mine.

"I don't ever want this to end."

"Oh, baby," she says as she moves closer to me. "Then let's make sure it never does." She nudges my nose with hers, then kisses me softly. "Let's go upstairs." She breaks from me and stands, holding her hand out so I can grab it. I follow her up the stairs to her bedroom. She holds my hand the entire time. Even when we sit on the edge of the mattress, she doesn't let me go. It's not until I decide to take charge that her hand slips from mine.

"It's my turn with you." I kneel in front of her and pull her to the edge of the bed. "Let's hope I don't give you a leg cramp. It does not feel good."

She laughs and laughs, then moans when I put my mouth on her warm center.

Everything about Emerson is everything I have always wanted in my life. A person who understands me and loves me *regardless*. A person who laughs at my stupid humor and also makes *me* laugh. A person who knows how to handle my emotions and gives the vulnerable parts room to breathe. She has completed me. She has taken the tapestry that is my life, the one I finally took a second to stand back and look at, and made it better. She's patched up the tears, added her own flair, and hung it on the wall for all to see.

Everything happens for a reason. And that reason was so I could finally find happiness. I'm so very glad that I did.

EPILOGUE

It's been a little over two years since that summer changed my entire life. Emerson sold her townhouse, and we moved in with Uncle Mark. He begged us to, saying something about how much he didn't want to be alone. Honestly, we are a perfect little family. Aunt Lisa started dating a trans man with whom she is madly in love. Uncle Mark is still single, but he seems to be the happiest he has ever been.

"Finnley, let's go. We are going to be late."

"I'm coming, sorry!" I pull my Northwestern University Volleyball T-shirt over my head and check my makeup. I look good. Damn, I haven't looked this good in years.

"Stop looking at yourself, and let's go."

I look at Emerson's reflection in the mirror. She's standing at the door to the bathroom, looking sexy as hell, in jeans and the same volleyball T-shirt I'm wearing. "Purple is a good color on you."

She shakes her head, a sly grin forming on her lips. "Yeah, same to you, my love."

"Do we have time?" I grin, and she rolls her eyes.

"No. Oh my God, we are going to be so late if we don't leave right now." She is all smiles, though, so I know she's not really mad at me. "Listen, if you're good, I'll fuck you in the bathroom between sets. Deal?"

I laugh as I turn and push her out of the bathroom. "Okay, okay, let's go." We head down the stairs, where Uncle Mark and Aunt Lisa are waiting in matching shirts. "Sorry," I say. "I'm never usually late."

"Um, you two are always late now," Uncle Mark corrects me. "I already threatened Emerson. We cannot be late today."

"I know, I know. Let's go then. What are we waiting for?" I open the door to the townhouse and head outside to the lovely September day. I check my watch. "We are going to be right on time."

"Yeah, you're lucky." Emerson reaches down and intertwines her fingers with mine after we climb into the back seat of a Lyft. Uncle Mark and Aunt Lisa climb in behind us.

"You all headed to the Northwestern volleyball game?" the Lyft driver asks with a chuckle.

"What gave it away?" Aunt Lisa asks; her question is as dry as a cracker. Uncle Mark smacks her lightly on the leg as the Lyft driver takes off.

∼

THE GYM IS PACKED. IT'S THE FIRST GAME OF THE SEASON. AFTER we find seats on the bleachers, I scan the players getting ready. Suddenly, a hand pops up and starts waving wildly.

"There she is," I say to Emerson. "There's Rory."

Uncle Mark and Aunt Lisa wave, as does Emerson. I do as well, but I'm also holding back tears. When Rory told me that she was going to Northwestern to play volleyball, I was so excited for her. But then she told me why she picked this school: "I gave Aunt Carla high school. I want you to have college."

Needless to say, I bawled like a baby. For someone who didn't want kids, I sure do enjoy having her in my life. I have had the conversation with Emerson a few times, and she always says, "Just because you didn't want to be a mom doesn't mean you are incapable of being important in her life." And she's absolutely right.

"She's the first starting freshman setter in the last ten years." I motion to the court. "She's like the third tallest person on the team. She's gonna be phenomenal."

"You worked her ass off this summer." Emerson's hand is on my thigh. She touches me, and my mind starts to race. It's bonkers that it's been two years, and she still gets me going with a touch.

I glance at her hand, then at her, at her profile, at the small smile on her lips. She knows what she's doing to me, and I love her for it. "I need to watch the game."

"Oh? I'm sorry," she says, followed by a light laugh. "Do you need me to move my hand?"

"No. I want you to keep it right there, and I don't want you to move it. Think you can handle that?" The benefit I have is that I know she wants me just as badly as I want her. Damn, it feels magnificent.

"Fine." She licks her lips and focuses on the game. I do the same because, after a few more seconds of looking at her, I'm going to have to pull her to the bathroom like she promised.

∼

THE GAME IS ABSOLUTELY FLAWLESS. NORTHWESTERN WINS IN FOUR sets. They were all nail-biters but so much fun. I had the best time watching Rory kick ass. We're waiting for her now outside the locker room.

"Never been a mom," I say, "but I sure feel as proud as one right now."

Aunt Lisa pulls me into her, her arm around my waist. "It's going to be a fun four years. You're both going to learn a lot about each other."

The locker room door opens, and a bunch of girls come flooding out. Then out comes Rory, her uniform still on, waving her hands like a lunatic. "We won! We won!" She jumps into my arms. "Thank you so much for everything, Finn. Seriously. I wouldn't have been able to do this without you."

"Oh, please. Yes, you would have. You're the one who got the scholarship. Not me."

"But you're the one who taught me everything I know about volleyball. I played soccer before all this. Oh, Emerson!" She leaves me and runs over to my girlfriend. "Did you see that sick hit I had?"

Emerson laughs as they high-five each other. "Hell yeah I did. You were perfection out there, kiddo. You're going to be unstoppable."

I watch them, their banter, how they laugh at each other. Tears are welling in my eyes, and I quickly look away so I don't start crying. I feel Uncle Mark's arm around my shoulders. He squeezes me close. "You did it, babycakes."

"Did what?"

"Found happiness."

"Yeah, I did, didn't I?"

"And so did I." He smiles while he's looking down at me. "Thank you."

"It warms my heart that two ladies in love living with you has made you happy."

He lets out a puff of air. "I mean, you two could keep it down, y'know?"

I laugh. "Oh, my God."

"But yeah…this family we've created is pretty awesome."

"My favorite family I've been a part of, honestly."

"Considering we've both had to deal with your mother, yeah, I agree." And we both start laughing.

We did it. Both of us. And I, for one, have never been more excited about my future, about my life, about my love, and about my family.

SIGN UP

Sign up for Erin's mailing list to be the first to hear about new releases. She promises to not spam you and to always try and make you laugh.

TUNE IN

Make sure to tune in to *The Weekly Wine Down* podcast where Erin Zak chats with her best friends Jackie D, Stacy, Stacey, and Julie (Jackie's sister). Find them on whatever podcast streaming platform is your favorite.

CONNECT

You can contact Erin Zak through her social media or her websites:
   Twitter: @erinzakwrites
   Instagram: @erinzakwrites
   TikTok: @erinzakwrites
   http://www.erinzak.com/

DID YOU ENJOY IT?

Thank you for purchasing The Tapestry of a Heart.

I hope you enjoyed it. Please consider leaving a review on your preferred site. As an independent author, reviews help to promote my work. One line or two really does make the difference.

Thank you, truly.

Love,

Erin

ALSO BY ERIN ZAK

Standalone Titles

Falling Into Her

Breaking Down Her Walls

Create a Life to Love

Beautiful Accidents

The Road Home

The Hummingbird Sanctuary

Guarding Evelyn

Novella

Closed-Door Policy

Co-Write

Swift Vengeance, with Jackie D and Jean Copeland

GLITCH, with Jackie D

Printed in Great Britain
by Amazon